C000007009

# WHEN
# GOD
# SAYS
# NO

REINA SASAKI

*When God Says No*

Copyright © 2021 by Reina Sasaki.
All Rights are reserved.

No part of this book may be used or reproduced in any manner whatsoever without written permission, except in the case of brief quotations embodied in critical articles and reviews.

ISBN 978-1-63944-082-5

# PART 1

# TRUST

RIE MITZUSADA

---

Imagine a person was drowning in the sea. She saw another person swimming her way. Together, they began swimming for the shore. What is strange about this picture?

Unless she figures this out soon, someone was going to die.

---

# SWIMMING LESSON 1

M y mother once said, looking at the sea made her feel sad. I never understood why until Ryoka came into my world.

The surf erased my footprints while retreating, leaving my bare feet to deepen in the sands. I removed my blue sailor scarf, then my blouse and pleated skirt, leaving only a swimsuit underneath. Then I walked over to where the sea formed as a straight line beneath the sky. The water reached my ankles halfway. The ground felt muddy under my feet. The steady rhythm of the sea, however, calmed me. The water reached my chest. I tasted the saltiness when a wave swept me underneath.

The world disappeared.

Down, down, I continued to fall. The luminous surface draws the distance away, the greenish-blue world darkened. I felt the vibration breaking through the silence. And I saw a figure coming from above. The water flooded my throat as I tried to speak, sharp pain cut through my chest, and my strength melted away like sea foam. I couldn't remember what happened, but a firm grip like an invisible hand from behind pulled me up.

I found myself awake, throwing up water. The sour, salty taste filled my mouth. I coughed, and coughed, found my hands grasping on dry sand. The late afternoon sun felt warm in the sky.

"What a show you put on out there," a voice said, making my head turn. "Were you trying to long-distance swim to Korea?"

"No," I said to the girl sitting two arms lengths away.

"Then, what were you doing?"

"Swimming," I rasped.

"Into the open water?" She responded with a chuckle.

"Are you a lifeguard?" I asked.

"No."

"Then you shouldn't have bothered," I said, "or do you always go pulling everyone out of the water?"

The girl looked at me with an intensity in her eyes, and I felt the air turn cold. I noticed a sweet fruit-like scent from here, sunscreen perhaps. She had thin arms, thin legs, and lips like razor blades. Here small eyes and the wet black hair draping over her shoulders made her look even more delicate, like tree bark with legs and arms. And she wore the same swimsuit as mine.

She was from my school.

"This is not a place to swim," she continued. "Others have tried to do the thing you just did. Not everyone survived. You did, though, so good job."

She got up first before offering a hand, but I stood up on my own. "Put out your hand," she said. "Come on. Any side would do."

I hesitated, though having no time to think, I held out my left hand. The girl undid something from her wrist and wrapped it around mine, securing its end with a knot. Pulling back, I saw a faded green ribbon dangling down my wrist.

"What is this?" I asked, holding the hand up.

"Protective Charm." She said before extending their hand, "I am Ryoka Namie. Nice to meet you."

I looked down at her handshake offering. "Rie Mitzusada," I returned the introduction while keeping my hand still in the air. "Miss Namie, I don't think I could accept this. I have no reason to."

"Keep it," Ryoka said with a little smile. "You need it to stay alive."

I made up my mind to forgot what had happened while leaving that beach, the sea, and her behind. Neither of them felt real but like a strange dream. I should be able to forget it soon, if not for the ribbon, which continued to remind me of the calm rhythm sea, its bottomless water, and her.

Saturday passed.

Monday, I got ready for school. My regular bus came at half-past six. Finding the seat next to the window, I looked at the vacant buildings passing before my eyes once the bus started moving. Houses from last year that owners couldn't afford to demolish had remained unsold. The Shinkansen had not reached Nagasaki, my hometown, during this year of nineteen seventy-four.

But though the town didn't change, the people had.

I had changed.

Last year, my aunt had sent me to study in Tokyo. If you love your child, send them to travel, she had said. But I hadn't been able to complete its first year. Something had happened. When I had returned home this August, my aunt had suggested if I should take time off. But I had insisted on enrolling immediately at the local high school, just half an hour away from home. Having to restart the first year had served as my distraction. These days, I found myself thinking less of the previous dormitory life, the big city, and people I used to know.

But I could never forget what happened.

Now, I was attending the public all-girls school, whose history dated back to the Taisho Era's beginning. The senior teachers still remembered how the previous buildings got burnt down by the bomb. The rebuilt main building consisted of four floors, higher than the last, with all the classrooms facing east, the auspicious direction. The second lower building was for gym classes, club activities, and events such as graduation ceremonies. The swimming pool was located in the west, next to the home economic garden. I had not gone there yet, as the swimming classes started during the second year. On the first day, my presence drew curious looks from my classmates due to my sudden transfer after the midterm exam. Luckily, we had the seat assignments around the same time, which diverted some of their attention away. I got assigned the third seat from the back by the window. A great seat, as the Nagasaki air feels pleasant around this time in autumn. Six days a week, I commuted between my home and this seat by the window. I arrived early and went home the moment school ended. I didn't miss a class and always handed in assignments on time.

My classmates had taken an interest in me when they learned I had been to Tokyo. But in time, they took notice of my indifference and left me alone.

No one bothered me, and I cause trouble to no one as my new life continued.

Miss Himura was reciting verses out of the Analects while moving through seats toward the front. Her precise intonation came to a sudden pause that drew a momentary silence from her class. "They said that the essence of Confucius was reciting the verses out loud until the wisdom committed to our memories." She spoke, "though as important as reading is, it's also important to learn from people around you. Think of your family members, your acquaintances, even the friends sitting next to you. Everyone here has their own stories, their wisdom, and experiences. To read is to learn, and to live is to learn from one another. You must learn to understand others to live."

I took brief notes, though Miss Himura's Confucius class was never simple enough that anyone might guess what would be on the exam. She gave fewer tests than the other teachers but was strict when marking the weekly essay assignments. So I made a reminder to later go over three chapters of the textbook. And that should cover everything.

My eyes turned toward the window. The sky looked pale blue, without a single cloud. The ribbon still hung beneath my wrist. The other day, when I walked into the sea. I had no intention to die.

I had only the curiosity if walking into the sea might kill me?

Something rushed through the air, knocking my head aside lightly. A thud fell over my notebook, and I saw an eraser there.

"Miss Mitzusada, please come back to us. "Miss Himura remarked, causing a roar of laughter. "Stand up and read the sentences I just mentioned."

I felt blood rush to my cheeks. Miss Himura was indeed a capable teacher, throwing an eraser across five rows of seats with sheer accuracy. Standing up, I held a copy of the Analects. Which sentence? I scanned over the lines before noticing the eraser still on my desk.

C 1:1-3 was written by Miss Himura's hand, in blue ink.

"Is it not pleasant to learn with a constant perseverance and application?" I read. "Is it not delightful to have friends coming from distant quarters? Is a person not one of the complete virtues, who feels no discomposure though others make no note of oneself?"

"Thank you, Miss Mitzusada," Miss Himura nodded toward me to sit down. Anyone have an opinion on what this means?"

My classmate with short hair, whose last name I remember only the first letter, stood up upon being called. "Miss," she said, "could the third line mean one shouldn't expect others to acknowledge her or his good deeds?"

"Or it could mean no one has the right to judge others," another girl said while still in her seat.

"Also, the second sentence said, how important it is the have a friend," said the one who was still standing.

Miss Himura could make even the most challenging subject became interesting. Her way of walking through the desk rolls, reading, then posing the open-ended questions, though strange in the eyes of many, had been well received by students. She didn't mind if they answer while standing or sitting, as long as someone answered something. The previous Confucius teacher only read from the book, according to others.

She used to tutor me the same way when I was nine and still living in Chiba.

Back then, she and her friends had been in the Social Working Club of the nearby high school and used to come doing volunteer work at my school. She had become my tutor during my elementary. Then after she had graduated, I had lost touch with her for a few years. The last time I had seen her, I had turned thirteen. She had come to my parents' funeral. Then, I had moved to Nagasaki and had not heard from her until my enrollment into this school.

I was still getting used to her being a teacher, wearing a black blazer and office skirt. She kept her hair short in a bob, however, like in her school day.

Miss Himura gave us homework to write a five hundred-word assignment. I decided to start early while the class continued. Finally, the bell rang, and school was over. I stayed to finish the task. Around four, my classmates on cleaning duty left when I saw Miss Himura waiting at the door.

"I'm ready, Miss," I said.

"Let's walk together."

It had been a few months, but we had never found a time to speak freely. A teacher being friends with a student would have caused unnecessary rumors. Besides, she had been busy.

"Congratulation, Miss," I said, leaving the school building. "You have become a teacher, as you said you would."

I chose to call her 'Miss' at school.

"I thought of coming to visit you when you gave me this new address long ago," she said. "I ended up finding an opening for a substitute teacher here, and I passed the interview. Sorry I haven't talked to you much until now. Lots of things happened that need my attention. It's nice to see you again, Rie. You have grown."

"It has been four years after all," I laughed a little. "Are you still in touch with the rest of the Club?"

"I still get New Year's Cards from Hiromi," she said. "And Makoto went to a medical school last time I heard."

Two students greeted Miss Himura outside the building, and I recognized one of them from the track team. The clock at the top of the school building said ten minutes past four. Students from sports clubs had already started their practices. I used to go to swimming practice around this time too, in my previous school. November had already begun, three months since I had last swum. Miss Himura bid goodbye to the students, and we resumed our walk.

"So, what do you think of my teaching?" she asked.

"Confucius suits you perfectly," I said. "Though most schools don't have the subject anymore. Somehow, I couldn't picture anyone, but you teach it."

"Have I always looked that old to you, Rie?" she said in a teasing tone.

"I wouldn't think of it that way," I said, "more like you found the job that fits you."

"I applied to teach Literature. Or Language class, or at least Home Economics," she said. "Then the Principal said that Mr. Tanikawa, who taught Confucius, was retiring, so if I wanted, I could take over his classes. Miss Kanae, who taught Home Economics, was also retiring. I wonder why I didn't get that post."

Probably because of how you look. The old fashion hairstyle, official clothing, and intelligent air made Miss Himura look like Shikibu Murasaki wearing a western suit.

"I recently started reading one of the English-translated German classics," said Miss Himura. "I would aim for the Language class once I could teach full time. So for that, I have been brushing up on language skills. I heard that in your previous school, there is quite a big department of language study, right?"

My hands gripped over the bag handle unconsciously when the conversation turned toward my old school.

"I heard from your English teacher," said Miss Himura. "He said you speak the language very well."

"Miss, I would rather not talk about my previous school," I said. "Not that I dislike this, you know. Getting to walk and talk with you again."

"I wouldn't have invited you if you already had a friend or two to walk home with," Miss Himura said as we continued at a slow pace down the narrow road toward the bus station.

"It's more fun talking to you," I said.

"When you were nine, perhaps," she said. "Being with someone your age and walking home with a teacher are two different things. Girls your age shouldn't even go home when it's this early, not five yet. They should be at the beach, eating cold noodles, or listening to the radio with someone. Once your youth is gone, you can never go back, you know. I am speaking from experience."

I chuckled. Miss Himura's ideas of spending free time came from ten years ago.

"Did something happen in Tokyo?" She asked cautiously, keeping her voice low.

I felt a cold chill running up my back and noticed Miss Himura had stopped walking. She was looking at me with the gaze of a teacher assessing her student. I fixated on the first button of her blazer. "Did my aunt talk to you?" I asked.

"Only that you haven't told her anything."

I looked the other way.

"Rie, do you still remember when we talked the last time, at your parents' funeral?" Miss Himura took one step closer. "You told me what you wanted to become in the future. Is that still your goal?"

My eyes lowered to the ground before I shook my head slowly. "I don't know," I answered.

"Unless you speak what is in your mind, no one will ever understand you." Miss Himura's voice grew intense.

"Miss, you know that I am a Christian, right?" I said.

"I still remember your mother," said Miss Himura. "She's the most devoted catholic, to the point that I admired how someone could believe in something so sincerely. And I remember your father. He's open about his wife and daughter taking the rosary while he was a Buddhist priest."

To hear someone talked about my parents in such a gentle manner increased my guilt for what I had become.

"Rie," Miss Himura called me with a soft tone. "Do you remember what you once said to me? Back in high school, when I was worried about my future. You said that instead of worrying about what next, I should live my present properly first. You were nine years old when you said that. Back then, I focused on helping you study and realized I wanted to be a teacher. So now, wouldn't you share your problem with this old friend?"

"Please, Miss, don't remind me of what I used to be," I said, feeling the strange emotion within that's causing me pain. "Because the way I chose to live, God has already said no to it."

"Since when, Rie, that happened?"

I kept the answer to myself—Tokyo, where everything fell apart.

"Forgive me, Miss. But my bus is coming soon," I said, "I should hurry."

"Before you go, Rie." Miss Himura opened her bag, taking out a notebook. "I am not in the same faith as you, so I can't say much about God or your belief. But I know a few things about being human, that so long as one lives, one is bound to have many thoughts. Some thoughts make you happy when remembered. But some thoughts make you suffer. And unless you let those thoughts out, you will continue to suffer. If you can't speak those thoughts, please write them down."

I stared over the green cover of the plain notebook, sold at the school store for five cents. I accepted it with both hands, feeling my fingers dig into the surface. "You want me to write a diary?" I asked.

"Is that a problem?"

"I have never kept a diary," I said. "I don't think I could write more than a sentence a day. Since every day is the same."

"Then write those same things over and over again," said Miss Himura. "That way, you might notice what you missed the day before. If it helps, think of this as an extra assignment. Teacher's order."

"When would you like me to turn it in?"

She looked thoughtful while glancing down at my hands, still holding the notebook. "On your graduation day," she said. "I expect good work from you, Rie."

~ ~ ~

I took out the notebook, once at home. Its first blank page stared back at me. I wrote my name over the cover, out of obligation, before leaving it on my desk.

Aunt Risa had just started dinner. I offered to help her, then insisted on doing the task myself against her protests. Although her cooking was good and reminded me of my mother's, she was slow. She always measured the rice at least four times and would spend an hour figuring from which angle to scale a fish. If her cooking started at five, we wouldn't eat until ten.

She gave up eventually and let me handle the dinner.

It had been three years since I had come to live here. This house had once belonged to her husband. It had two floors, with doors so small, as if to fit the Meiji Era's average height. The living room had wallpaper, green twigs, and purple mukago patterns of my aunt's choosing. Aunt Risa had no children of her own and seemed happy to have me living with her. I remembered seeing her husband only a few times when I had been little. So most of my knowledge of him came from her. A good man he was, she would say. He rarely drank, always hard-working, always rushing off to work early and rushing back home in the evening.

He passed away only seven years after their marriage, I recalled.

I made a simple fish dish with takuan and for the sides. The miso came out reasonably well, and the rice was well cooked. We ate together at the table behind the kitchen, silently. I forced myself to swallow the rice, feeling her eyes from across the table.

Aunt Risa had never asked me why I had come home. But apparently, she had been talking to Miss Himura.

I had never wished to cause her to worry.

"Have you gotten used to school?" She asked.

"Yes, Aunt Risa," I answered.

My aunt's creases deepened beneath her eyes. Her smile reminded me of my mother, with the kindness behind them. "Rie, I don't hold it against you, you know," she said, "that you have returned home suddenly. True, it was unfortunate. But I am happy to have you around again. Still, I wonder, are you alright?"

"I am fine," I said, playing with the rice between my chopsticks. "I will work hard. I won't disappoint you again."

She shifted her position, like she wanted to say something, but didn't know how to put it into words. I finished my dinner, feeling no taste of it. Aunt Risa said she would do the dishes herself. So I was going back to my room when she caught up with me on the stairs.

"Rie, I once thought I shouldn't pry." She spoke, standing at the bottom. "I used to think that by giving time, you would return to being yourself eventually. But you seem to grow worse, so why don't you tell me—?"

Please, don't ask me.

"What happened in Tokyo?"

My palms hurt as I dug my nails into them. My legs shook. I turned my back toward her, slowly, and continued walking upstairs.

# Swimming Lesson 2

---

The train station platform looked flickering under the white neon light. The warmth of the August air and the smell of damp grass near the rails felt real, despite this being a dream. A person stood there with a worried expression.

I came out of hiding.

I woke up. The pain cut through my chest, and I bit into the blanket. My heart pounded as if trying to tear itself out. I waited, waited until it passed. Getting out of bed, I turned on the light, and my room appeared before me. My bed, its light blue sheet, the deep blue carpet, the framed Virgin Mary image was sitting in the corner of my desk, next to my parents' photo. The twelve-inch wooden cross hung on the wall above.

That night, the person waiting at the train station was gone. I was alone.

I gripped my pajamas, afraid to return to sleep. The sudden chill brought in the salty scent of the sea. I moved to close the window when my eyes stopped over the desk, where the notebook was left open.

I sat down and began to write.

The following day, I forced my eyes to stay awake until school was over. Collapsing on my desk, I felt the warmth on my back. The sun felt strong, although the light had already moved to the other side of the school. Calm wind soothed me. I tried to get a little more sleep while three of my classmates were hanging around the nearby desk.

"There's a new café opened on Uonomachi," one said. "The waiter is so cute. Let's go together."

The others sounded agreement before going silent.

"What say we invite Rie, too?" The second girl spoke. She used to sit next to me before the seat assignment, and I long forgot her name.

"Should we?" The first said.

"She helped me with the English homework," said another. "She translated the whole thing like a pro. She's alright."

"Let's ask her then," said the first.

"You do it," said the second, who brought up the café.

"Why won't you do it?"

I ignored their whispers. I didn't want to go. If I gave it enough time, they would give up. I wished my existence to remain just as it was, neither being seen nor talked to. Please don't notice me. Please, leave me alone.

I want you to learn by interacting with the people around you. This Swimming Association that I have put your name in. Please, consider it another step forward, to learn how to live."

"But—"

"Having friends, Rie," she continued. "Two are better than one because they have a better return for their labor. If either of them falls, one can help the other up."

"Is that Confucius, Miss?" I asked.

"No," she said, "it's from the Bible."

~ ~ ~

School was over, yet for the first time since returning from Tokyo, I felt like there was nowhere for me to go.

Yesterday, when that girl showed up with the tissue pack order, I was afraid that Miss Himura learned about what I had done, walking into the sea. But she had not mentioned it. So it was safe to assume that her pushing me into this Swimming Association was unrelated to the incident. That gave me some relief. Still, that girl had seen me. And the thought of me getting close to her gave me discomfort, like my sins were exposed to the world.

Would it be possible for me to pretend like nothing happen? At least, until Miss Himura gave up her wish?

I knew that would not be possible.

Miss Himura had put her hands together, leaning her face down, with her elbows on the table. She only did that when she was serious. Years ago, one of her friends had told me that she used to be very quiet and didn't speak her mind. So they taught her that pose to trigger her confidence whenever she was about to speak.

Once Miss Himura said something while in that pose, no one could change her mind.

There was no way for me to get out of this.

Aunt Risa had still not returned home. She might not be home until after six. She mentioned that we had run out of soy sauce, so she would likely go shopping. And her trips to the supermarket often resulted in her buying more than we needed. Once she went to buy salt and returned with a whole sack of garam masala, and she spent the next two days achieving a new curry recipe. Putting away my bag, I reached for the Bible I found last night, hidden away at the bottom of my traveling bag. I found the words Miss Himura had mentioned, *Ecclesiastes 4:9*.

I reread it over and over until pain began to throb in my chest. The pain transformed into a fear that I had never known existed within me.

The fear of being alone.

I rode off on my bike toward the direction I had been a few days ago. I wanted to get away, anywhere but home.

A narrow beach stretched before my eyes, empty as if all people had vanished from the world. Sand got in my shoes as I stumbled down the slopes. So I removed my footwear before proceeding toward the shoreline. The setting sun felt warm over my face, and its red tone set the sea ablaze like William Blake's illustration of hell. I paused over the compacted sands when the calm tide washed up toward my feet, wiping away my footprints—an extended shadow cast behind me.

Should I step forward, or should I go back?

I began to walk along the shoreline, watching the sun setting in the distance. Ever since I was little, never once had I doubted God's existence. The sand existed beneath my feet, the water, the air. Someone must have created them. Therefore God existed. Because we lived, thus God does also, a priest who taught math in my elementary school had said once. And I had believed, I had always believed.

Once, I even heard God speak to me.

But since then, nothing.

"Found you!" Ryoka was waving behind me.

I kept walking. Ryoka's voice was calling me, again, in the distance, then closer. I sped up.

"Hello!" She said in broken English. "May I talk with you, Miss Rie?"

I paused. "Why are you talking in English?"

She caught up. "Oh," she said, "you speak Japanese well."

"I am Japanese. And your accent is all wrong."

Ryoka was wearing a loose white shirt, with pants cut far above her knees. Her legs were revealed. I felt my face turning red, though I had seen this as the upcoming fashion in Tokyo. Around here, she would give the wrong impression.

"Ryoka, are you like—" I paused, "a friend for hire?"

"Is there a job like that?" She responded with a shrug. "Does it pay well? I always need a good part-time job."

"Are you stalking me?"

"I've come to see you," she said with a casual tone. "Please, won't you come just once for swimming practice?"

"No. Quit following me," I said. "I am not interested."

"Why not?"

"Can't you just leave me alone?" I raised my voice. "I can't. Go look for someone else!"

"Can't what? Swim, or spend time with me?" Her fox smile appeared as she spoke. "Swimming is a good way to pass the time, you know. You can take your mind off things. And at our school, you would feel like you had the whole pool to yourself. You could learn to swim better and wouldn't have to worry about drowning again."

I turned away but felt her hand grasping mine, just over the green ribbon.

"Please," she said, "it has to be you."

"No!" I jerked away.

"Like it or not, you are the official member of the Association," she said, stepping in front of me. "Look, Rie, this predicament is causing me as much trouble as you. So I understand your frustration. But there's nothing I can do either. So what do you say we make this easy. You come for one practice, and then we see how it goes."

I stepped aside, but Ryoka shifted into my path.

"Please, move," I said.

"No," Ryoka said, with her arms spread out.

"Ryoka, let me go."

She stood, blocking my escape.

"So if I am in this Association," I said, "how do I quit?"

A thoughtful expression came across her face for a while. "I can't let you," she said. "Unless there's grounds for it. If you and I compete, and you win, then you'd prove you no longer need me to train you. How does that sound? Tonight, seven sharp at the school pool. Win a race against me, and I will leave you alone."

"And if I say no?"

"Then I will come every day," she said, her smile twisted like a demon mask. "I will come to your class, to this beach, to everywhere you go. I can be very persistent. That's just who I am. You can push me away a thousand times, and I will come at you ten thousand times. Unless you beat me first, I will never let you go."

Her voice rose at the last sentence. I couldn't see her expression, as the sun had already set. Pretending to go right, I moved instead toward the left and passed her blockade.

"Your answer?" she shouted after me.

I nodded, only to get away. Collecting my shoes and socks, I walked up the slope toward where I had parked my bike. My heart pounded, so fast that my breath felt short.

"Seven sharp, at the school's pool tonight!" Her voice floated on the wind. "I will be waiting!"

When I was eight, I read the **Turandot**, the story about a Chinese Princess who gave three riddles to the men who proposed to her. And if they couldn't answer, she cut off their heads. Then came Calaf, the nomad Persian Prince who fell in love with her. He solved her riddles and married her, a happy ending. Ever since I finished that story, I grew obsessed over a porcelain doll on top of a cabinet in my father's office. Her skin looked pure white, eyes painted black, and lips pink. Her gown was painted blue like the sea.

I wanted to touch her. The urge filled me with an emotion, like love.

I found a stool, stepping on it, trying to reach for the doll. But my fingers slipped, and she fell. A single bang sounded across the room. And she lay shattered under me, her blue gown scattered like white ashes. Her face broken in two. Those painted eyes looked empty now when separated from her smile.

My breathing remained calm, like an icy surface undisturbed by wind.

Piece by piece, I picked it up, then sensed a prick. A giant red bead popped out of my thumb, then dropped over the white ash. I rubbed my fingers together and felt the pain, but no sadness. The doll I loved lay shattered on the floor. Yet, my heart was empty, as if my soul had turned pure white. And that's when I realized I could never be the Prince who solved the riddle. For I was the Princess whose finger pointed, and all died under her.

# Swimming Lesson 3

I dreamed of the train station in the flickering light and the person standing there. The clock above the ticket office said thirty-five minutes before seven. My hands felt the weight of the traveling bag as I watched from my hiding place. The person looked worried. I stepped into the light.

The figure spoke, but the coming train shrouded the words.

I woke up.

Then the pain struck. I clung to my blanket against the surrounding darkness. My breathing felt hot as my heart continued ramming against my chest. The sound of the wheels continued squealing in my head. The pain subsided eventually, leaving me drenched in sweat. Turning on the light, I spotted the clock on my desk. Twenty minutes before seven.

Aunt Risa caught me at the front door, putting my shoes on. I was still in my uniform, with my old sports bag hanging from one shoulder.

"Are you going out?" She asked.

"I forgot something at school," I lied.

"I will leave your food on the table," she said. This evening, she had returned home with four packages of pasta, so she would make seafood pasta with the canned fish in the cabinet. Noticing her wet hand, I knew she probably was still working on how much water she needed to boil the noodles.

If I stayed, I would end up causing her to worry again.

"I will be back as soon as I can," I said, then ran off. The bus arrived at ten minutes past seven. Despite better traffic at night, I arrived at school more than half an hour late. The security let me in after I wrote down my name and the purpose of my visit. Running past the home economic garden, I saw the outdoor pool from a distance, surrounded by a wired fence, with the light on inside.

Back in my previous school, I used to go for night practices. My last team had a long tradition of competing against school rivals. So all members and newcomers alike had worked hard to be promoted to regular competing members.

I had fast enough timing to be selected for the competition. But I left the school before the actual decision was made.

The front gate made a creaking noise when pushed. I couldn't open the door to the changing area. So I turned the corner and found myself before the twenty-five-meter pool, lit in turquoise color by underwater lights. Ryoka was sitting at the far corner, her legs in the water, her face turned in my direction. She caused large ripples when getting up. Water dripped down her legs as she approached.

"Yaa," she greeted me from a distance, raising one hand.

I focused on not seeing her legs.

"To start, get changed," she said. "Then, we will go over the basics."

"I already know the basics."

"Rie, your attitude," she bent her face closer, like trying to examine a strange-looking fish. "You don't look it, but you have an audacious spirit, don't you?"

"I just want to go home."

"To what, hide under your blanket?" She pointed to her head, making me self-conscious of my bed hair. "You will follow my instruction. I am the instructor, and you are the learner. Now go get changed."

I let out a huff, then moved toward the shower area inside the small building. My stomping felt loud over the marble floor. I found myself disliking Ryoka with her strange pale skin, her strange sunscreen scent, and her smile that looked forced. Miss Himura wanted me to make a friend, but that goodwill already smelled like a failure. The showers appeared under a flickering light when I turned on the switch. Six shower stalls total, the sinks with mirrors had traces of moss around the corners. I felt the nostalgic smell of chlorine. The path on the right side led toward the locker area. I put my bag in a locker, noticing the faded nametag stuck to its door.

This school probably had a swimming club once. Until, it got demoted to 'Association,' due to the small numbers of members. Just two now, according to Miss Himura's tissue pack.

My uniform was reek with sweat, so I went for a shower. Showering before and after practices had been my habit since the previous school, as no one would want to be teased for coming to class in the morning smelling of chlorine. After getting out, I patted a little water on my head in front of the mirror to get rid of the bed hair before putting my swim cap on. I noticed how my front bangs had become long.

Come to think of it, it felt strange that Ryoka had no chlorine smell on her.

Ryoka saw me coming out, and I continued to pass her toward the water. "Wait, you're supposed to warm up first!" Her voice sounded behind me.

But I'd already sprung off, feeling the water rupture around me in a deep burst. Once the white foam melted away, the sight of blue water came into my view. I pulled the water beneath my stomach and pushed forward with both legs. My eyes followed the black line on the tiles below. Reaching the other side, I did a flip turn and started swimming back. I felt my arms and legs moving like they used to. My speed remained as if I had never taken an absence.

Reemerging, I saw Ryoka standing above me, holding an expression I couldn't read.

"Let's race," I said. "If I win, I can quit, right?"

"Rie, there's no need to rush," she said, crouching by the pool. "Won't you relax a little? I can give you a pointer or two, how to do arm strokes better—"

"Just letting you know," I interrupted, "I was on the top lists for a promotion to a competing team."

Ryoka lowered her head, shadowing her expression. Her shoulders shook with laughter.

"What's funny?" My voice raised.

"Rie," she said while laughing, "what is with that crappy attitude? Aren't you a funny one?"

"Please, take this seriously," I spoke, feeling my temper warming up against the water. "I came tonight to quit this. But if you are going to keep treating it like a joke, then there's no point of me staying."

"Alright," she spoke before getting up. "Since you want it so much, I'll just have to show you your place, don't I?"

Ryoka took off her top, revealing the school swimsuit underneath. She kicked away her pants before tying her hair back in a ponytail. Without a word, she moved toward the other side where the jumping platforms were located. Ryoka was doing her warm-up routine when I got out of the water. She raised both arms close to her ears and stretched backward.

Then, she lifted each leg and pushed back, bending forty-five degrees forward, till her body looked like a Y shape. Her thin body allowed such outstanding flexibility that I could only watch.

"Four hundred meters, freestyle. Is that alright with you?" Ryoka asked, once she'd finished.

I nodded before stepping up to the platform. The pool felt small before my eyes, without lane ropes and only the black lines over the blue tiles as a guide. I pretended to adjust my goggles while observing Ryoka on the left. She had neither a cap nor goggles, which would put her at a disadvantage in the water. Fastening my goggles, I gave her a ready signal.

"On three," Ryoka called.

I clenched my toes over the tip of the platform to add power to the jumping start.

"Set!"

I bent downward, feeling the familiar silence before the race.

"Go!"

I plunged forward, feeling the water blast past my body before all noise disappeared, leaving only the steady rhythm of my heart. My arms and legs moved as if possessing a life of their own. I shifted aside to breathe, ten seconds before a flip turn, and bounced off the wall with my feet. Ahead of me, Ryoka had already increased the distance. Her slim body sped like an arrow.

I still had a half-lap left after Ryoka finished hers.

She was standing over the poolside when I touched the finish line. "Well played," she said while I was exhaling into the water. "You are not half bad. Now relax, I will come up with a practice routine—"

"One more time," I said.

The look of pity in Ryoka's eyes made me feel like I could hate swimming at that moment. Ryoka agreed to a second match, and we went through the same process again. We dove into the water at the same time, but by half the first lap, she'd pulled ahead. Ryoka beat me, this time leaving a whole lap behind after she finished.

"Please, one more time."

She beat me the third time.

The fourth time.

The fifth.

"Give up, Rie," Rie said, squatting above me while I caught my breath. "You have already lost five times, and five times you stay a member."

"One more time."

Ryoka sighed before she got up. "Don't overdo it, Rie," she said, "you will get hurt."

"Please," I said, blowing bubbles into the water.

"Rie."

"Didn't you hear me?" I spoke, with my eyes raised toward her. "One more time!"

Ryoka's expression in the blue light looked as if she was enjoying the situation, and her lips curled into a faint smile. The sight disappeared once I wiped the water off my face. I was still exhausted from the last race. My saliva tasted bitter with a chlorine taste mixed in. But my pride wouldn't allow me to stop. I wanted to get out of here.

I wanted to return to that beach.

The race started, and once in the water, Ryoka pulled ahead again. I chased after her, trying to close the distance. But she kept her lead throughout the first two laps. By the third lap, however, something felt strange. Like, you see something five times, and the sixth time felt off. We were halfway through the race, and I could still spot her ahead. Ryoka wasn't as fast as before.

Our distance continued to shrink.

A sudden cramp paralyzed me. I gaped, swallowing a full gulp of water. I struggled to stay above the surface, but the pain gripped my left leg and dragged me downward. My voice turned into white foam, and my strength faltered.

I felt death coming to take me away.

~ ~ ~

I vomited water. My stomach felt like a swirling mud pool—the sour acid taste of chlorine filled my mouth. My head hurt, trying to remember what happened. I saw Ryoka an arm's length away, leaning back with the support of her palms.

"You are a handful, you know that?" she said, "don't worry, I did CPR, the no kissing version. You haven't lost your chastity yet."

I felt my lips with the tips of my fingers.

"What? Would you rather have the mouth-to-mouth version?" Ryoka said, laughing. "In your dreams."

"Why did you save me?" I muttered.

"Save you or let you drown. Are those my only choices?"

I rubbed my mouth with the back of my hand, again and again. My sight turned blurry with nausea. I felt Ryoka's movement beside me, then saw a palm-sized tangerine handed over my way. "Eat," she said, "it will wash the bad taste from your mouth."

She dropped the fruit into my hands like she was afraid to let her fingertips touch me. She moved away toward the poolside and sat down, with her legs dipped into the water. Her back silhouetted in the pool's light. The musty tangerine scent made my stomach growl. I dug my fingers through the middle, peeling off its skin, and tried a piece.

Its sourness brought my eyes to fully awake.

"Sorry, was it too sour?" Ryoka asked, leaning back against her arms.

I swallowed while I chewed. My stomach turned calm. Though I wasn't fond of sour food, tangerine was an exception. In my old team, the senior members always stressed over how citrus fruits contained the alkalines necessary for sports. We also had the superstition of eating soba with lots of vinegar to gain strength. I licked off the sour juice from my palm, and my stamina was restored.

"Come sit with me," Ryoka said, observing me. "Please, if you pass out again, Miss Himura will kill me."

I left the fruit skin on the pool bench before moving cautiously closer to her. The turquoise surface stood still, without a sound. I felt as if the world had reduced to this small space of the twenty-five meters pool. Sitting beside Ryoka, I dipped my legs in the water, disrupting the surface into ripples.

"Now lie down on your back." Ryoka said, leaning back, "just do it. This is also training."

I leaned back, supported by my elbows. The hard ground against my back made it difficult to relax at first. I rested my head, and the sky came into view, exposing the few stars scattered there.

The pool in Tokyo was indoors, so such a sight was impossible.

My sense of discomfort vanished. I began to kick the water slowly and felt calm ripples brushing my legs.

I was swimming in the sky.

"I have wanted to ask," Ryoka spoke, "is it the fashion in Tokyo to wear a swimsuit underneath your clothes?"

"It's just a habit. So I won't take time changing before practice," I said. "You, too, do the same."

"My case was to not overspend on clothes that wouldn't even show," Ryoka said in a laughing tone, which then turned thoughtful. "I see. Good to know I haven't suddenly grown a fashion sense."

I continued watching the stars.

"Are you angry that I beat you?" Ryoka's voice came.

"You are better than me," I sighed. "It was a fair race."

"Would you like me to throw the match?" she asked.

"No," I said, "if I have to do something, I will do it with my own power."

I felt Ryoka's eyes toward me for a moment. "Then I won't," she said, "so you will always have a reason to come here."

"That won't do either," I said. "I don't plan to stick around."

"I heard shaving your legs could improve speed. I saw your leg hair earlier."

"I don't have hairy legs!" My voice raised as I felt my face turn red.

I didn't, did I?

"Just kidding," she said. "You looked so tense, so I felt like teasing you a bit. Sorry."

My head turned, seeing Ryoka's gaze fixed toward the sky with an intense look. I caught a whiff of her scent again, now that my nose got used to the chlorine smell. Mango? No, sweeter.

"I heard that you barely talk to anyone in your class," Ryoka's face turned toward mine. "What's that about, social phobia?"

"Things feel simpler that way," I answered while looking into her eyes. "Why do people even need to talk to one another, anyway? Life feels less complicated when I am left alone."

"Connecting with someone means you are abiding to fulfill others' expectations," said Ryoka. "You have to listen to stories you don't care to hear, laugh at jokes you don't think are funny. You can't do what you want, or like what you like, if it doesn't agree with everyone else. Those dilemmas make life complicated."

"Why me?" I asked, feeling a sudden warmness. "If you just wanted a new member, you could have asked anyone. Did Miss Himura ask you to do this?"

"Yes, partly," she said. "If I told you it had to be you, would that answer be good enough?"

"That's no answer at all."

"If you want a reason," she said, "it's because you can't swim. That's why you have to be here."

"I can swim," I said, "not the best, maybe, but not that bad."

"Then why did you nearly drown the other day?"

"That was—" I chose my words, "unintentional."

"Maybe that's a problem," said Ryoka. "Tonight, too, though you are good at technique, you weren't very good at swimming."

"What does that mean?"

"I can't put it into words myself," said Ryoka, "except that when I saw you earlier, I got the feeling like you wanted to drown."

I blinked.

"That's not true," I said before turning my face away. Ryoka got up, causing the water to stir, before moving toward the staff office. I sat up, watching the light turning on inside the office for less than a minute.

She returned, holding something in each hand.

"Look at this ball. And look at this rock." Ryoka said, sitting down, a tennis ball in her right hand and a black rock in her left. "Now watch."

She tossed the rock first toward the pool's middle. A giant plop sounded. It sank immediately and hit bottom with a resounding thud, leaving rings across the surface. "And now the ball," Ryoka tossed the second item over the same spot. A splash sounded upon the impact, the ball bounced over the surface, causing new ring patterns inside the previous ones. After a few seconds, the water finally calmed. The rock lay still at the bottom while the ball continued floating, pushed by an invisible force toward the pool's opposite side.

"Rocks sink. Balls float," said Ryoka. "You sank."

"What are you suggesting?"

"I once had a friend, who said that swimming lessons have three parts," she continued. "First, there must be trust. You have to trust me. Second, we must work on the instructor and learner relationship. It might take time, but it is necessary. The third is the final process of letting go. I will let you go the moment I am confident that you won't drown on your own."

I watched the tennis ball moving away, closer to the poolside.

Ryoka's legs moved in the water, causing a stir. "So what do you say?" she asked. "I am offering you a chance to learn how not to drown. My only condition is that you work hard and come for practice two times a day, six days a week. The morning practice starts at six, and the afterschool session continues until six. You can keep competing against me. Or you can just enjoy yourself, anything you want."

Six days a week here, I would have time for nothing else.

I couldn't return to that beach.

"Rie, there's nothing wrong in wanting to be alone," said Ryoka. "But don't you think it sucks, being alone all alone? It may be easy to say that you want to interact with no one. But to actually be left on your own can be a painful thing. If you would continue to come here, I offer to share with you this space. You can do whatever you like, and if you want lessons, I will offer them for as long as you need. So long as you won't drown on me. This is my swimming lesson."

Ryoka extended her hand, like the other day, when she'd first offered the handshake. The ball touched the poolside while the rock remained where it had been.

I remembered the sound of a coming train.

I slapped her hand away.

# SWIMMING LESSON 4

R yoka had come to my class on Thursday afternoon, my classmates told me. Ever since that night, I started arriving at school five minutes before the first period and left once school was dismissed. Then on Friday evening, the phone rang. I remained under the blanket, feeling my back soaked in sweat. Aunt Risa picked up the phone. She talked for about fifteen minutes before she came up to my room, saying Ryoka called.

"Please tell her I am busy," I said.

Aunt Risa had a puzzled look, watching me from the light at the entrance. Eventually, she closed the door, leaving me in the dark.

The same thing repeated on Saturday, I avoided her at school, at home, then I went to sleep.

The sound of the rails crushed beneath the train woke me up. My head felt as if split opened. I bit into the blanket until my headache, and the chest pain subsided.

Sunday.

My desk clock said two minutes before six when I got up. Aunt Risa usually slept till late when I didn't have to go to school. I went downstairs to the kitchen to make toast, eating it with strawberry jam. I left some on the table for her, so she wouldn't have to waste half an hour trying to plug the toaster in safely.

Returning to my room, I changed into a white dress for Mass and left for the bus.

I arrived at the church half an hour early, before the eight o'clock service, seeing its gate already opened. Sitting down at the bus station, I gazed across the street over the tall white building, with its roof in a triangle shape. The cross stood on top, looking tall under the sky. Strangely my chest felt heavy toward the sight. The church was built at the end of the war, I heard. Its external wall had undergone repainting at the same time I had left for Tokyo. However, that new color had already faded into a grey-white after only a year of withstanding winds and rains. I watched people arrive as they were going inside.

The clock under the triangle beam struck eight. And the gate closed.

I hadn't come here since I returned. Getting up, I crossed the street toward the closed gate and sat down on the ground, leaning against the door. The hymn came through its wooden surface. I leaned over to listen to the voices singing in unison. Through the corner of my eyes, my gaze caught sight of the angel on the stained glass window. She dressed in a red robe, her skin pale as porcelain, white wings on her back, bending down. She offered charity to children who reached for her hand. I had always thought the window looks in discord with the church, the excessive decoration provided by wealthy patrons. The singing finally stopped, and I heard the priest blessing his congregation before starting the story of Jonah, the man who had run away from God only to be swallowed by a fish.

I spotted Ryoka's wave from across the street before she came over.

"Yaa," she greeted me with a hand raised.

"Are you a Christian?" I asked.

"No, I'm an atheist," she said. "But there's no law saying non-believers can't come to church, right?"

Ryoka took a seat at the top of the steps, where light reflected off her hair, like a halo. She wore a red shirt so thin I could see the shape of her swimsuit underneath. And she still wore those short pants that exposed her legs. I sensed her usual sunscreen, the sweet fruit scent that today mixed with the burning smell of the sun.

"I have a joke to tell," Ryoka said, clearing her throat. "Do you know, there are only two types of nurses, glasses and no glasses nurses."

I waited.

"Strange, it sounded funny in my head," she said, scratching her neck.

"Maybe if you add the punchline?" I said.

Ryoka leaned back so that her long hair touched the ground behind her. "So you are religious," she said. "Do you think Santa Clause might be real, too?"

I pressed my ears to the door.

The ground felt warm over my legs, through the white dress, although I was sitting in the shadows. Ryoka, on the other hand, seemed to prefer her spot in the sunlight.

"I know a few things, you know," continued Ryoka. "I had a teacher in elementary who liked telling stories about a naked couple, who got kicked out after stealing an apple from their landlord."

"Is that another joke?"

"They're nice stories for children," she said. "I'm rather fond of the story of the carpenter's son turned sorcerer, using magic to heal and raise the dead."

"What are you doing here, Ryoka?" I said, wanting to know how she found me.

"I've come to see you," she said. "You never returned my call, even though I gave your aunt my contact number. She's so nice, beautiful too, from what I imagined. She even shared a cooking recipe. I called your home this morning since it's a nice day for swimming. And she told me that you would be here."

I continued pressing my ear to the door. The sermon was about the finish.

"Rie," said she, her face hung upside down, over her shoulders, "teach me how to pray."

The hymn started again on the other side.

"Please, Rie, evangelize this lost soul."

"First, you need stillness," I said, "then speak what you want, quietly."

"Like this?" Ryoka joined her hands, eyes closed, and began to move her lips. She reopened her eyes a few seconds later, with her head up toward the sky. "Nothing, no sugar candy raining. Could your God possibly be sleeping?"

"Why are you ridiculing my faith?"

"Does your God not like jokes? No wonder you are so afraid of him." Ryoka sat up. "Hey, just a question, what kind of relationship do you have with Miss Himura? She looked ready to go through a lot of trouble for you."

"I've known her since I was little," I spoke slowly to calm my temper. "She used to tutor me from time to time."

"I see." Her face turned away, gazing up directly to the light. "Doesn't that make you feel guilty, making her worry about you?"

"That's not your concern."

"Oh, have I just stepped on a landmine? My apology. Let's talk about something else, say, what do you want to do in the future?"

"What do you mean?" I asked.

"We will graduate in less than three years," she said. "We will have to think seriously about it, eventually. Have you ever thought about what you want to do after graduation?"

I felt like I'd heard that question recently. "Did Miss Himura send you to ask that?"

"Her? No, that was me. I am genuinely curious about what normal people think when someone asks them about the future. Even I've been asked once or twice. So it would help me if I could have some kind of reference."

I looked down over the white dress that covered my knees, no longer trying to hear the sermon.

"You don't happen to have some embarrassing dream that you can't tell anyone, do you?" Ryoka said with a laughing tone. "Like wanting to be an actress or musician."

"I can't even play piano," I said, "it's too hard."

"So, what is it then?"

"That's—" I paused, "not important."

"Rie, are you incapable of being honest?" Ryoka's gaze turned sharp as she spoke.

"I haven't lied," I said, lowering my eyes, "I just don't want to say it."

"Not saying is worse than lying," Ryoka said. "Come on, I am not going to laugh, whatever it is. Just tell me already."

"You won't laugh?" I raised my eyes.

"I won't. I won't." She raised one hand, "I swear to die if I ever laugh at your dream."

I felt my lips freeze, and my voice caught in my throat. My heart started to pound in a deep tone. I took a short inhale, then the answer came through my mouth in a stuttering whisper. "A S—"

"A, what?"

"A Sister," I said, "after graduating from high school, I planned to take a vow and join a convent. I wanted to become a Sister."

Ryoka's lower mouth dropped, for a second, before she turned the other way, covering her mouth. "I am not laughing," she continued to shake until she finally calmed down. "See? I am not laughing. Sister Rie, that fits you. And your parents are ok, letting their daughter join a religious order?"

"My parents died when I was thirteen," I said. "My mother was a Catholic, and I made her a promise then that I would devote myself to God. I told my aunt, and she sent me to a private Catholic school in Tokyo, so I could learn about the world before I made a final decision."

"And right now, are you still serious about becoming a nun?"

"I am not sure," I said, shaking my head, surprised at myself for feeling comfortable confessing this to Ryoka.

"Rie, could it be that your being religious is just your way of pretending that you are not on your own?" said Ryoka, moving closer into the shadow. "You lost your parents, a tragedy, and you have my condolences. But do you have to go as far as sacrificing yourself for an imaginary friend?"

I felt such a rush of anger, that my hand raised to strike.

"If you slap me, I will give you the other cheek," said Ryoka, "but did you notice that when you talked about your dream, you sounded like you have already abandoned it? You aren't sure anymore, are you? That's why you stay out here instead of going inside."

My hand dropped in the face of Ryoka's eyes, feeling as if she was staring into my soul.

"What happened, Rie?" she asked, "what kind of apple did you taste that made you feel so guilty?"

I braced my knees, averting my eyes.

"Did someone break your heart?"

I shuddered at the memory of the train station.

"So it's a heart matter," Ryoka said, sitting cross legs before me. She straightened her arms forward once while her eyes continued to fix over mine. "Did you fall in love with someone and become heartbroken in Tokyo?"

I hid my face between the knees. "No," I said, "that's not it."

Ryoka made a long sound in her throat. "Only heartbreak could make someone doubt their God," she said, "what else could it be?"

"You don't know anything," I said, with my face still down.

"I don't. But since you're not telling me anything, I can't help but keep guessing."

My teeth gnashed together, feeling Ryoka's presence less than an arm's length away, her smell like a sun.

"Or," her voice came, "may be you broke someone's heart?"

I raised my face.

"Is that why you stop believing in God, because you hurt someone?"

"Go away," I said, lowering my head. "Go away, please. Just go."

A grip took my wrist, and the sudden pull caused me to fall forward. The green ribbon fluttered before my eyes. I felt Ryoka's breath over my wrist. "You still keep this," said she. "I'm glad."

I tried to pull away. But Ryoka was stronger, despite her thin hand.

"Come back to the pool, Rie," she continued, letting go so suddenly that I stumbled back. "You don't really want to be here, do you?"

I turned around toward the gate and heard the hymn. I used to love the sound, but now it caused me pain. "I don't know what's happening to me," I said, turning my side away from Ryoka. "I used to think that as long as I had faith, everything would be fine. Even if everything else fell apart, so long as there is God, everything would be fine. God is good, I believed. God is kind, the priests taught me. And God always answers prayers. Sometimes God has to throw us into painful situations, but God will always save us in the end. I believed this, and so I prayed. But why? Why is it that when I pray now, all I hear is a silent no?"

I wiped the tear away before it flowed down my cheek.

Ryoka gripped my shoulders, forcing me to face her. "Rie, just tell me honestly," said she, "when you pray, has your God ever really talked back? Or are all those answers just made up by you?"

I glanced down.

"Rie, you may think me a devil for saying these things," she said, "but please, listen anyway. A God with any decency wouldn't throw his child down a painful path just so that he could save them. If a God like that existed, hell, I wouldn't feel guilty pissing on the cross. And here I am blaspheming your God, is lightning going to strike soon? What is he waiting for? Stupid God! Idiot, Useless God! Hey, where is my lightning? None! So what is this telling you? Except that God doesn't exist. He never has."

I felt what little strength I had left being sapped away.

"If your God told you to die, would you let yourself drown? Or are you going to swim and survive? Which is it?"

The hymn started behind the door, the tune that called its participants to accept the communion. I raised my eyes toward Ryoka. Her grip continued to hold my shoulder.

"I want you to live, Rie," she said.

At Ryoka's voice, the sound of the hymn faded away. The heaviness in my chest felt as if being lifted off. She offered me her hand, and I felt the unbearable urge to grasp onto it, afraid that should I refuse, it would disappear. I glanced at the stained glass angel, then at Ryoka. The two bore such an expression of kindness that I couldn't tell them apart. I finally took her hand. And my soul felt light like a feather when she pulled me to my feet.

I felt peace as Ryoka led me away.

~ ~ ~

We arrived at the pool before noon. The janitor had just finished the shower area and said he would return around three to add chlorine to the water, so we should leave before then. Ryoka led me in an exercise routine by stretching my arms and legs until I felt the tension ease up.

The cool water brought my senses to alert. I swam two laps and felt myself warming up inside.

"Not a bad start," Ryoka said, squatting down by the pool when I reemerged. She showed me her stopwatch. "Thirty-seven seconds is your current timing for fifty meters. Set the goal in your mind to go two seconds faster."

I exhaled into the water, then took a deep breath.

"When you breathe, picture your tension moving to your chest area, and relax your stomach," continued Ryoka. "Shift a little more to your side so that you can get more air in, ok? Left, right, left, right, it's all about keeping the balance. Now, let's try again when you're ready."

I pushed with my feet off the wall, swimming for the other side. I did a flip turn, returning, and felt the water brushing against me. Then I thought of the other day, swimming out into the sea. The opposite side of the pool suddenly felt far away. I dove downward, reaching out for the pool bottom. Its tile surface felt warm, reflecting the sunlight. The water surface looked transparent above me. I closed my eyes and braced my knees to stay still, like the black stone.

I felt Ryoka's gaze from above and heard her voice calling for me.

The surrounding water felt heavy. Nausea rushed through my head. I reopened my eyes and saw the water had turned red. A sharp pain gripped my legs. I gasped and tasted the chlorine, mixed with the saltiness of my blood. My head pounded as if trying to escape, and a veil of blackness clouded over my eyes. I felt strong vibrations breaking through the water as my arms and legs gave up the struggle.

Death felt close.

I woke up and felt my stomach squeeze, making me vomit the bitter and sour water. I felt a warm salty taste on my lips, and when I wiped my face, I saw blood mix with the water on my hand.

"Just lie down and keep your head raised," Ryoka's voice came. She was leaning next to me, her hair and the red top soaked wet, even her shoes. "Sorry, your God didn't save you. So I did."

A hot rage rushed up to my face. "I didn't ask you to save me!"

"Lie down, Rie, your nose is still bleeding—"

"I quit." I stood up, feeling a wave of nausea as I lurched sideways. My hand grasped the ribbon on my wrist in an attempt to tear it off.

"Please, don't do that." Ryoka's exhausted tone raised a little.

Its knot continued to elude me, and I ended up crying out in frustration. I started walking away. A grip seized my arm from behind.

"We had a deal," Ryoka said. "If you want to quit, beat me first."

"I'm not bound to you!" I screamed, the emotion clouding over my eyes. Then I saw Ryoka moving backward in slow motion, and the water burst where she fell. Confusion replaced the anger, and I found myself asking, why was Ryoka in the water? Then I saw my arms stretched out in front of me. And then pain, caused by guilt, was cutting through my chest.

I ran.

A force took my arm and pulled me around. "Where do you think you are going?" she said, water dripping down her face. "You're not done here!"

"Let me go!"

Her fingers dug into my arms, sending pain through my body. "Why won't you swim?!" She screamed. "Do you want to die that much? DO YOU!?"

I would never forget Ryoka's expression.

Her head fell over my chest. "I didn't sign up to watch you die, damn it," she said, more like to herself. "I want you to live. Is that too much to ask?"

"Why?" The sound came through my lips. Part of me was still making sense of what had happened. "I just pushed you into the pool."

Ryoka raised her wet face, and her small eyes gazed through her damp hair. "Rie, you may fight like a shark. But my skin is as thick as a whale. You will have to do more than push me into the water to get rid of me."

At her words, I felt my shoulders shake as laughter erupted from inside.

"Ah, this sucks. This sucks." Ryoka muttered as she let me go. She crouched over her feet, hands over her head. "I am just too bad at this. Why can't things go the way they should?"

I got the feeling that she forgot I was even there, for a moment.

"Let's go camping, Rie." She said suddenly, looking up as if the idea had always been in her mind, but she'd just now remembered it. "We need a change of pace. What do you say? Tonight, seven sharp at the beach. I will treat you to a picnic. After what you did, you better not bail on me."

I couldn't help but notice that Ryoka said 'seven sharp' a lot.

She waited for my answer.

The image of the beach came to me, its water, and the roaring waves, the place where I tried to disappear. It felt like fate that Ryoka should suggest we go there now.

I gave her a nod in reply.

# SWIMMING LESSON 5

I ate what Aunt Risa had cooked for lunch and finished on time for dinner. She was preparing the water to wash dishes when I told her of my plan to go out tonight.

"With a friend?" She asked from the kitchen, turning around with her arms still in the sink.

"Yes," I answered after a short pause, thinking she would show signs of concern. Instead, a look of relief came to her face.

"Have you started swimming again?"

"Yes," I said, realizing I must still smell of chlorine. "There's a Swimming Association at school that I go to sometimes."

From the time I had returned from Tokyo, Aunt Risa had always had a look on her face. As if she had taken notice of something about me, and it caused her to worry. Until this evening, when I spoke of Ryoka as a friend, and swimming again. Aunt Risa let out an expression like she just obtained a moon. "Are you still going to be home for tonight's dinner?" She asked after turning her head back to focus on the dishes. "Or should I wrap it away for breakfast?"

"I will be home," I answered after some hesitation. "I might be a little late."

The realization that I had just lied to her felt like nails in my stomach.

I struggled to finish my food and brought the plates to her, finding my eyes lowered to the ground. Aunt Risa finished the washing and moved toward the grocery bag to start dinner. At that moment, it crossed my mind to confess everything that had happened in Tokyo. She noticed me still in the kitchen. And I turned away in panic, stepping out of the room. My heart pounded, like after having run a long distance.

Ryoka was right. Not saying was worse than lying.

I took a quick bath and changed into a one-piece cotton blue dress. Aunt Risa had just finished peeling half a daikon and looked to be preparing ten samples of broth for tasting. She told me to ride my bike carefully. I left the house, glancing back toward the window to watch her one last time, setting up a pot with enthusiasm. I unlocked my bike and took off, my direction guided by a few street lights as I rode. The sun had set an hour ago. The salty scent felt strong in the air when I got closer to the destination, then came the sound of the sea roaring a short distance away, as if expecting me.

I arrived.

The vast sea looked black, lying beneath the night. I noticed a spot of flickering light on the beach that I realized was a campfire. And I saw Ryoka standing about twenty feet away, where the water reached her, before retreating. I looked on from a distance. The black water formed a wall that was rushing toward her. Its formation broke when it got closer and scattered into white foam. Ryoka remained unstirred as the water washed over her feet, then retreated once more to where it came.

I tiptoed closer to her. And she turned around as if she had eyes in the back of her head.

"Yaa there," she said in an energetic tone. "Come, I've got everything ready up at the campfire."

She walked past me before I could return the greeting. I followed her back toward where the fire stood and sat down. The sand felt warm next to the campfire and still held the smell of daylight. A yellow tent stood only a little distance away, looking large enough for two people to sleep comfortably. Ryoka squatted down, feeding another piece of wood to the fire. She wore a pink shirt tonight, with the short pants that I had gotten used to by now.

I averted my gaze to watch the fire consume the piece of wood, turning it into charcoal.

"Hungry?" she asked before climbing inside the tent. She came out soon with a lunch box which she offered me. The four board cutting sandwiches, stuffed to the brim with filling, gave out a strong scent of fish and cucumber. "I don't know what you like to eat. But no one should dislike fish and cucumber. Look, I even removed the crust."

"I don't mind the crust," I spoke in a mutter, holding one sandwich and biting into it. Its flavor burst in my mouth, the freshness of cucumber with the slight sourness of salad dressing, providing a rich taste to the regular canned fish. "This is very good."

"That's a relief," Ryoka said, holding up the box after I finished the first piece. "Go ahead, feel free to have the rest."

"Aren't you going to eat too?"

"I have already eaten," she said. "It makes me happy to see someone eat my food for once."

"This may be rude of me, but thank you for the food," I said before taking the second piece. Eating someone's food all by yourself was a quick way to lose a friend. But because of all that had happened since morning, I felt like eating anything offered to me now. "Do you cook a lot?"

"I have to since I live alone," said she.

"You're living by yourself?" I asked, "what about your parents?"

"What about my parents?"

"I mean, aren't you living with them?" I asked.

"Oh," Ryoka voiced, "no, they are too busy. So I got an apartment. It's not that bad since it's closer to school."

A high school girl living by herself in an apartment, I intended to ask further. But something in Ryoka's expression said that I should change the subject. "The tent," I said, "where did you get it?"

"I managed to borrow it out of the school's storage," said Ryoka, the fox smile returning. "Watch out, Rie, rumors say ghosts from the war haunt it."

"I am not afraid of ghosts," I said. "There are things in the world much scarier."

Ryoka looked my way. "I heard you were living in Tokyo. What was it like?"

"Please, Ryoka, I don't want to talk about that."

I ended up finishing the whole box of sandwiches. Ryoka put the box aside. I observed her calm expression, reflected in the light. Part of me felt she knew more about me than I had let her, yet she pretended not to. Despite my refusal to talk, she had not pushed the subject. As if I could continue keeping my secret until the end of my days, and she would maintain her distance. Her act of courtesy put me at comfort.

"Is there something on my face?" Ryoka asked.

I ducked my head. Ryoka got up, walking down toward the water to wash the lunchbox. My legs had lost feeling, staying in the same position, with my arms squeezed around them for the past ten minutes.

Ryoka returned.

"Do you know," she said, sitting down, "in the beginning, two hundred forty-eight thousand and five hundred fifty species were living in the sea. I read it in a book once. Humans were just one of those who chose to walk out of the water. Amazing, don't you think?"

I nodded.

"Do you like the sea, Rie?" Ryoka asked.

"Not really," I said.

"What's wrong with it?" Ryoka sounded surprised. "It has water for swimming and all."

"I don't dislike it, but I have never found a reason to like it, either," I said. "My mother used to say, though, that looking at the sea made her feel sad. I never asked her why."

Ryoka leaned back with her arms supporting her, and her back facing the campfire. Her legs stretched forward. A thoughtful expression came over her face. "Probably," she said, "because the sea tastes like tears."

My gaze turned toward her.

But she continued to look out toward the dark horizon, with an expression that I couldn't see from where I sat.

"What about you?" I broke the silence. "Do you like the sea?"

"A friend of mine did," she answered. "once, long ago."

"Is your friend no longer around?" I asked, using this chance to move over, and sit down beside her.

"You could say she's gone far away."

"Like, overseas?" I asked.

"Well, she's a half American, now that you mention it." Ryoka paused. "But no, somewhere farther than that."

Ryoka's tone changed, strangely colder. Her face turned my way, bearing an intense look.

"What is it?" I asked.

Ryoka's hand raised, her fingertips brushed over my bangs. "Do you cut your own hair?" She asked.

I nodded.

"You aren't doing a good job," she said. "You cut this side too much, and your face looks like it's falling off to the right."

I covered my forehead with one hand, as Ryoka explained. "Aunt Risa usually cut my hair," I said. "But I haven't asked her lately."

"I could cut it if you like," her voice sounded excited. "I cut my hair all the time. Can I?"

As soon as I agreed, Ryoka went inside the tent. She came out with scissors, which made me wonder if she always carried those. "I can trust you, right?" My voice grew stern. "Please, don't let my eyebrows show."

"Do you not like your brows?" she said, "they're the perfect shape."

"Just trim a little around my bangs, please."

"Trust me," she said, snapping the scissors. "So long as you don't move too much, I promise you won't end up like a Buddhist nun."

I moved close to the fire, where Ryoka pointed me to, feeling my head over my left arm.

She knelt before me and held my bangs between her fingers. "Close your eyes," she said, "you don't want hair to get in."

I let my eyes close, feeling Ryoka moving closer. The clipping noises caused my brows to knit together until I felt her fingers combing down the bangs.

"Done," said her voice.

I opened one eye first while Ryoka was still brushing off the excess hair with her fingers, a look of satisfaction on her face.

"Your hair is long in the back, too," she said. "It just needs a little trimming. Can I?"

I made a sound from my throat, then a slight nod. Ryoka got up to brush sand off her legs before getting down on her knees behind me. My body jolted at the touch of her fingers.

"Sorry, I've got cold hands," she said. "It will take a moment to get used to."

"It's nice," I said. Ryoka's hand felt strangely cold but didn't cause me to startle. I just got ticklish around the neck. "Your hands feel nice and cool."

Her hands paused for a moment before they resumed the work of gathering my hair together. I closed my eyes, breathing comfortably while her fingers were running down my neck. The scissors continued their work with quick, efficient sounds. I became aware of myself sitting still for a while now. So I stretched my neck a little to get rid of the ache. "Don't be scared," Ryoka said, mistaking my movement for tension. "I am quite proud of myself, you know, never having to waste money for a haircut. I even tried getting a part-time job as a hairdresser since it pays better than my current job. But they wouldn't hire anyone without a high school degree."

"You do part-time jobs? But I thought it was against the school's rules."

"If you get a teacher's permission, then it's fine," she said, running her fingers through before resuming her work. "I thought about going to Tokyo one day since lots of people say you can earn better money. But I heard that it is a scary place, with scary people. Is that true?"

"I don't know," I said. "I spent most of my time between the school and the dormitory. I only went shopping in Mitsukoshi when someone invited me."

"Did you get this dress from over there too?" Ryoka asked about my blue one-piece dress.

"This one was handmade, actually," I said. "I used to help out around the handicraft club. Its president liked to go out surveying new clothes, and then she bought materials to make them with different colors. She gave me this one as a thank you for being her mannequin."

"What kind of duty was that?"

"I stood very still for her while she tried different colored garments on me, let her stick pins in me like a pin cushion. Sometimes it lasted a whole hour, sometimes three."

"Sounds like you earned your dress," she said. "And did you learn things like sewing, too?"

"I helped out with small stitching sometimes," I said. "The president said once that I could sew so fast, I should try becoming a surgeon."

"Sister Rie, the surgeon," Ryoka said with a laugh. "Watch out. You might kill someone."

"I think I hurt someone already. Unintentionally, but I still did."

"You mean that boy who got heartbroken by you?" Ryoka's hands became slower before gathering part of my hair up as she continued trimming.

"It's my fault."

"Heartbreak is painful, to both those who get their hearts broken, and the one who broke it," she said. "That is just my thinking, though. After all, I've only known you for a week. What happened between you and that boy, anyway?"

My mouth opened, but something within me snapped shut.

"Done!" Ryoka said, running her fingers through my hair one last time. "I must say, I am very proud of myself now. Next time you see yourself in the mirror, I am expecting lots of thanks."

The crackling of the fire filled the silence, followed by the distant sound of the roaring sea. Ryoka put away her scissors and let my hair fall across my shoulders. She blew over my back and gave a quick slap to brush off the excess hair.

My feet had turned numb, my eyes down between my knees while listening to the waves rumbling in the distance.

"Rie, listen to me." Ryoka knelt before me, holding my hands in hers, as the green ribbon fluttered in the wind. "I don't know what happened in your past, but you are no longer there. So you hurt someone, but that's over. Your past is gone, Rie, forever. You are here, and I know some people are happy, knowing that you are safe and still around. I might sound arrogant for saying this, but you even have me now. So let's not cry anymore. Let bygones be bygones. Let's live on, won't you?"

I gazed over her faint smile, dancing in the light. Her eyes awaited my answer. "It may be easy for you to say anything you want, Ryoka," I responded. "But you have never been hurt, nor hurt anyone, have you?"

Ryoka's grip became fierce, before gradually loosening.

My gaze avoided her until she stood up. Ryoka was walking away toward the water to wash her scissors. Through the corner of my eyes, I noticed the fire begin to weaken. And the salty scent grew strong in the air, raising within me a feeling of cold despair. I closed my eyes, attempting to pray. But even praying now caused me pain. I reopened my eyes and felt the world was darker than before.

The waves sounded in the distance, like a coming train.

# SWIMMING LESSON 6

---

This was a dream, I knew, and yet it felt as if time had stopped. The train station flickered in the white neon light. The smell of the grass near the rails felt sweet amidst the summer night. I watched the person standing there. The clock above the ticket office said five minutes from seven. I gripped the handle of my traveling bag before stepping into the light.

"You came," those lips moved before the coming train enfolded away the voice.

I felt the ground shaking beneath my feet, and my hesitation disappeared under the clashing metal sound—the silence resumed. The air vibrated with the sound of rumbling engines. The train's door opened, and my feet moved forward.

We got on the train together.

The scenery rushed past my eyes outside the window. I had slept, and now it was morning. I saw few buildings outside the window, only the greenery, and the endless sky—my companion, still asleep with exhaustion, was at the window seat next to mine.

I leaned my head over that broad shoulder, closing my eyes, a peaceful smile on my lips. Nothing else in the world mattered, but this moment, my journey with the person I loved, toward our unknown future.

"Leave."

My eyes opened, as the voice filled my ears. The vibration rushed through my body as if struck by lightning.

"Leave," the voice spoke, "and never look back."

I sat up. An attendant came closer with a tray, offering food and drinks for sale. Some passengers were waking up. I struggled to breathe—the smell of air conditioning above me and the coolness covered my face. The voice, too, felt real. The prickling sense over my skin hurt like a thousand needles piercing my pores.

A voice stirred from the window seat.

I looked at my companion and felt warm tears gather at the corner of my eyes. The scenery outside the window looked as if being mixed with a heavy tone of blue. The voice had gone silent now, but its impact continued. I felt like a vase, with its content emptied and replaced by different emotions. The familiar feeling I used to experience while praying in church. And this new pressure continued to increase. I must obey, lest I would break to pieces.

The train stopped.

My hands clutched over the handle of my bag. I slipped through the door and continued to move away from the train. Despite being only a few hours into the morning, the sunlight felt strong. I felt it showering heat upon me, like a rain of fire. And I remembered the Bible passage of Lot and his family fleeing from Sodom. God had told them never to look back at the burning city. But Lot's wife had looked, and she got turned into a pillar of salt.

I looked back at the window.

The train door closed, the rumbling engine shook the air. The light reflected off the window, blinding me for a short second. I felt as if something within me had died. Time felt as if frozen, and the train departed. And my senses ceased.

I woke up. The stabbing pain forced my eyes to shut. With an inhale, I reopened them and saw the yellow ceiling above me. It was a dream. It was a dream, I whispered to myself while clutching my chest, fighting against my own heart, that continued to cause me pain. I turned toward the side and attempted to exhale before taking in another deep breath. The salty scent then made my body remember where I was. The pain finally began to calm. I closed my eyes once more, and when I finally got up, my eyes got used to the dark.

Ryoka was sleeping on her side, facing away from my feet. Her one hand gripped the thin blanket. She shivered like she, too, was having a bad dream.

I unzipped the tent and got out, not bothering to put shoes on.

The campfire had only black charcoals left, cold, with a burning scent lingering in the air. The sea looked closer now. Its water swept over the shore before retreating, leaving the ground flattened. My feet paused when my eyes came face to face with the rumbling sea. Its black wall rose in the short distance and came crashing down as its formation broke.

I closed my eyes, feeling the cool sensation wash over where I stood. Before the water reversed, grains of sand brushed against my toes. How ironic that the face of death could feel this peaceful. Amidst this darkness, I brought my heart to silence. And I tried once again to pray.

God, please God, speak to me again as you did that day. I had not wanted to leave. So why did you tell me to? I've never asked for anything selfish, but to be happy with the one I love.

So why did you say no?

"It's a bit late to go swimming."

I opened my eyes, feeling Ryoka behind me in the darkness.

"Rie, come back," Ryoka's voice said. "It's dangerous when the water is rising."

"Please, Ryoka, leave me be," I said.

"So you can't sleep either," she said, stepping over to my right side. "It gets cold during the night, doesn't it? So why don't we go back? Try getting the fire started. Let's stay up all night and talk. What do you say? Anything you want to talk about, I will listen."

"Please, Ryoka, don't make me say anymore."

Ryoka went silent, but I could feel her eyes toward me. She came before me, then, took my left hand. Her gaze focused on the ribbon. "Don't do it," she said, "the thing you are trying to do."

I tried pulling away. Ryoka raised her face, a glimmering look in her eyes.

"Don't go," she said, "please."

I felt something run down my cheek. It tasted salty, around the corner of my lips, like the sea.

"Let me tell you something about drowning, Rie," she continued, "you get surrounded by water. Your head feels so blank that you can't think, and your feet no longer feel the bottom. Then, your instincts kick in. You turn around. But the shore looks far away. You start to panic, your arms and legs begin struggling, but the current continues to sweep you aside. You get tired, and your body can't keep up. It becomes hard to breathe with water in your mouth. You can't even scream anymore. Finally, the water pulls you down. According to a book I read, in the sea, you probably would last only forty seconds. Once you can no longer hold your breath, the water floods down your throat and fills your stomach. Your lungs bloat up like balloons, and it hurts. Your head screams in pain until boom. You pass out in shock. And you die."

My hand pulled free. I stepped backward, away from the water.

"Rie, you may not have said much about yourself. But I like to think myself good at reading people, you know." Ryoka said, then after a pause, continued, "you and that boy were eloping together, weren't you?"

I looked downward.

Ryoka's gaze caused my toes to hunch over, and I felt the sharp sand between my toes. She guessed right, mostly.

"Why?" Ryoka asked. "Please, Rie, help me understand. What is the reason for leaving someone you love behind?"

"I was told to leave," I answered.

"By who?"

It took all my strength to raise my face and look past Ryoka's shoulder toward the horizon. "God," I told her.

Ryoka's expression blurred through my tears.

"Do you understand what it feels like," I continued, "when something you put faith in suddenly turns against you? It feels like the life I have lived until now was a lie. I tried to return to the life I was used to after returning here. But something's changed, and I don't know what. It's like the sky that's always been blue, now has dark clouds only. It's like planting flower seeds, and seeing weeds grow out in their place. It's like, living in a town with my favorite place just around the corner. But now, when I turn the same corner, nothing is there. It's like I believed that someone would never hurt me. Then one day, they did. Why must I get hurt? What have I done wrong? It's not fair. And before I realize it, anger fills me. I become filled with this ugly feeling. But against whom? Whom should I get angry to? I can't bear myself feeling this way. I can't stand living in this body, with this ugly feeling spilling out of me. My head and everything about my life, hurt. I can't pray. I can't sleep. I can't go to church. I can't go outside without feeling like being burnt inside out. And I just want all these things to stop. I just want to—"

"To die?" Ryoka finished my sentence in a whisper.

Sounds disappeared in the rumbling sea.

Ryoka sighed, moving closer, her hands gripping my shoulders. "I think I'm beginning to understand you a little bit," she said. "You are a selfish person, aren't you?"

I shivered. Ryoka's hand felt cold.

"You want the world to be as you wish, don't you?" she said. "And you want God to give that to you? You can't, you know. No one in this world can have everything they want, and you are no different."

I felt something within me that had been dead, return to life when Ryoka let go of me.

"Rie," Ryoka spoke. Something changed in her gaze. "I don't care what reason your God had for saying no to you. But if you die, it's all over. You will be dead, Rie, forever."

"But," I said. "If I can't believe in God. What reason have I left to live?"

The glittering light in Ryoka's eyes looked like a religious image of a saint, which I used to have as a prayer card when little. The expression of calm, yet, with passion, as the saint gazed up to heaven. "If you can't find a reason to live." She said, "then let me be your reason. For I want, more than anything, that you live."

The water retreated from under my feet, and I felt the presence of death backing away.

"Why?" I asked.

A shadow came across her face as she lowered her eyes. Seconds passed as she searched for a response. She took my wrist in both hands and lifted it up. The ribbon fluttered in the wind. "I want you to live, isn't that a good enough reason?" she said. "Live, live, and live on. Until one day, when you look back, you can tell yourself that it was all worth it. Who knows what will happen in your future? What kind of people will come across your path? Life can take a surprise turn beyond your imagination. So long as you keep living, something or someone will present you with a chance that you don't have today, a chance to be happy again. So live on, Rie, stubbornly, until you learn what value life has. And once you can do that, then—"

The sea expelled a roar that cut part of her sentence.

"Please—too."

Once, my parents took me to visit our relatives in Kyushu. The place was close to the beach. So they brought me a beach dress, a peach-orange dress with flower embroidery around the shoulder. I put it on immediately and let everyone look. I thanked my parents, said I loved the dress, with a smile. Then that night, when everyone went to sleep, I took scissors to the bathroom and made a hole in its back.

When I finally looked up, the face in the mirror looked like something that had the mask of a human on. And the mask slipped off.

I forced a smile, that concealed my real face.

"What happened to the dress?" My cousin asked when I came down the following day before he snapped a picture.

"Don't tease her too much," said the girl, who came out suddenly from behind. "If you hit on her too much, I might get jealous."

I let her pull me the other way. The camera sound snapped one more time before we finally got far away from the house. She then took me by the hand, and I followed her while looking downward. Her full legs were revealed under the short pants that cut far above her knees. And her cantaloupe scent sunscreen smelled strong under the sun.

We reached the beach.

"So you didn't like the dress," she said in a whisper.

"I hate the color orange," I said while looking out at sea. The blue surface reflected the sunlight, like a cold glass surface.

"Tell me then, what to get you for your birthday?" She asked with a genuine smile.

"Give me a sunscreen that smells like yours," I said.

She looked at me with her eyes narrowed. Then a tiny laugh came through her lips, and she opened her arms. "I'm here, come."

I went, and she embraced me.

"Anything you need," she said, next to my eyes, "you know I love you, right? No matter what you are."

Even though we were the same age and height, somehow, I always felt that she was taller. There was a time when I thought that the reason she had everything I lacked, was because somehow she had stolen them from me. And now, all warmth and kindness condensed within her. When she held me like this, I felt as if there existed a hint of my humanity somewhere within reach, like a spark from whetstones that only needed something to burn.

"Got you!" My cousin's voice was heard for a second. Then the warmth disappeared.

"Takeru, stop!" She laughed as he carried her off toward the water and threw her in. Her smile from a distance looked like a puppy barking happily, playing with her master. He took out his camera and began snapping pictures.

The two of them had been dating for a while now. I found out for myself not long ago.

They had been together since little, my cousin and her. And when their relationship had come to the knowledge of the adults, all had nodded in approval. He was in his last year of high school, being a President of the Photography Club, and already got accepted to Toei University to pursue art studies. They were perfect for each other, like a house and a light, as the grown-ups said. Looking at them from a distance, I felt, at that moment, the spark of my emotion finally finding its fuel. And it burned.

The next thing I knew, I opened my eyes and saw her face above me. My cousin stood nearby. The sand felt cold beneath my back.

"Could be the heat," he said.

"Can you get us some water?" She said.

He ran off, leaving us alone.

She looked, until he went some distance, then her face returned toward me. Her eyes looked like two pieces of clear marble in the shadow. "You faked that, didn't you?" She said.

I glared back at her.

What did my face look like in her eyes, I wondered.

"Please never let me go like that again," I said.

She gave me a smile like one would to an abandoned pet. "Grow up," she said. "We weren't born joined at the hip, you know. And I can't be with you forever."

My cousin returned just then, and she got up, leaving me for him.

I closed my eyes, then inhaled. And I felt something within me take form, like fire, but with a firmness-like sensation, same as what I had felt last night when holding the scissors.

Don't take what's mine.

In my imagination, I shredded my cousin to pieces.

———◇———

# Swimming Lesson 7

---

Ryoka had saved me. Looking back at that moment of my life, I wished it marked 'The End' of my story.

But such an ending was never meant to be.

Eight months passed, following that night at the beach. My second high school year started in April, and I worked to keep up my grades up while attending Ryoka's swimming practices. By the time July began, the weather had turned so warm that the water no longer felt too cold for morning practice. Ryoka had set a goal for me to swim two seconds faster for the fifty-meter range. The other day we had gone over my swimming posture. I needed to swim more to my side, Ryoka said. Unless I did so, my timing would never improve.

But I didn't care about swimming, better or faster.

I just wanted a reason to spend time with her.

The clock on my desk said six when I woke up on Sunday. The weather forecast predicted no rain. I looked out the window and saw the sun was already up, over the cloudless sky. I still had an hour left before my appointment with Ryoka. Instead of swimming practice, we would go shopping together in the morning, then catch a movie in the afternoon. A week earlier, I had found two tickets in the mailbox for a scheduled feature of the *Death in Venice* at the Morimachi local theatre. I thought Aunt Risa might have won them from the newspaper lotteries that she kept entering. Even thought she said she knew nothing about it.

So I had invited Ryoka, since we never did anything together apart from the swimming lessons. When I asked her, she agreed upon hearing the movie's title.

I pushed aside my white dress and picked another out of the closet. The cross over the wall caught my glance for a moment. I turned my back toward it, away from my desk, where the framed image of the Virgin Mary lay facing down.

I hadn't gone to mass since last year.

I no longer read the Bible.

I no longer prayed.

I no longer had the dreams.

I ate a tangerine for breakfast before running to catch the bus. Sitting down near the back, I glanced outside the window when the bus finally took off—the sweet-sour taste of the fruit still filled my mouth. The sun hung over the pale blue sky, feeling warm on my face. But beneath my chest, I felt the icy cold.

Ryoka had promised to be my reason to live.

Once I remembered this, the emptiness within me became full to the brim.

I got out at the Seafood Market, where Ryoka had suggested we meet. She needed to buy something, she had said. I looked at my wristwatch, just above the green ribbon. I arrived early, watching another bus come across the street, filled with office workers and those who worked on weekends.

As I was about to sit down, I spotted Ryoka among the crowd.

For some time now, I'd had the feeling that even if a thousand people were crowding together, I would still be able to spot Ryoka right away. I had never understood why until now. Ryoka had always had this presence, like when you gazed at a billboard painted orange, and you noticed one white spot of paint. It wasn't even noticeable until you knew it was there. Then, you kept looking at it, no matter how hard you tried to look away. The billboard, thus, transformed from a plain orange surface into an exhibition of the white spot in its corner. From across the road, I could see Ryoka was even starting to draw the eyes of bystanders. She was wearing a thin yellow and white top with a vertical pattern that emphasized her slim form. Her long legs were exposed under the short pants, like a doll wearing the wrong clothes.

She leaned back against a pole as if running out of energy suddenly. Her pale face bore an exhausted expression.

I crossed the road to her. "Ryoka," I called out. "Are you alright? You look as pale as a ghost."

"Oh, Rie," Ryoka said before lifting her hand. "I've been feeling a bit dizzy this morning."

"Are you sick?"

"No, I will be fine later, probably," she said. "This happens from time to time."

I felt her forehead to check the temperature. She looked ready to pass out. "Ryoka, have you eaten properly?" I asked, "sleeping enough hours?"

"I have been on night shifts at my job for the last three days," she said, "and I had a cucumber for breakfast yesterday."

"Are you saying you haven't eaten since yesterday?" My voice raised.

Ryoka's head dropped over my shoulder. I sensed her sunscreen extra strong today. "I will take you home," I said, "tell me the address. Or your phone number, I can call your parents."

"No, no home, please. I finally got out of there."

"Ryoka, you aren't making sense," I said, then remembered that Ryoka lived alone.

"Just take me somewhere," she said, "anywhere but here. I will get better once I sit down, please."

Another bus arrived. More people stood around now, and more eyes were looking our way. Ryoka struggled to even stand. "I see, somewhere to sit, right?" I said, looking around. "I have an idea. Follow me. I will get you medicine."

I gripped her wrist and started walking, feeling Ryoka's light footsteps behind me. The market area began buzzing with people who continued to arrive. The air filled with smells of fresh fish and recently caught prawns. Large king crabs and purple-shaded octopuses were put on display, covered with ice. I stopped before the place across from the vegetable stalls, where I saw a light on inside. An old-fashioned wooden sign with faded ink calligraphy stood next to the entrance.

An *Open* sign hung above the door.

I pushed aside the Noren curtains and felt the warmth inside the wooden structure. The soft aroma of boiled soup warmed the air. The old man and his wife raised a 'welcome' in unison from inside the kitchen as I led Ryoka toward the empty seats at the bar.

"One ramen, please," I ordered, "light soup, thin noodles, extra garlic, extra egg. And one extra rice. What about you, Ryoka?"

Ryoka looked at the menu for over five seconds before whispering, "the same, but no rice."

So I ordered another bowl for her.

"This," Ryoka spoke, "is medicine?"

"It's the only place that opens from five in the morning," I said. "The owner came from Shizuoka. They eat ramen for breakfast over there. I eat here whenever I help my aunt shop for seafood. You have to eat, Ryoka. You look ridiculous, like a sketch of some horror cartoon walking out of the page."

"I guess it wouldn't be so bad to eat out for once," Ryoka spoke in a tone of surrender. "I got paid last night, so let me cover the bills."

"What are you talking about?" I said. "I'll treat you."

"Please, Rie. Let me keep some pride. After I had to rely on you for taking me here. Let me thank you properly at least."

The radio inside the kitchen started playing Mari Amachi's *Koiwa Mizuiro*. Then, the weather forecasted that today's sky might get cloudy in the late morning. Another customer came in just then, a worn-out-looking salaryman who might have just finished a night shift. I waited until he finished ordering and left to take the seat. Then I took a plastic mug from the end of the bar, pouring two cups of tea. Its white smoke smelled like what they served in a Chinese restaurant. I offered one cup to Ryoka, who sat still, looking like she'd been led into another world. Then I filled a small container with spicy beansprouts and took two disposable chopsticks, giving one pair to Ryoka.

"The tea and beansprouts are free," I said, placing the sprouts between us. "Can you eat spicy food?"

"I like spicy things," she said, "and really any hot cooked food."

Ryoka broke apart her chopsticks unevenly and took a few sprouts into her mouth. A pink blush glowed over her paled cheeks before she blew a little air over her fingertips. My bowl of rice arrived just then. I put some sprouts over it and ate a small mouthful.

"Won't it make you full, eating rice before the ramen?" Ryoka asked.

"I always like to have rice when eating noodles," I said. "Don't you think ramen is just a side dish? With beansprouts, it's also delicious. Here, try some."

I offered the bowl of rice to Ryoka. She took a bit with her chopsticks before adding the sprouts into her mouth. Her eyes grew wide. I urged her to eat more.

A gray cat came toward us from outside before she could do so. It stopped, peering up at me first, then Ryoka.

Then, it jumped over onto her lap.

Ryoka took some of the rice, blew a little, and put it in her hand to feed it. "Thanks for being with me," said she.

"Of course it likes you," I said, glaring at the cat. "You just gave it food."

"I am talking to you." Ryoka raised her head.

I felt my face blush. So I took a sip of the still-hot tea. The grey cat turned my way, its yellow eyes unblinking. The owner's wife noticed and said in a laughing tone that the cat always came around at this time. And their business thrived as if the cat had brought them good fortune. Ryoka added more rice and let the cat munch out of her hand.

"Why did you want to come here, and so early in the morning?" I changed the subject, "you said you needed to buy something?"

"I just wanted to have a meal with you," she said.

"Did you?" I asked in surprise.

"Oh, sorry. I was talking to the cat this time," Ryoka looked up. "What did you say?"

The cat sat up and jumped off Ryoka's lap. It turned around toward me before walking off through the gate with its head held high. Ryoka wiped her hand with the disposable paper offered at the bar. "I want to buy some sugar," she said as if my earlier question had just reached me. "The convenience store near my home ran out yesterday."

I looked toward the gate. The smell of fish faded away after the owner lighted a stick of cinnamon incense. Sugar, here? I wondered if Ryoka might not go grocery shopping often.

"Rie," Ryoka spoke, "have you been happy?"

I didn't understand her sudden question.

"Do you still have the dreams?" She asked.

I glared downward at my chopsticks, paused halfway toward the bean sprouts before retreating. "Not anymore," I answered, wondering why she'd raised the subject. "Not since last year."

"Does that mean you got over it? You and that person, I mean."

"I haven't thought much about it these days," I said, seeing Ryoka glance my way, her brows closed together with a skeptical expression.

"So, everything is fine?" She asked, "I was worried when you suddenly said you wanted to hang out. I thought something might have happened."

"That wasn't it," I said, half-relieved. "No, nothing happened to me. I just wanted to see you properly, for once."

"But we already hang out, six days a week, at the pool."

"That's not what I mean," I said. "We've known each other for months and still haven't even had lunch together. All I ever do is show up for practice and leave once it's done. You're always helping me. And I just wanted to do something for you in return, by spending more time with you."

Ryoka looked the other way with a sigh. "Ah, this won't work."

A glass broke in the kitchen. Ryoka's low voice sounded like the whisper amidst the chaos. And when the air turned calm once more, the only thing I noticed was that my tea had gone cold.

Ryoka took another mouthful of beansprouts before putting down the chopsticks and turning my way. She reached her finger across my back. "Your hair is getting long again, and your bangs are crooked," she said with her usual smile, "you are hopeless, Rie."

"It's your fault for not cutting them again," I responded.

Somehow, it felt like a very long time ago since I last saw Ryoka's smile.

Our food arrived, two bowls of piping hot ramen in a light-colored soup, with dried sardines for topping, kelp, and boiled eggs on the side. I added vinegar in mine before trying the soup with a spoon. Ryoka, on the other hand, took a bottle of cayenne peppers and sprinkled an amount over her noodles.

"Can I have some?" I asked.

Ryoka passed me the bottle before tasting a spoonful. Her face blushed in satisfaction.

I shook the bottle over my bowl, but nothing happened.

"What's wrong?" She asked, noticing my struggle.

"It's not coming out," I said.

"Let me see." Ryoka took the bottle and shook it before peering down the holes. "The peppers are stuck together inside. We just have to knock it hard."

She turned the bottle upside down over my bowl and banged its bottom. The cover made a slight cracking noise before plopping out a pile of red powder. "Sorry!" Ryoka cried after gaping. "Spoon, spoon, hurry!"

I got to my spoon first and began working to skim out the top—Ryoka managed to take a little more out. But the powder had already mixed with the soup around the bottom.

"I'm sorry, Rie. I'm sorry."

The tea-colored soup turned a deep red.

"Let's switch. I will eat this myself." Ryoka said, dropping her spoon. She took my bowl and gave me hers. Using the chopsticks, she stirred the soup before taking a chunk of noodles, now glazed with red powder, and slurped them into her mouth. She paused for more than three seconds. Her eyes looked like they were about to cry, and her face blushed in a deep pink tone.

"Ryoka."

"I'm fine. I'm fine." She turned, laughing with tears in her eyes. "It's delicious."

"Don't force it," I said. "Is it that bad? Let me try some."

I used the chopsticks to pick up a small chunk of noodles and slurped, feeling the hot flavor burning like an iron, melting my inside. "What is this!?" I cried, "it's hot. It's hot!"

"Water! Water!"

I drank a whole cup of nearly cold tea, only to feel the pain worsen. Ryoka reached for a jug of cold water beside the tea, poured herself a glass, and finished in one gulp. She poured another cup for me then, which I swallowed like I hadn't drunk for days.

More than half of the noodles were still left in the bowl.

"We just have to take turns at it," I suggested to Ryoka, whose face looked as red as bell pepper. "If we eat one bite each, then swap with this other bowl, we can finish them both."

Ryoka nodded, blowing out air. She took a slurp of noodles from the less spicy bowl. Then, she chopsticked up the red noodles and ate them in one quick movement. My turn came, but the salty dried sardines and the added vinegar acted like salt and acid to a wound. I ate some rice, letting Ryoka have some, too. We cut the boiled eggs with chopsticks and licked at their cores to ease the spiciness. Then we drank about half a cup of water before encouraging ourselves to repeat the process.

We finished them, the noodles and the soup.

My stomach was burning by the time we stepped outside, arms crossing each other's shoulders. The grey cat stood by the curb, glaring through its yellow eyes, before licking its paw and walking away. Passerbys glanced our way, with questions, about the two girls supporting each other who looked like they'd just swallowed red hot charcoal.

I looked over at her, and her face turned my way at the same time.

"It might sound strange to say this," said Ryoka, "but give it a week or two, and I might start craving for that again."

"Are you kidding?" I said, "forgive me, but I'll pass."

"I liked it, honestly. Thanks for the food, Rie."

We laughed despite the pain.

"Let's go, Rie." She said, wiping tears away with both hands. "how about getting something sweet this time? My treat."

The market was crowded with people this time, and more fish continued to pour over the stands. Ryoka led me by the hand in the direction of the tramcar station. Near the exit, she stopped at a food cart selling taiyaki. The sweet aroma of freshly fried dough and beans flooded the area. Ryoka paid the money and received two paper bags of the smoking hot sweet. "A friend of mine likes this," she said, giving me one bag before taking out her fish-shaped food and biting into its stomach.

I took out mine too and blew first before biting through its tail.

"So you eat taiyaki from the tail," Ryoka commented, still chewing hers.

"I like the crispy flour part," I said, covering my mouth. I took another bite and felt the creamy sweet red bean paste. "This is delicious. I never had taiyaki freshly made before. How did you know this place? You said something about your friend, right?"

"I did?" Ryoka said, looking more focused on her food than my question.

"You mentioned it once, too, long ago." I said, "about your friend who was half-American, or something like that."

Ryoka's eyes raised toward me.

"This friend of yours, does she or he have a name?"

"Saki." She said before going silent.

"I was blowing the steam out of my mouth when I noticed Ryoka staring my way with an intense expression. Her eyes grew wide, looking over my shoulder. I turned around to follow her gaze and saw a figure coming through the crowd.

The girl had long brown hair that gave the impression of gold in the sun. "Yaa, Ryoka," said she, with a wave, "long time no see."

Ryoka looked like she'd just seen the devil.

# Swimming Lesson 8

---

T he next day, I still couldn't stop thinking of what happened at the market. While listening to Miss Himura reciting Confucius, she passed by my desk toward the front, and my eyes turned toward the window. This year too, I had been assigned to a window seat. The warm air of July disappeared once a cloud moved in the way of the sun.

Yesterday, too, the sky looked this way.

The taiyaki had fallen out of Ryoka's hand. Her face turned white like porcelain, facing the newcomer. "Cat got your tongue, Ryoka?" the girl said, lowering her hand.

"What's with the 'Yaa' thing." Ryoka's voice came in a whisper. "You are not — Saki, right?"

The girl's expression changed, as if the sky suddenly grew dark, casting a shadow over her face. She stepped closer, then paused an arm's length away from Ryoka. "Look closely," She said, "who am I?"

Ryoka blinked, her mouth opened. And I heard a small noise like she had a blade stuck into her tongue.

"Just because Saki is my twin. It's rude of you to mistake me for her."

"Sayo," Ryoka finally spoke. A painful look cut across her face. "You're Sayo."

"Bing bong!"

I felt the sweet red bean taste stick in my throat. Sayo's smile replaced her dark expression. Then, she turned my way as if she could hear me gulp. "Ryoka," said she, "why don't you introduce me to your friend?"

"Oh, Rie, this is my—" Ryoka paused, making a face like about to spit something rotten. "Acquaintance."

"Sayo Odani, nice to meet you." The girl extended her hand my way, which I shook while looking into her blue eyes. She had a Japanese-looking face and spoke the language fluently, with only a hint of a foreign accent. She had a light orange t-shirt on, with long jeans. She wore makeup, slightly heavy on the lipstick, which made her smile look as if permanently plastered to her face. And she wore overly strong perfume, that in my opinion, didn't suit her.

"How do you know Ryoka?" I asked.

"My sister used to be close to her," Sayo said, turning back toward Ryoka. "Isn't that right, Ryoka? You haven't already forgotten her face, have you?"

"Is that a joke?" Ryoka's tone became stern as she looked at the other girl.

"Maybe," I said, shifting, "I should leave you two to catch up—"

"Why?" Ryoka's face snapped my way and grasped my hand. "Who said you have to go, just because she shows up?"

I bit my lips. Ryoka's grip hurt a little.

Sayo let out a small chuckling sound. "Ryoka, your friend is just like a schoolgirl, who doesn't want to be a third party," she said. "I see that you have managed to find a good friend. Even after what happened."

"What do you want?" Ryoka's eyes dilated as she spoke, and I felt her hand trembling.

"I have come to take back what belongs to my sister," Sayo said, glancing my way before her eyes lowered to my wrist. "Could you please return my sister's ribbon?"

I moved closer to Ryoka, instinctively, to hide behind her. My mind still struggled to understand what was going on.

Sayo's eyes narrowed at my movement, as if I'd unintentionally hurt her. "It's not normal for two girls to be hanging out when one of them has indecent intentions." She spoke to Ryoka. "What do you think you're doing, letting someone else wear Saki's ribbon. You have gone too far."

"What's wrong with two girls hanging out together?" Ryoka pulled me out of hiding. Have you been making a habit of going around, chastising every pair of girls you find together?"

"You haven't changed at all, have you, Ryoka?" Sayo spoke, with her voice through her teeth like a hiss. "My little sister has been gone not a year, and you already found a replacement. And even though I am asking nicely for the last token of my sister, you are going to ignore it?"

Ryoka's hand softened a little around my wrist the moment the mention of the ribbon came. Something came over her face, and she looked sad.

The silence felt like time had just stopped, for a second.

"Find your own ribbon, Sayo," Ryoka spoke, with the intonation on the last word.

"Grow up, Ryoka," Sayo said, "unless you need another repetition of what you have done."

I startled a bit when Sayo's glance moved my way. And this time, her eyes paused over me for a full five seconds, like she was an antiques dealer assessing a piece of ware. Her lips moved, indicating she'd just spotted the tiniest fracture. And her lips broke into a smile of pity.

Meanwhile, Ryoka looked like she had been holding her breath.

Sayo finally moved her gaze away, back to Ryoka. Her eyes transformed into two shards of ice. "You will regret this, Ryoka," she said, "when the time comes, and you lose everything, and you will have only yourself to blame."

I watched as Sayo took a step back and turned around. She soon disappeared into the crowd. The taiyaki had gone cold in my hand. And I felt the air warm suddenly, so that I looked up. The clouds were moving away, revealing the sun halfway up the sky.

"Rie, just now—"

I turned toward Ryoka. She had just let go of my wrist. Her eyes continued to gaze in the direction where Sayo had disappeared.

"I think I just saw a ghost." She spoke in a broken voice.

Ryoka continued to look possessed throughout that afternoon. Until the movie, I didn't think she would be in the mood for it. To my surprise, however, I found her sitting up straight in her seat. *The Death in Venice* featured the story of Gustav von Aschenbach, a middle-aged male protagonist who had fallen into infatuation over Tadzio, a young boy he had come across in Venice. The movie was based on a novel by the German author, Thomas Mann, adapted into the musical. The theatre seats remained almost vacant, and a few audience members walked out halfway. Ryoka, on the other hand, remained focused on the movie until the end.

When we finally emerged from the theatre, Ryoka looked as if she'd had a nightmare.

I heard a 'psst' and saw a note drop on my desk. Miss Himura was writing on the blackboard. I hid the paper in my hand, forgetting to breathe for a few seconds. Our teacher continued to lecture as she wrote the verses on the board with white chalk. The girl at the next table had gone back to pretending as if nothing had happened.

I unfolded the note.

*You look cute when staring out the window.*

My head turned toward the back door, saw it partly opened, and Ryoka hiding behind it. I hadn't seen her at practice this morning since she had called last night, saying she needed a morning rest. Ryoka covered the side of her mouth, and her lips moved—

*Let's – cut – class.*

"I can't," I mouthed back.

*Come – over – here.*

"It's class Time." I accidentally made a sound at the last word.

*Who – cares?* Ryoka shrugged. *Study – sometime – else.*

"Miss Hirasawa, please stand up and read this out loud," Miss Himura called out a girl from the front row before turning around to face the class. The girl stood up, taking a moment to go through the chalk-written verse before slowly reciting, "therefore I say, the perfect man has no self. The holy man has no merit. The sage has no fame."

Miss Himura nodded at the girl to sit down, then glanced my way.

My heart raced, and I felt like I couldn't breathe when her eyes moved toward the back door. "Anyone have any idea," she asked the class, "what Zhung Xi meant when he spoke of the 'no-self' as perfection?"

A girl from the middle row raised a hand and stood up. "Miss, could this mean that no one is perfect?"

Our teacher responded with a comment that I couldn't bring my focus to hear. She found another piece of chalk and faced the board once again, writing the next verse. I turned toward the back door and saw Ryoka still there, waiting.

*Hurry — Up!* Her lips mouthed. Her hand was beckoning.

I looked toward the front of the class, where Miss Himura continued to explain, as she wrote the history of Confucius and the relationship between the Chinese Tang Dynasty and the Japanese Heian Era. I gathered my books and stationery, putting them inside my desk. I would have to return for them later. As quietly as I could, I moved my chair and stood up, holding my school bag in one hand. The girl sitting next to me glanced in my direction, then back toward the front of the class.

At least six other girls near the back, too, pretended not to see me moving toward the door.

Ryoka broke out a little smile as I got closer.

A whizzing sound cut through the air before exploding into white powder next to Ryoka's face. I froze. A small thud sounded as the broken chalk fell amidst the sudden silence. One of its halves rolled to stop against my shoe. I turned toward the direction it came from and saw Miss Himura with her hand still in the air, bearing a dark expression.

"Miss Mitzusada, Miss Namie," Miss Himura's voice filled the room. "I am sorry for getting in the way of your friendship. But where do you think you are going?"

A roar of laughter burst through the room.

~ ~ ~

I received a summons to go to the counseling room after school. Ryoka had already arrived before me, sitting in a folding chair with her head down. Another chair had been set beside her. Miss Himura stood behind the table, facing the open window. I made my way to the empty chair and waited.

"Sit down," Miss Himura said.

I sat, feeling like I could see her frowning from the back of her head. Despite the ventilated air, the room filled with a depressing feeling. Miss Himura finally turned around. Eyes turned wide. "What were you thinking?" She said, "you both are already in your second year. Have you not learned yet, how to act better as a good example for one another?"

"Miss, I'm sorry," I spoke, hearing another voice say it at the same time.

Ryoka's head almost touched the table, and I found myself pausing. "It's my fault," she said, "I was forcing Rie to come with me. She was just being nice and—"

"Both of you are responsible for your own actions," Miss Himura said, ignoring Ryoka. "You are capable of thinking and doing things without needing anyone to force you. You could have been a good influence on one another. Instead, you encouraged each other to skip school!"

I bowed my shoulders and head.

"You two have failed to keep yourselves in check," continued Miss Himura. "Not only would you lead yourself into trouble, you even involved each other into the matter. Is this the result of what you have learned since last year?"

Through the corner of my eye, I saw Ryoka trembling. Her eyes dilated, and her mouth looked as if sewed together.

"It has been a year since you two started the Swimming Association, hasn't it?" Miss Himura's voice turned calm. She moved away and pulled the window shut. "It's time you showed me the fruit of your work. Go and get ready at the pool in half an hour. I will be there shortly."

She left the room once the instruction was given, leaving us seated in the chairs. Ryoka's head continued to stay down for almost ten seconds before she finally sat up with a blank expression. She took her chair, folded it, and turned to me in surprise as if forgetting I was still in the same room. I stood up too, and a single question came to my mind —

Was Ryoka afraid of Miss Himura?

Although at some point, I had suspected the two of them shared a connection that had led me to meet Ryoka in the first place. But since I had never seen them together, I had not paid too much thought to it until today. The two of us left the room together and made our way toward the pool. Something we had never done before. We always met at the pool, where Ryoka usually arrived earlier than me. Ryoka was walking few steps ahead, and I sped up to walk by her side. But then I saw her face, wearing an exhausted expression, even worse than I'd seen yesterday. Her eyes looked as if seeing the world without color.

I continued to walk behind her in silence.

The distance from the school building to the pool lasted less than ten minutes. But that day, it felt like the longest road I'd ever walked.

I went for a shower, leaving Ryoka to change in the locker area. I kept the goggles around my neck while bundling my hair up, putting the swim cap on. Ryoka appeared to be taking her time, so I decided to go wait by the pool. Coming out, I spotted Miss Himura near the poolside, sitting on the bench with her legs closed together under her black office skirt. She had taken off her blazer and was focused on the clipboard on her lap. The turquoise water looked crystallized under the sunlight. And the stone ground felt pan-hot against my bare feet.

Miss Himura looked up, noticing my approach.

"Are those my swimming records?" I asked, recognizing the outline of the papers.

"These are Ryoka's," she said, unclipping the board and swapping the front papers with those in the back. "These are yours. From the looks of it, Ryoka has been doing a good job of keeping track of your progress. So let's see, you have been practicing fifty to one hundred meters. And four hundred meters on Friday and Saturday."

I looked at her, flipping through the papers.

Miss Himura had been below average at sports back in her school days, and I had never once seen her at a swimming pool. But she was skilled at organizing, that the badminton team once asked her to act as their manager. It's all about the numbers, Miss Himura had said, how many times you hit, and how you may increase results by adjusting the practice routine. She finally placed her hand over my swimming records, then looked up to me.

"So, Rie," she spoke, "we haven't talked much lately, have we? It has been just you and Ryoka since last year. You must be lonely. If you like, I heard there's an opening for a part-time job as a swimming teacher nearby. I can recommend you."

"I'm not looking for a job right now, Miss. But thank you."

The idea crossed my mind once if Ryoka might want to gather more members. But since she had not shown any interest, I had never bothered to mention it. Besides, unlike the usual school clubs with at least four members, Association could exist with less numbers and less pressure from the school. Back in my old school, if the Swimming Club failed to produce results like winning at competitions, it might lead to some questioning by the teachers. Associations, however, had more freedom to set up their own measure of achievement. It usually started when a student or two would like to borrow the school's space or practice room. The Classical Music Association at our school had only two members using the piano in the music room. And the Haiku Association, I heard, had only one member sharing space with the Photography Association. Maybe, I used to think, Ryoka just wanted to keep things as they had always been.

I thought it's fine the way it was now, too, just the two of us.

Miss Himura looked at Ryoka's swimming record again, as if comparing her timings to mine.

"Ryoka had someone training her swimming, too?" I asked.

"She did, long ago."

I had never thought of that, seeing that Ryoka had never once swum since last year.

"About Ryoka," Miss Himura spoke after finally put aside the clipboard. "How has she been doing?"

"She's been helping me, Miss."

"Has she?" Miss Himura said, elbows over her closed legs. She joined her hands together. "And what improvement have you made with her help?"

"I—"

Somehow, it felt like whatever answer I gave, would be wrong.

"Ryoka had set a goal for you to swim two seconds faster, didn't she? How's that coming along?"

"Swimming faster is not as easy as one thinks," I answered, attempting to smile. "I guess even I have my limit."

Miss Himura made a long sound in her throat, relaxing her hands, placing one on top of the other. "Are you sure you haven't been holding back?"

I linked my hands together behind my back while I shifted my feet to avoid the heat.

"You were always too kind, Rie." She said, "remember once when we played badminton, and you kept letting me win. I really was mad at you when I found out—"

"Miss, I still owe you a thank you." I interrupted her unintentionally. The words simply came out of my mouth. "Last year, when I returned home. Something within me had gone missing. And I was confused, not knowing what to do. But Ryoka helped me. Somehow, I feel like I've managed to get something back, after what I lost. I am fine now. So thank you."

Miss Himura closed her eyes for a moment, and when she reopened them, her expression looked as if I just told her that I believed all crows were white. "Let me told you a story, Rie," she said after a momentary pause. "Imagine a person was drowning in the sea. She saw another person swimming her way. Together, they began swimming for the shore. Think, Rie, with this picture in mind. What is strange about this picture?"

I blinked before shifting my feet again.

"There's an old say, Rie. So long as there is a worshipper, even a sardine head can become a God. Have you ever thought for a moment that you might have overestimated Ryoka?"

"I don't understand, Miss."

"Do you like Ryoka?" Miss Himura asked, with gentleness in her tone, while her eyes looked into mine.

"She is my friend," I answered.

"Then shouldn't you finally take this seriously?" She said, "I know what condition Ryoka made when she pulled you into this Association. You two have made an agreement, haven't you? Don't you think it's time for you to honor that agreement?"

I had forgotten it, the promise.

No, I had not forgotten it. I just didn't want to remember it.

Ryoka had told me, if I could beat her, I could leave this place. But if I was to leave now, where would I go? As if the answer had been lying in wait, for a split second, I felt a chill running up my back—the memory of the compacted sand under my feet and the sound of rumbling waves. My saliva tasted salty. And the pain, as if for a moment my chest came close to splitting open. But when I touched my chest, the wound was not there.

"Is it a bad thing, Miss," I asked, "to keep things the way they are?"

Miss Himura lowered her eyes, sighed, then stood up. She balled her hand in a fist, pointed down over the top of my head, and down the middle. "Hard, so hard-headed, you always were." She said. Then, her hand relaxed, and I felt the warmth through my hair. "Rie, when you let yourself became overly focused on something, it's the same as filling a tub and drowning yourself in it. You then see nothing else that's going on around you, and that could be a very lonely thing."

She let go of my head. Her eyes looked past me.

I turned around and saw Ryoka coming out of the shower area. She walked straight toward the water before stopping by the poolside.

"Try giving it your all to beat her today," Miss Himura spoke next to my ear in a whisper. "You can't let Ryoka continue to guide you forever, can you?"

Miss Himura held a stopwatch in one hand and the clipboard in another. Ryoka wore a cap and goggles, unlike the last time. Both of us had finished our warm-up routine, and at our teacher's instruction, we would start a race of one hundred meters. We stepped up to the jumping platform at the "Ready" provided by Miss Himura. I returned my focus toward the black lines under the water, bending down and reaching my fingertips to touch my feet. My toes hunched around the tip of the platform.

"Set."

I listened to the final second of silence before the race.

"Go!"

We jumped into the water at the same time. Ryoka sprinted off, and I put in the effort to catch up, to an extent, until the result already became clear. I allowed then the distance between us to increase. Seeing Ryoka passing me back to the other side, I felt nostalgic. Once, long ago, I might have contested this established result.

But now, I didn't mind losing to her.

Miss Himura stood above me when I resurfaced. She clicked the stopwatch, then took a few seconds to examine the numbers there before comparing them to the record. I let out a long exhale in the water while peeking through my goggles at Ryoka beside me.

"Let's change things a little," Miss Himura said, crouching down. "This time, I want you two to keep swimming, no fixed distance. Whoever lasts the longest win. Any questions?"

Ryoka's expression remained hidden beneath her goggles, except her mouth that hung open without a sound. She didn't turn toward me. But I felt her eyes behind the dark film staring back for a second before she got out of the water. I lifted my goggles to see clearer.

But Ryoka continued to keep her face hidden.

"Ready," Miss Himura raised her voice when we were back on the platform. I refocused my sight over the black line below me.

"Set!"

I inhaled.

"Go!"

I sprang forward, feeling the impact blast over my body, then like a switch flipping inside, energy flowed through me. My eyes focused past the blue water. I pulled the water beneath my stomach. Ryoka had already moved ahead, and her kicks left the water stirred behind her. She did a flip turn and swam back, passing me. I bent my body downward, turned, and pushed off the poolside with my feet.

Swimming to my side, I raised my face over the water after two strokes, feeling the cold fresh air replenish my stamina. Because of this being long-distance swimming, I needed not push for speed. By swimming in a moderate rhythm, with only enough energy as needed, my nerves became fully awakened. And a sensation like joy flowed through my body.

I could swim like this forever.

Ryoka did the seventeenth flip turn and swam toward the other side again. She still maintained her lead, though I felt a change in the water vibrations. Reaching my arms forward, I saw my distance from Ryoka continued to draw closer.

Her legs appeared to be struggling.

She saw me catching up and increased her speed, pulling ahead again. But her lead lasted only for a moment before I passed her. I got ready for another flip turn when I saw a hand in the water. I touched the poolside and resurfaced. Miss Himura's face greeted me with a faint smile before she stood up. I exhaled into the water first before turning to see that Ryoka had stopped in the middle of the pool.

"Ryoka forfeited." Miss Himura's voice spoke. "That's it for today. I will leave. You can relax now. But do ten breaths into the water before you get out."

I turned around and saw Ryoka swimming toward the other side. Miss Himura took her blazer from the bench and left through the gate. I exhaled into the water before lifting my goggles, wiping the water from my eyes. Then the knowledge that I alone remained in the water erased the exhilaration I had felt while swimming. The pool water felt as if turning into ice. And Ryoka was nowhere within sight.

I struggled out of the water.

The sound of the shower turned off when I arrived inside and caught a glimpse of Ryoka moving toward the locker area. I got into one stall and let the hot water run over me. I tried not to slip over the wet floor when following her into the next room. Ryoka was changing out of her swimsuit without seeming to notice me enter. I looked away and reached for my locker on the opposite side. I took a deep breath and waited until my heart to calm down. I looked again out of curiosity. Ryoka put on two unmatched underwear, a flowered pattern, and a pink bra. My face felt like a hot water bag.

Ryoka still had not talked to me.

"I didn't win." I broke the silence.

Ryoka made a sound as she turned, surprised for being talked to. And I saw her little smile, with her eyes narrowed as if she was looking at a stranger.

"You've been busy and not had a chance to swim yourself," I said. "I just swam as you have taught me."

"Rie, what are you acting all worked up for?" Ryoka said. She had put on her blouse and was zipping up her skirt. "It's just a race, and you won."

"I didn't." My voice came out in a whisper.

Ryoka was focused on tying her sailor scarf while looking the other way. I took this chance to take off my swimsuit and change as quickly as I could. Ryoka had not spoken for almost a minute. She busied herself by putting her wet swimsuit in a plastic bag.

What would happen now?

"Yesterday," Ryoka's voice ended the silence. "I am sorry, Rie, for what happened. I have been wanting to say that, but didn't know how to break it. Hanging out with you was fun. So I am sorry that it got weird in the end."

"So," I spoke, "if I ask, you will still give me swimming lessons tomorrow?"

"About that," Ryoka's voice paused when she pushed the locker shut. "I can't do it this week."

"Oh?"

"I planned to tell you earlier that I would be busy until next Monday." Ryoka turned around, "so let's move our lessons till then."

"Do you have something else to do?" I braved myself to ask after a moment. Somehow, Sayo's face came to my mind.

"You could say it that way," Ryoka answered in a whisper, her eyes averted as if in deep thought. "Tomorrow, I am going to see my old friend."

What is feeling? To me, it's like a flick of lighter next to a pile of hays, and it burns. That day, at the sight of my cousin with that girl, I felt like I could burn anyone, destroy everything if I wanted to.

The next day, my parents forced me to stay home, to rest, after they heard that I fainted while on the beach. Then, after the adults left for their business, that girl stayed home to take care of me until I told her that I wanted to eat ice cream. There was a shop just nearby, but I asked her to go to another place. The place nearby didn't have what I wanted for sale, and I wanted another. "Please, please," I begged her, "buy me that ice cream."

She left eventually. It would take her half an hour walking there, so I had one hour before she returned.

I left my bed and found my cousin in his room.

"Are you feeling better?" He asked, adjusting his glasses upon seeing me at the door. His blush suggested his being uneasy, seeing me having only a thin-strapped top and a pair of jeans.

"I want to thank you for yesterday," I told him. He turned around in his chair as I stopped before his desk. The instant camera that he always had around his neck rested in the corner. "You took lots of pictures of your girlfriend yesterday. Can I see them?"

"Why?"

"Uncle and Aunt always praised how talented you are. Are you not?"

His bare chest rose and fell. His blue beach top looked pale compared to the tan of his skin. It made me jealous that I couldn't have been born with this same feature, that girls seemed to go for. "Here," he took the photos out of a drawer. "It's not that grand, you know."

I took them and looked through them one after the other, taking time to study each, but not too much time. "Wow, you're so talented," I said, then bit my lips so hard that I began to feel pain.

"What's wrong?"

"You know, I shouldn't say this. But we are cousins. We must be honest with each other. I talked to your girlfriend, you see, and she said horrible things about you. She told me that you bored her, with your talentless photos. And you always take her pictures, like you're a lecherous old man."

"Come on, are you joking?" He adjusted his glass and looked the other way, like he was trying to hold in his laughter.

"It's horrible, I know. Your girlfriend went too far, I admit it. But I'm telling the truth. It took me all my courage to come face you like this. I don't want to keep a secret or lie to you, so please don't hate me for doing this."

A knot appeared between his brows. And a hard look came to his expression as he continued to avoid looking my way.

"Let's not pretend, shall we?" I moved closer and placed my arms around him slowly. "You also notice everything, don't you? How she doesn't always treat you right. Then, you start thinking, God, she must be stupid. It's alright to feel this way. You are too good for her. She's so lucky to even have you, and yet she talks about you behind your back. It's cruel."

His gulp sounded like something moved inside him, the doubt taking hold.

My hands over his chest felt his heartbeat rising. I moved around to sit on his desk. Before he could look the other way, his eyes already got caught on my small hips. "I'm sorry if I have said too much," I said, holding his face to look up. "Let me do something to help you. How about you take pictures of me?"

———◇———

# SWIMMING LESSON 9

A unt Risa found me making breakfast in the kitchen. She asked me if something had happened and I told her how my swimming lesson had been postponed. I felt her eyes on my back for a long second. I could imagine her brows knitted together. She knew that I looked forward to starting each day at the pool, and she knew I was disappointed.

I hated myself for causing her to worry again.

The first morning class of mathematics went by, then came the second class of history. I tried to focus on the lecture about Emperor Kanmu, taking notes of what might be on the midterm exam. I finished my math homework by lunchtime, out of habit, before realizing that I wouldn't have to go to the pool today. How long had it been since I didn't have anything to do after school?

Ryoka had said she was going to meet her old friend. Strangely, this bothered me.

Why?

Mr. Kogawa, the English teacher, was reciting some easy conversation dialogue out of the book with the wrong accent. I attempted to put my mind onto the lesson when the image of Sayo formed within my mind, her brown hair with hints of gold, the perfume, and those blue eyes. Sayo had smiled at me the other day. The way one did when she sympathized with another. The image of her face felt clear now, in my mind, like mold over a bathroom ceiling that went unnoticed at first. Until the spots increased. Now, as I continued to question, why had Ryoka canceled her plans with me, each 'why' came with a glimpse of Sayo's face, and the smile of pity on her lips.

Why? Why? Why?

I was leaving the classroom after school when I spotted Ryoka in the distance. She had not turned my way but was rushing down the stairs. I paused for a second, then found my feet going after her, hiding among the students leaving through the building's exit. Ryoka took a left turn outside the school gate, toward the bus station.

A bus arrived, and Ryoka got on.

I waited until a few other students went in through the back, then I followed. Paying the conductor, I squeezed myself into a seat. Ryoka was sitting toward the front, next to the exit. She hadn't seen me. I kept my head low behind the chair, drawing some attention from passengers close by. The bus was only half full when its door closed. Two girls from my school, carrying musical instruments, were standing next to me. They would offer me extra cover in case

Ryoka turned around. The bus began to move. Ryoka turned her head toward the window, once or twice each second, looking restless. She was going to meet her friend. This thought alone helped me focus. Part of me acknowledged what I was doing was wrong, but I kept telling myself that I could no longer back out. Ryoka had been acting strangely, and I wanted to know why.

Ryoka got up suddenly. I ducked before hearing the bell sound and felt the bus pulling toward the curb.

I peered across the seats and saw Ryoka leaving. Getting up suddenly, I bumped into the two girls as I rushed for the door and got out only a split second in time. My feet turned numb after a quick jump. My eyes scanned left to right, recognizing the shopping area, with old-fashioned-looking hairdressers on the right end corner. Only a few people stood waiting for the bus. A postal box stood over to my left, the direction where I spotted Ryoka walking back my way.

I moved to stand next to an office worker waiting for the bus. His height shielded me as Ryoka moved past me from behind. My heart pounded like a taiko drum.

Ryoka looked lost.

She took out what I recognized as a pack of tissue and looked at the advertisement's cover before checking the hairdresser's address number. She then turned around the corner. And I sped over the same direction. I saw Ryoka stop in front of a flower shop from a distance, examining the various colors of flowers on display outside. A woman shopkeeper wearing a white apron came out to greet her, and Ryoka responded with something I couldn't hear. I noticed the shopkeeper's expression change into one of sympathy before returning inside the shop. Ryoka waited for about ten minutes until the woman returned with a bouquet that looked freshly wrapped. I couldn't name the giant orange flowers, but I recognized the many small white flowers to be chamomiles.

Ryoka was returning my way.

I slipped inside the hairdresser and waited until another bus of different numbers came, which Ryoka boarded. I got on the bus at the last second and found an empty seat in the back. I could count only eight people altogether taking this bus, including me and Ryoka, who sat near the front. Ryoka's restlessness from earlier disappeared, and was replaced with the air of calm. Her face had not looked up once from the bouquet in her lap. Until we reached the destination.

The bus stopped in an area of town, which I recognized to be a high-end neighborhood.

I peered through the window as Ryoka got out. Then I stood up, cried to the driver to reopen the gate, and left the bus, finding myself surrounded by houses twice the size of mine. Ryoka had already walked some distance away, carrying her school bag in one hand and the bouquet in the other, as if she knew this area by heart.

She finally stopped in front of a house.

Its roof looked the largest compared to the others around it. The western-style gates stood ready to topple her as her hand reached for the bell. She looked hesitant for a moment before finally pressing it in a quick motion, letting out a short ring.

I hid behind a wall around the corner.

A minute passed.

Ryoka pressed the bell again, longer this time, before stepping back. Her head raised toward the top of the sharp-looking fence. Her legs shifted after another minute passed without an answer. Then she pressed the bell a third time, keeping her fingers there for three seconds. Before she retreated.

Her arms squeezed so hard some chamomile petals fell around her.

Ten minutes had passed when the gate finally opened, automatically. A woman came out. She looked to be of middle age, wearing glasses. She wore black hair that was cut short above chin level. Her white blouse and blazer looked expensive. Ryoka put down her school bag before bowing toward her.

I tried to listen.

But Ryoka spoke in a low voice while the woman kept her arms crossed. Finally, Ryoka extended the bouquet in front of her with both hands. Then it happened. I blinked at the sight of the flowers flying backward, the white chamomiles scattered mid-air. Ryoka's face turned aside as she moved one step back. The woman's hand was still raised in the air, while Ryoka clutched her face with one hand. A look of pain came, then, to her eyes.

The plastic wrapping fell with a thud, followed by quietness. The orange flowers lay still as if dead, and white petals scattered across the ground.

"See anything interesting?"

I almost screamed when a hand gently pressed over my mouth.

"Don't make a sound," the voice whispered close to my ear. "You don't want Ryoka to know you were stalking her, right?"

Once I recognized the accent, I nodded. The hand released me. As I turned around, the perfume caught my nose. Those blue eyes were looking at me. I sensed that Sayo could be two or three years older than me, but she looked much older with those jeans that added to her height. And the intimidating smile, that bore an amused expression.

"I need to talk to you," Sayo said in Japanese, which sounded abrupt in an American accent. "Don't worry about Ryoka. She'll survive."

I turned around to look at Ryoka once, to see her standing alone. The wrapped bouquet lay unmoved nearby. The woman in glasses had already gone.

The gate stood shut.

I wanted to go to Ryoka. But Sayo was waiting for me at the other end of the path. Ryoka's legs were rooted on the spot as if time had stopped for her. A part of me was still confused about what I had seen, while another part couldn't find the courage to show myself now. Not yet, not until Sayo explained this to me.

My fingers turned numb, clutching the school bag. Sayo continued leading me in the opposite direction, then turned left toward a small park.

She stopped.

"I am sorry," I decided to speak first, with my back bowing forward ninety degrees. "I didn't mean to pry."

"You're just curious. Anyone would be curious if placed in your situation. You meant no harm, right?" Sayo spoke. Her smile showed a glimpse of teeth. "I am kind of thankful for having run into you. I have always wanted to talk to you."

"To me?"

"I have been observing you, you know."

I raised my head to see her eyes fixing down toward me, like an inquisitor gazing at a heretic.

"You don't have to be scared. I won't bite," Sayo said with a good-natured laugh. "Miss Himura and my mother know each other. You could say my family has been like a patron to your teacher. So I have heard things about you."

"Oh."

"So, Rie, may I call you that?" Sayo said, "what do you think of Ryoka?"

It was the second time someone had asked me that. "Ryoka's my friend," I said.

"A 'friend'?"

"Yes," I responded, disliking her intonation. "Ryoka is my friend."

Sayo's eyes narrowed. "And you?" She continued, "what are you, to Ryoka?"

"You should ask Ryoka that yourself," I managed to answer, after a moment of surprise. "Would you be able to entitle yourself as something, based on your imagination alone? I wouldn't do that unless Ryoka herself said what she thinks of me."

"You are an interesting one," Sayo said after a blink. "Miss Himura was right about you, always keeping your head on your shoulders. Maybe there is still hope for you yet."

"What's going on over there?" I decided to ask. "What was that about? Ryoka came here with some flowers and got slapped. Why? Things started to get strange the moment you showed up. Ryoka said she came to meet her old friend—"

"Hold on. Stop, please." Sayo said the last two words in English, her hand raised.

"Something is going on," I continued with a calmer tone. "You might think of me as an outsider who doesn't know anything. That is true. But Ryoka seems to have some kind of trouble, and I can't ignore it completely. So please, help me understand."

Sayo took a deep breath, then held and released five seconds full of air. She raised her hand then and pushed, causing me to stumble backward. "Feel that?" she said, "that's the feeling when you lose the person you love."

I was still rebalancing myself when she grasped my wrist and pulled me closer. The green ribbon moved before my eyes.

"And this," said she, "is when Ryoka picks you up. That's what's going on."

I stepped back, rubbing my wrist after she let me go.

"I hired a detective to look into you," said Sayo. "Don't get me wrong. I needed to understand the situation. I will apologize for disrespecting your privacy if you want. But from what I have heard, you caused quite a tragedy back in Tokyo."

I felt my breath stop.

"Do you want to know what happened after? To that one you left on the train, I mean."

My legs went weak.

"Don't worry, no one is dead. But that poor heartbroken soul quit school and returned to hometown, to start a new life. I can give you the contact info if you want."

"I already have that," I said, looking aside. "I know the address, the phone number, everything."

Sayo blinked. "I see," her smile grew softer. "So you have some sense at least. Knowing that now, I can sympathize with you. Please believe me when I say this, that I feel for what you had to do. It's not easy, going against the one thing you want the most. It could almost feel unfair. Once, you might have believed that as long as you wished for something sincerely and were positive about it, everything would work out somehow. But then, it didn't. It's like the world crumbled down on you. And amidst the chaos, Ryoka showed up. It must feel as if being lifted from the ground by someone like a saint or an angel."

Something within me stirred as if waking up, causing pain like a sharp cut across my chest.

"But Rie," Sayo gazed down at me. "Ryoka is no saint, nor angel, nor any such miracle as you are trying to picture her. She is just a human, and she has her limits. So I have asked you, what are you to Ryoka? Are you ready to answer yet?"

My breath grew quicker.

"You are her burden, Rie."

My lips hung open, my tongue felt dry.

"You are a perceptive person, so you should have realized this too," she continued, "how you have been relying on Ryoka's emotional support. I could empathize with that, at first, considering your past. However, when the life you have known suddenly ends, you should reflect on the experience. By learning from the past, you can move on to the future. But what have you been doing? Instead of learning, you distracted yourself by clinging to Ryoka. You might think this alright. You might even fool yourself into thinking that Ryoka can take it somehow, no matter how much you put on her shoulders."

The sun was setting behind Sayo, her shadow casting my way. "What do you want?" I let out the question.

"Distance yourself from Ryoka," Sayo said, her face cold, like a Greek statue with a piercing glare.

"Are you telling me to stay away from her?"

"You don't need to abandon her completely," she said. "I am saying that you should allow some distance while you deal with your own troubles."

"And if I refuse," I asked, "would you turn Ryoka against me?"

"Do I look like that kind of person to you?" Sayo responded, "to make or break a friendship is your job. Please, don't cast me off as a villain simply because you have no courage to correct your ways. Besides, if I had to lower myself to do something like blackmailing you, that would mean you are a worthless human being, who's not worth saving in the first place. But you have a conscience, don't you? You haven't gone looking for your lost love, even when you could have all this time, because you have an awareness that they are better off without you. The reason I even bother to talk to you, is that I believe in you."

I had to get away. Sayo's presence was hurting me inside, like there were bugs in my stomach.

"Don't you want to be free from your past?" Sayo's words stopped me. "Sincerity would grant you that. Start by confessing everything to your Aunt."

My resistance snuffed out at the mentioning of Aunt Risa.

"Confess, and the truth will set you free. I believe that's what the Bible says. Your past, Rie, as well as your guilts, are yours alone. If you keep running away, they will just come after you. Stop acting like a victim and bring yourself to face reality. Confess, and let the flow take you where it will. Until you do that, please stay away from Ryoka. In case you have not noticed, Ryoka, too, has her own weight to carry. And she can't handle any extra. Ryoka is no saint. If you keep relying on her, she will break. And you will have only yourself to blame for forcing your ideal onto her, based on your imagination alone."

Sayo walked past me and put distance between us.

"Wait," I called.

She stopped without turning around.

"What are you to Ryoka?"

Sayo turned. The evening light revealed the glittering in her eyes. "I am," said she, "whatever Ryoka would think of me, be it the angel of luck or misfortune."

"And Saki," I spoke, "what is she to Ryoka?"

"Saki." Her voice carried the sound of the name. "Saki was—"

The sound disappeared once the final word came. My eyes dilated, and I forgot to breathe for a second. Until the scent of the evening brought me back. And I gazed after Sayo, who had already walked a long distance away. Her words continued to echo in my mind.

"Saki was Ryoka's burden."

~ ~ ~

Aunt Risa asked if I had eaten the moment I returned home. She had finished the cooking, she said, having worked on it since this morning.

"Go put your bag away, then we can eat."

I tried putting away the thought of the evening as I sat down at the table. But the event had already made its way into my mind, so that now when I gazed down at the table, I could see Sayo's pitying smile in every curve of the table lace cloth. I could remember her voice so clearly that, if I was to write it down now, I would be able to capture every word. Even her perfume imprinted to my memory as a reminder of something that symbolized sincerity. Aunt Risa came out of the kitchen, just then, carrying a pot of nikujaga. She had also cooked rice with the right amount of water, so that each grain came out glossed white like fragments of pearls with a soft smell.

Aunt Risa sat across the table. And we began to eat.

I couldn't eat more than three bites before feeling sick to my stomach. The thought of Sayo took over my senses. As if by some gift, she had gotten into my head.

"Have you been hanging out with your friend after all?" Aunt Risa asked.

"No," I responded. "I just went for a walk."

"Oh?"

Could it be? Because she thought I would have nothing to do this evening, that she spent the whole day making this food?

"I need your opinion, Rie," she continued. "I've been thinking of getting new curtains for the living room. What color do you think would look best?"

I gave her an answer but made a mental note to talk her out of the project later. Aunt Risa always thought of changing something once a month, be it curtains, wallpaper, or bathroom tiles. She had swapped the old tablecloth into this current white lace one when

I wasn't looking. Though I admitted that Aunt Risa had good tastes, the new cloth just didn't match the surroundings. Once she heard my opinion, Aunt Risa began suggesting her choices of color, either pink, orange, or something of a similar tone. If her plan came to pass, the living room would turn into something between a Valentine and Halloween decoration.

Things were fine the way they were.

But some things couldn't continue as they had before.

"Bring your plates when you're done." Aunt Risa had finished her food first, while I still had about half left.

"I can do the dishes," I said. "You cooked, after all."

"You should rest more, Rie." She said, "you have been working hard, right? Don't worry about me all the time."

The rice usually tasted sweet, after chewing it too long. But tonight, it tasted bitter.

I made myself finish it all.

Aunt Risa accepted my dishes and said goodnight as I left the kitchen. She finished all the cleaning in less than five minutes. She was about to go to the living room for her usual television program when she found me still sitting at the table.

I inhaled before raising my face toward her. The silence felt as if it would continue forever.

"Auntie," I finally said, "I need to tell you something."

# SWIMMING LESSON 10

M y body felt as if it was moving back in time as I told Aunt Risa about my past. The train station's image, the warmth of that night in August, the smell of grass. The person whose smile expressed relief upon seeing me.

"You came." She said before the rest of her voice was eroded away by the coming train.

My thoughts felt like a movie rewinding backward, to where it began. I had met the girl during April, about two weeks after my enrolment to the school, and I'd finally settled down over the thought of me living in Tokyo. Unlike Nagasaki, I heard that snow would last more days in the big city during Christmas. I never had the chance to see this come to pass. The school consisted of five main buildings—four, which had been built at the start of the Meiji Era. The latest Western building was made of stone, equipped with modern facilities, including cafeterias and an indoor pool. Most of the teachers were nuns. The only male teachers were foreigners employed for language classes, like Herr Schumann, who taught German, and Monsieur Pierre, who taught French. The majority of the students came from well-to-do families. There had been a shared feeling of being sheltered in this all-girls school where they adopted the Catholic virtues as its core. I felt freedom within this traditional atmosphere, participating in reading passages before homeroom, following rules such as no extra accessories and strict dormitory curfews.

In no time, I adapted to my new life far away from home.

About ten minutes' walk from the Western building, there stood a small church where I had gone every day after school to pray. I heard it was built long before the land around here got purchased to build the school. Its bell tower was still in use. The sound could be heard even from a distance away. I imagined how people in the old days woke up to the bells, ready for mass, and the sun rising behind the church served as the first sight of their morning.

A cross stood behind the white altar as I entered.

The dim brightness inside gave me a calm atmosphere. I heard my own footsteps, moving toward the front. The images of Saint Hildegard surrounded by hydrangeas over the stained glass felt real, with the slight smell of incense and fresh flowers near the altar. I took a moment to observe the quietness before crossing myself and kneeling over the marble floor.

I joined my hands together and felt every word within my heart being listened to.

Minutes passed in silence.

I was getting ready to leave when I heard a sound from behind and saw a girl sitting up from among the pews. She stretched herself, waking up, before looking my way. The first thing I noticed was that her hair was trimmed short like a boy. Her shoulders looked broad, like the statue of the Roman goddess Artemis. She possessed a height that looked tall from a distance. And once she noticed me, she glanced my way, in the manner of someone who was annoyed for being awoken suddenly. She turned around and left the church.

The next day after that first meeting, she didn't come.

But a few days later, on my way to the church, I found her sleeping on a bench under a Camelia tree, with a book covering her face. I saw her there, too, over the next few days. Until the fifth day, I decided to approach her.

"Why are you sleeping here?" I asked.

"Because you took away my napping place," she said.

"It's a church, not a place for sleeping."

"It's quiet, with many empty seats and books large enough to make a good pillow," she said, lifting the book off her face. "Are you going to claim this spot as well?"

My eyes glanced over the book cover to ignore her tone. Dostoevsky's *Crime and Punishment.* "Are you reading that?" I asked, "or you just use it for sleeping, too?"

She sat up. Her eyes looked blue like the sky. "I was reading it," she responded after a moment.

"Is it interesting?" I asked, realized I might have offended her for staring too much. She had natural gold hair, also. Could her father be a foreigner? Or her mother?

"Better than the Bible."

"Oh, which part do you like the most?"

"The crime, and the ending," she said. "I don't like the detective that much, though. And I think Sonya better leave that good for nothing man to rot in Siberia."

"I could recommend a good book," I said, sitting down next to her.

"Are you from the Scripture Discussion Club?"

"No," I said, laughing. "I got invited once, but I said I was already signed for the Swimming Club. Not that I have anything against them, there're lots of seniors there that I respect. But something about it just feels like I wouldn't fit in around there."

"Why's that?" She sat up now and placed an arm over the bench, behind my shoulders.

"It would complicate things if they knew," I began, then felt like I might as well confess it. "My father used to be a Buddhist Priest. I grew up in the temple in Chiba. It's shut down now after my parents passed away. My mother was a Catholic, though, and I took after her. With this background, I sensed it would be awkward if we started discussing things like God is the only truth and other faiths are all heretics. Or, something along those lines."

"Don't you think that way?" the girl spoke.

"If I started saying things like that, it would be like bad-mouthing my own father." I said, "everyone is different, and we can choose which way is best to save our own souls. I believe in religious freedom."

Her lips moved a little around the corner. But no voice came.

"So, the book." I realized I had been the only one talking. "How about *The Tale of Genji*? We read the abridged version in class last week. And right now, there's a long queue to check out a full version at the library. Do you know, the author Shikibu Murasaki was rumored to write the story, using her best friend, Lady Fujiko as a model for Prince Genji—"

"Why do you care what I read?" She interrupted.

"I want to make peace," I said, looking into her eyes, "for taking away your spot. You will be here every day, right? And I will have to walk this way every day, so don't you think it would be a good idea if we settled our hostility as soon as possible?"

Her eyes narrowed.

I felt my face warm.

"No religious talk," she said finally, "and you are free to do what you want."

I sighed in relief. "One question, though." I decided I should ask this before I got too cowardly to ever mention it. "What's your name?"

The name, little that I knew then, would become a sound that caused me pain. Night after night, I'd wake up from nightmares, and the memory of her name would cut me like a shard while my mouth gaped for air. Then, when the pain finally ceased, a single line of thought fell upon my conscience.

How I wished we'd never met.

Months passed since our first meeting, and I adopted this new routine to stop and talk with her on my way to return from church. We began to meet during lunchtime, on the days I had to go to swimming practice in the evening. We liked to sit together, on the bench, or in the library. She read her books while I read mine. As time passed, I found my eyes observing the curve of her neck, the tips of her hair that hung across her eyes, the round shape of her shoulders, her lips.

"Why are your eyes blue?" I asked her one day. "And your hair gold?"

"My ancestors happened to mingle with the Dutch," she said. "I heard that my great great great Grandmother was also born with blue eyes and golden hair. Why? Do you have a problem with how I look?"

"No," I said.

She appeared dissatisfied with my answer. Back then, gold hair was used to depict troubled people. Like back in the Edo period, when blue eyes symbolized demons.

"It suits you," I continued. "Your hair looks like leaves in the fall."

The intensity in her eyes softened, then she returned her focus to the book in her lap. She continued to read the same page over half an hour later.

Three days after that conversation, she took me behind a building where the music room was located. The sound of a hymn from the Choir Club came within a short distance. "Can I embrace you?" She asked, "if you don't mind."

I said I didn't mind.

Her arms wrapped around me—her flat chest against mine. And I rested my face over her shoulder. The scent of her body reminded me of sunflower seeds. Her hands moved down around my waist. Strangely, I found myself used to her touch as if our bodies had always meant to be this way, long before we had met. My heart and her heart, beating together in the same rhythm.

June approached, and rainy days became frequent.

We began to spend more time in the library. One day, after we got inside, I was looking outside the window where the rain was pouring down. And I placed my hand over its cold surface, feeling the water dripping down on the other side. She had gone and returned with a book. And we found a place to sit, at a long table that faced the window, next to each other. I had already finished preparing for the midterm exam and brought out a Bible.

"How can you read the same book over and over and not get bored?" She asked me after a while.

"I guess because I already know how the stories go." I answered, "I feel comfortable knowing the endings."

She went silent for a few seconds before closing her book, as if she'd lost interest in reading any more. The book cover, I noticed, was Dostoevsky's *Demons*.

"Say there was a book that had your whole life written in it," she said. "Maybe it's a book of fate, written by God. And on the last page, it predicted your bad end. The description said that whatever you try to do, all efforts would be in vain. No matter how much you prayed or how sincere your devotion was, God would, in the end, say no. If you were to come across a book like that, what then would you do?"

Her question echoed within my mind as the sound of rain continued to fill the silence. I tried to return to my reading, but something changed in the lines of the page.

"Could you," I said, "embrace me?"

We went to the part of the library, where only the dim light was turned on. And she placed her arms around me while I pressed my face over her chest to feel the warmth. The thought that one day I might lose this warmth gave rise to a cold feeling in my heart. Never once in my life had I found myself wanting something. Never once, had I thought I could feel for someone this way.

I wanted her.

But if she was to disappear. What then would I do?

I was afraid to answer the question.

Until the answer came, less than a month later. One week before it happened, we had kissed, and someone must have seen us. We received a summons to the Guidance Office. I remembered standing there with her by my side, her hand holding mine. The Reverend Mother sat behind the table, staring at us with a cold glance. "It's a sin what you two did," she said. "How could you be so arrogant, thinking this was acceptable?"

The words didn't cause me pain. Until I saw that it caused her pain. That I had caused her pain.

For a few weeks after the summons, I tried to distance myself from her. Until she found me at the church. She embraced me, and I didn't resist her. "Let's run away together," she said. "We could go to my relative in the countryside. I could find a job, and we would make this work. I would make you happy, Rie. Meet me at the train station tonight, at seven. I will wait for you. Even if you don't come, I will continue to wait for you. I will wait for you forever."

Back then, I didn't say no to her. But God did.

I finished the story up to the point where I left her on the train. I didn't tell Aunt Risa about the voice, however. Then, I raised my face. My aunt sat opposite the table, her shoulders drooping, and she let herself lean back against the chair. Her eyes looked as if she was counting the lace stitchings of the tablecloth. Creases deepened beneath her eyes, and her brows knitted together. She was shivering.

"I am sorry," I said with my head down, touching the table. "You sent me to school, trying to give me a future. But I chose to throw it all away. I know I have disappointed you, even though you have always been kind to me. I betrayed you, and I don't expect you to forgive me—"

"That's not it, Rie," Aunt Risa raised her head, sighing. "Maybe this is karma."

A heavy silence fell, following her admission.

"The truth is, I too, once left someone." Aunt Risa said, then wiped something from her eyes.

I felt the cold air over my dried lips. And for a moment, I felt like seeing a faint image of Aunt Risa without those creases. The look in her eyes when she finally spoke again the innocent appearance of a young girl.

"Yumie Oe was her name," she began. "Like you, I met her while attending a high school in Tokyo. She was a kind, strong-hearted girl, and I had feelings for her. I confessed to her, and she told me she felt the same.

Then, we, too, planned to run away. There was no other choice. That's what I had been telling myself. We would go on the day of our graduation. The two of us planned everything, detail to detail, what to pack in our bags, where to go, what to write to our families once we settled down. We tried to think of ways to be together, and I felt hope that it would work out somehow. "

I held my breath.

"On the day before graduation—" she continued, "Yumie said to me, I will see you tomorrow. And that was the last time I ever saw her."

Aunt Risa's face turned away as if looking at something I couldn't see. "After the graduation ceremony, I returned home and was ready to leave with my bag. But then the rain started to pour outside. I was waiting for it to stop. Then your Grandmother said that she wanted to speak to me. First, she sat me down, congratulated me on the graduation. Then she told me that she had found me a suitor, a good man she wanted me to meet. That man was your uncle. At this point, you might already guess what comes next."

"Why?" I asked her.

"You know our family situation, Rie. Your Grandfather had lost the entire fortune because of the war. Your mother worked till her bones were breaking to send me to school. She had to quit her nursing study to work and support me. She sacrificed her future for me. If I married your uncle, I would finally set her free. I couldn't betray your mother or our family."

A tear flowed down her face. And she no longer bothered to wipe it away. "I didn't go to meet Yumie," continued she, looking into my eyes. "And that was it, no explanation, no goodbye. I simply turned my back and ran. I cruelly shoved her aside and never returned to Tokyo."

"Do you know what happened to her?" I asked.

Aunt Risa looked away again. Her eyes looked empty, like glass. "I wonder," she said. "Even now, sometimes I still have a lingering wish, that she didn't catch a cold because of the rain that day."

In my way, I understood her. Aunt Risa's choice to leave her lover and to accept the pain that came.

"Rie, there were times when I found myself thinking, what would have happened if I hadn't broken my promise with her," Aunt Risa spoke, as she wiped under her eyes. "If I hadn't chosen your uncle, would I have been happier? For a very long time, I have found myself trapped within these thoughts. So I would like to ask you now. Rie, would you rather quit the life you have now and go looking for that girl?"

Her eyes held kindness when looking my way. "If you do," she added, "I will support you. But if you don't, then let that be the final answer. You have suffered enough, Rie. It's time that ended."

I lowered my eyes.

The answer had been within me all this time. Tears brimmed over before streaming down my face. "It would be better," I said, "that I don't see her again."

If I had never met her, I wouldn't have had to hurt her. And none of this would have happened.

"Cry, Rie," Aunt Risa came to embrace me. "It hurts, I know. We have decided, and yet it hurts. Even though we know that crying won't help, we still want to cry. Because that's the only thing we can do to ease the pain just a little. People like us have to bear the pain that we have caused others. And so we deserve to cry as much as we want. You are not alone, Rie. I'm glad you finally opened up to me. I am glad you returned home."

At Aunt Risa's words, I found myself finally being set free, to cry, and cry, and cry.

It was finally over.

He took one picture of me, at first, with his instant camera. I looked away, in the manner of showing him a better angle, while the corner of my eyes took notice of something that stood up in his pants.

"Let me see," I said once the photo came out, and he shook it in the air. The image, my picture, I held into the light. It wasn't bad, but neither was it good.

I always hated having my photo taken.

"Come on. You must be joking. Is this the best you can do?" I threw the photo back. Its tip hit his bare chest. He stepped back as if he'd been pricked by a blade. "You disappointed me, you know. I thought you might have talent. But she was right. I overestimated you."

"What's wrong with it!?"

"Do I have to point it out? Mind, would you like me to guide your finger too?" I said as laughter burst out of me in a sharp tone. "Oh well, I suppose I could help out a bit—"

I pushed one strap down my shoulder with my finger, then sat on his bed and lay down. I watched his eyes dilate. A red color appeared around the corner of his eyeballs before he raised his camera and shot consecutively.

"No good," I said, after a glance over one photo and the next. "No good, no good, this is boring."

He stood as if lost, looking at the photos I threw at his feet. Then, I heard a sound from downstairs. I pulled the string of my top over my shoulder and moved for the door.

"I don't want some third-rate photographer to take pictures of me," I said before leaving, "bye, bye."

That evening, I told everyone I was sick and would not leave the bedroom. That girl looked at me with her eyes unblinking, like she was observing a strange-looking creature. It felt as if she was asking me, with her eyes—you are hiding something. You are hiding something, aren't you?

So I pulled a blanket over me and said I wanted to sleep.

Yet, I continued to sense those eyes tearing in through the sheet, to the point where the warmth under the blanket began to grow. And sweat formed over my back.

I waited until later that night when she returned after dinner. She slept on her side, facing my way. After many hours, her eyes finally closed, and there came a soft breathing sound. I left the room for my father's room. Mother was downstairs, talking with Aunt. Uncle couldn't handle liquor and always passed out first. Father, on the other hand, was always up late at night to read a book, no matter where he went. He looked up as I entered the room, and was about to ask me what was wrong when I threw myself at his lap.

"Father, he, he's scaring me," I cried.

He asked me who, and I gave the name after some hesitation.

"He was acting weird this morning," I continued. "He called me to his room and told me to lie in his bed. He said he wanted to take pictures of me. I said no, but then he threatened to hurt me. I didn't understand why. He's always quiet, and I used to like him. But now, he said he's going to hurt me. He said he dreamed of hearing me cry. And the way he's looking at me, it makes me sick. Please, Father, you must help me. I'm afraid of what he might do to me. I'm telling the truth, look in his room if you want proof. He must still have the photos."

# SWIMMING LESSON 11

I heard the television turn on in the living room. Aunt Risa's regular cooking show had long since ended. The weather forecast predicted continued hot weather for the next few weeks, a suitable time for swimming in the sea, it said.

The dark green telephone sat over a single cabinet in the hallway, next to the stairs. I felt my hands go cold, hanging down my sides.

I had to confess to one more person.

I could wait until tomorrow, or next Monday when we met at the pool. Ryoka had given me her number, though I had never once called her. From the living room, the opening music of a late-night television series was starting. I finally picked up the receiver and turned the rotary dial. Then I waited until I heard the ringing start.

One ring, two, three.

I planned to give up on the fifth ring.

"Hello?"

I almost dropped the phone. Opening my mouth, only the sound of air came out.

"Hello?" Ryoka's voice spoke, "Rie? Is that you?"

"I'm sorry. Maybe I should call later—"

"Wait!" her voice burst, then went silent for a second. "It's alright. I couldn't sleep anyway."

My hand relaxed around the receiver. I remembered then of earlier this evening, the bouquet, the big house, and what had happened. "Ryoka," my voice came out in a whisper, "are you well?"

"Why do you sound like I am dying?"

"Don't say a thing like that," I said, sitting down on the stair step. "It's just a general question."

"I'm fine," she answered, "never better."

Until that day, I had never known Ryoka to be a good liar.

"So, what's up?"

"Ryoka," I let my voice drag out the sound of her name. "Can we talk? About last year, I still owe you an explanation, about what happened—"

I told her everything, from beginning to end, all except the girl's name. Ryoka had gone silent even after I finished. Aunt Risa had forgiven me, I added. But I couldn't hear her response as if her breathing had stopped.

"So your aunt wasn't angry," Ryoka's voice finally came. "Aren't you glad?"

"Ryoka, there's something I want to say," I spoke, twirling the phone cord around my fingers. "I've wanted to say this out loud for a very long time. I have been thinking about the voice I heard, and every time a question came. Could that have been just a dream? It's like when you are about to take an entrance exam, and you have a nightmare that you've already failed. Back then, though I had agreed to go with that girl, I knew that I was running away from responsibilities. I would betray the promise to my mother that I would join the convent. And I would betray my Aunt, who supported me. The guilt was so much that it consumed me. So could it be that the dream was just my creation, to leave that girl and justify it as an act of God?"

Ryoka had not made a single noise during all this.

"I have her phone number, her address, everything." I continued. "And yet I have never tried to contact her. Neither would she contact me when there are ways she could get my information. And secretly, I was relieved she didn't. Why is that? I think she knows, like I do, that we might end up hating each other, if we ever met. For a long time, I left things in the air, unable to admit that I left her because I couldn't abandon everything else for her. I was the one who said no to her, and I blamed God for it. And I tried to walk into the water because I couldn't bear the guilt. It's all my fault that she got hurt. I brought pain to many people. It's my fault."

A deep tone came, like a hand squeezing around the phone. "What will you do now, Rie?" Ryoka's voice finally came.

"Ryoka, you were the one who pulled me out from where I'd fallen in. You helped me believe in life again. And now, I could finally reach the point where I could live on with my strength. I am ready to move on, making my way forward into the world. No longer shall I let the past hold me back. For all your help, Ryoka, thank you, thank you for everything."

The green ribbon hung around my wrist, the treasure that I had received and would hold onto. It felt like forever since I felt this genuine gratitude, to life and all its hardships that led me to this point, to Aunt Risa, to Miss Himura, to Ryoka.

I even felt grateful to Sayo.

"Rie, would you like to hang out?" Ryoka spoke, "if you like, you could come to stay over at my place for a night."

My finger paused, then released the phone cord. "Your place?" I asked.

"We can go somewhere else if you don't want to."

"No, that's not it." I grasped the phone with both hands, "I want to see where you live."

It had been a long time since I last visited a friend's home.

"Alright then," Ryoka spoke in a final tone. "I will call you this Saturday to confirm the time. Talk to you later, goodnight."

I responded with a quick goodnight, then heard her hang up. Struggling to stand, I placed the receiver back on the phone before my thoughts finally caught up with me. We could meet tomorrow on a school day, so why wait till the weekend? Could it be that she had something she must do? The thought of her getting slapped returned to me. She wasn't going to get herself into that kind of situation again, was she?

The next day, after school, I visited her class. Ryoka had called in sick, according to her classmates. I considered staying with her at home. But she had not given me her address yet.

Ryoka didn't return to school for the rest of the week.

I began to scare myself, thinking about the worst scenarios. But then I received a phone call on Saturday, the moment I got home. Ryoka sounded like she had just woken up when she asked if I had a paper and pen nearby. I took something out of my schoolbag, scribbled down the address as she gave it, and the time I should come.

Another phone call came later that night when I was about to go upstairs.

"Hello?" I picked up the phone.

"Yaa."

At my recognition of the accent, I felt my heart stop for a moment.

"Hello?" The word came in English, "Rie there, isn't it? I recognized how you always hold your breath whenever you're surprised."

I swallowed.

"Have you talked to Ryoka lately?" Sayo continued, "I heard she hasn't come to school. She isn't sick or anything, is she?"

My breath became steady after I let out an exhale, the way I did in the water after swimming. "I was going to meet her at her place tomorrow," I said. "If you have something you need to tell her, would you like me to pass along the message?"

The silence went on for almost five seconds.

"Sayo?"

"Did she ask you to go to her place?"

My lips felt as if frozen. Then, I noticed myself holding a breath.

As Sayo's next sentence came, my ears felt as if covered in ice, preventing her words from escaping my head. Her voice transformed from the earlier cheerfulness into something else, as if spoken by a different person. Then the phone line went dead. And I placed it back on the receiver. I continued to stand there, staring at the phone, hoping it might ring again.

But it didn't.

That night, I dreamed of the beach. The sun looked high in the sky, yet strangely, the air felt cold. I looked and saw someone in the distance, facing the sea. The long dark brown hair fluttered in the wind. I stepped over, placing my hand over her shoulder, and made her turn around. The girl with a face like mine spoke with Sayo's voice.

"You still don't get it, do you?"

~ ~ ~

In the morning, Aunt Risa was flipping through a interior design magazine before starting breakfast. She took a liking to a forest green table cloth with an elaborate vintage pattern. I distracted her by asking what was for breakfast. I boiled some eggs to eat for lunch, then went to my room to finish packing, putting my bed gown inside a bag, and checking that I didn't forget my toothbrush.

I left the house at four.

Ryoka's place appeared closer to the school than mine. I checked the address and remembered her description of the area. I saw a convenience store opposite the one-way road from the bus stop, leading deeper into the alley. I continued walking straight along the old-looking walls, both sides thick with trees. Finally, I saw the five-story apartment building, which seemed to be the oldest among the surrounding houses.

The elevator didn't work, as she had said. So I took the stairs on the side of the building. Ryoka lived on the third floor, the last door at the end of the corridor. I found the place and checked the number.

I had arrived.

The vacuum sounded from inside. I pressed the bell, and the sound stopped. The door opened, and Ryoka stood before me, in a blue t-shirt and her regular short pants.

"You're here," she said with a smile, "was it hard finding the way?"

"No, not at all," I said with a little bow. "Thanks for having me today."

"I'm still in the middle of cleaning," she said, looking behind her with a nervous expression. "Well, come in. Just wait for a bit, five minutes, ok?"

Ryoka stepped backward to let me in, and she showed me where I could leave my shoes before running back inside. The vacuum started again. I found my eyes scanning the vacant area before me, of what was supposed to be the living area. The kitchen area was a little distance away. Behind a bar, the refrigerator looked to be the only piece of furniture here. I put down my bag before removing my shoes, placing them over the newspaper pages by the door. Ryoka had only two pairs of shoes, from the looks of it, one for school, and she seemed to use the school-provided sports shoes for all other occasions. Something smelled, from the kitchen, like old vegetables. I stepped over the bar and saw a half-eaten cucumber with plastic-wrapping still hanging over one side. A bowl stood next to it, half full of white sugar.

The vacuum stopped, and Ryoka found me standing before the refrigerator.

"Do you mind if I look inside?" I asked.

"Go ahead," said Ryoka, with a shrug.

I grasped the handle and pulled. An already opened milk carton tilted a little at the force of the door opening. A bag of tangerines sat at the bottom. The top shelves looked pack full with cucumbers. "Ryoka," I said, "don't tell me you have eaten nothing but cucumbers and sugar?"

"I eat something else too," Ryoka said as I closed the refrigerator, "like milk."

"Ryoka, you are going to get sick, like the other day."

"I know, I know. I am planning to go shopping soon. Anything you like to eat? I can make sandwiches and tea later."

"I have eaten for the evening," I said, being honest, "Aunt Risa's breakfast was delicious."

Ryoka didn't realize it was a joke.

"Come on, don't just stand there. I'll show you my room." Ryoka said, moving away. So I took my bag and followed her. The door to her room was opposite the bathroom. The vacuum machine was still plugged in and left beside the entrance. Coming inside, I spotted first the queen-size bed that took up half the bedroom. A writing desk stood next to the opened window with a large tree outside. It swayed in the wind, causing scratching noise against the frame. Her school bag sat against the wall, next to books, newspapers, and old magazines piling up both sides of the desk. And I could see her wallet, left on top of the pile.

This room alone felt ventilated, with the warm air of July.

"You can put your bag here," Ryoka opened the closet on the right side of the door. "I'm going to the convenience store for a bit. You can have a shower if you like. There's no bathtub, though, sorry."

I let Ryoka walk past me toward the bathroom. The sound of water turned on. And a feeling came to me that something felt off about Ryoka today. Like, she was missing something.

But what was it?

Ryoka returned. Her unruly hair looked better, with water patted onto it.

"Do you need help?" I asked.

"That's alright," Ryoka spoke while moving quickly across the room. She took the wallet and put it in her pocket. "I will be back as soon as I can. Just make yourself at home."

Ryoka left the room, and soon I heard the front door shut.

Silence fell.

I put my bag inside the closet. It would get dark soon during this season. I took out my sleeping gown, thinking of having a shower as Ryoka suggested. A large wind caused the tree branches to brush against the window. I left my bathing kit on the towel and went across the room. A few leaves fell in as I tried to push the branch away and pull the window shut.

A book set at the end of the desk, and I picked it up. *Death in Venice.*

The book had a school library card. The returning date was June of last year. I flipped through the pages and saw they were marked with blue pen. I stopped over a page. "Tadzio was more beautiful than can be expressed in words," I read out loud the underlined sentences. "And Aschenbach again felt pain about the inability of words to honestly describe beauty instead of just praising it. "

I paused at the handwriting underneath the paragraph —

*Aschenbach made Tadzio his saint.*
*Now he would die if the saint left him.*

The book snapped shut between my hands. And I realized I had been holding my breath.

A feeling of guilt rose within me as if I had just read someone's diary. I placed the book back and adjusted its angle to the way I remembered its position being. Then, I left the room. I helped to put the vacuum out of the way. And I went into the bathroom and found the switch. A yellow light appeared without a flicker. The pink bathroom tiles made me blink, and I felt the strong scent of sweet fruit. A sunscreen bottle tilted over the washing basin. *Cantaloupe Scent*, I read, before placing it back. I turned on the water, splashing some over my face before checking my bangs in front of the mirror. Ryoka was right. They were getting too long.

My eyes paused at the sunscreen bottle again, and I realized why Ryoka had seemed off earlier.

She wasn't wearing her sunscreen today.

I hung my towel over the rail next to hers, taking only the soap into the shower. Turning on the water, I waited till the water got warm in my hands, then stepped in. White steam fogged up the shower stall. The feeling of steaming water against my body calmed me only a little. A feeling of unease had been wriggling within me. Something terrible was about to happen. I could sense it with intensity. Like, when you were walking down a familiar road in the morning, and something dark loomed over your head, warning you of an approaching predicament. You couldn't see where it would come from or what form it would take. You could only wait until it happened.

I was wiping my face when I noticed my wrist was bare. A second passed before the realization settled on me. My legs weakened, and panic took over.

The ribbon was gone.

The drain groaned as the water disappeared down the black hole. On my knees, I gripped the drain's opening with my fingers. The steaming shower continued to rain over me as I cried.

I heard the front door open.

Ryoka was calling my name. Her footsteps were moving toward the bedroom. I didn't know how long it was before she started calling me again.

"Rie?" She called after knocking two times. "Are you in there?"

I wrapped my arms around the legs and hid my face between my knees.

"I am coming in."

The sound of her footsteps stopped outside before the stall got opened with a creaking sound. "Rie, what's going on?" Her voice asked, and I felt her bending over me.

The shower stopped, and a wave of cold struck my naked back.

"It's gone," I said.

"What's gone?" Ryoka asked.

"The ribbon you gave me," I answered, "I'm sorry, Ryoka."

The whirlpool got sucked down the drain, causing a croaking sound before silence returned. "What?"

Ryoka's voice came as a whisper, "don't worry about it, Rie. That thing wasn't really—"

"I'm sorry, Ryoka. I'm sorry."

"Rie, it's no big deal." Ryoka spoke, "it's just a piece of ribbon."

I sensed her crouching before me, her hands grasping my naked shoulders. I looked up slowly. Ryoka's expression looked hard, her lips pressed together in a single line. And there was another feeling in her eyes that I couldn't read. A shiver came over me when she let go and stood up.

"I will go downstairs to check around the drain," she said. "If we're lucky, it will get stuck around the end of the pipe. Just dry yourself off, Rie. I will be back soon."

Ryoka left, and soon I heard the front door shut again. The bathroom entrance remained open, letting in the cold air. Struggling to get up, I felt Ryoka's stern tone still echoing in the room, telling me to dry myself. So I reached for my towel and worked it around my shoulders first, then my hair. I put on my sleeping gown and returned to the bedroom, where I saw two plastic bags left on the bed. Ryoka had bought chips, biscuits, and green tea bags. The second bag had bread and canned fish, which reminded me of the sandwiches she used to make.

She tried to make something I liked. Sitting myself down on the bed, I felt the silence. Outside the window, the tree branch hung still.

Ryoka had already been gone for more than ten minutes.

They say you could never know the value of what you had until it was gone. I grabbed my wrist where the ribbon had been. And I remembered what Ryoka had said, that night, on that beach—

*"If you can't find a reason to live, then let me be your reason."*

Those words had comforted me, and the ribbon had been its reminder. It had worked as a seal that held me together. Now that it was loose, my heart became flooded with emotions, like dirty water. I was scared. I had always been scared. Even though I had confessed to my Aunt and freed myself from my past, something remained unchanged.

Ryoka was my reason to live. And if I was to lose that then, I think—

"I would die." The words came out loud.

Wait. What was I thinking?

The front door opened, followed by her light footsteps. I stood up, waiting until she finally appeared at the door. Ryoka took notice of me standing there. Her arms looked wet with black-colored water.

Did you find it? I wanted to ask.

She shook her head, as if knowing my thoughts, before retreating from the door. I heard the bathroom door close quietly. I let myself sit down again, listening to the sound of the water turning on. She stayed there for almost half an hour.

If Ryoka came out, saying that tonight was already ruined and telling me to go home. What would I do?

The sound of water went off, and I heard the door open a few minutes later. Ryoka appeared at the door, with her hair damp. She was wearing a light orange shirt, with the same pants, and had on her scent of cantaloupe. It felt stronger than usual, somehow. Her face held the relaxed expression. "Quite an evening, isn't it?" She said, coming to take one of the plastic bags, "help yourself, Rie. I've got lots of chips and sweets."

I felt able to breathe again.

Ryoka made tea using an old metal pot on a gas stove. And we opened the bags of snacks.

"Up for a game?" Ryoka took out a pack of cards from one of the bags. "I can play Seven or President."

Ryoka took a chip in her mouth before jumping on the bed and started shuffling cards. The feeling took me back. Back in the Tokyo dormitory, when the worst thing you could do was hold a private snack party after curfew, I had become the host of some of those events. Especially after exam season, and we had only wanted to throw a well-done party. My former roommate had always provided us with confeito candies, and I made yaki udon with the goto udon that Aunt Risa sent me. The others had brought snacks, like senbei or specialty sweets. And because we couldn't afford to leave any evidence that a dorm monitor might catch, we had never put food on the bed. Instead, we stacked textbooks in the middle of the room and put newspaper over them to make a table. The paper could then be wrapped and disposed of anywhere on the school premises. To see Ryoka eating food in bed, without regard, felt like a significant change, so I forgot the tension from earlier.

I was overreacting for nothing.

By the next morning, however, I would regret that line of thought.

Ryoka placed two Queens, and I then won the round with two Aces. "You are good at this," she said.

I couldn't tell. Either I had always been a good player and not known it, or Ryoka just didn't do well at games. "You shouldn't play the strong cards too early," I said. "You're supposed to let go of the low numbers first, then work your way up."

"Sounds complicated," she said, "sorry, I just have no patience."

President wasn't that complicated a game.

"How about we play something else? Like, Old Maid?"

"Are you being too kind, Rie? Sometimes I think that's mean of you." Ryoka said, in a teasing manner, "what say we turn this into a penalty game? The loser must answer anything the winner asks?"

"Ryoka, you've been losing this whole time."

"So what?" Ryoka looked straight into my eyes, "don't you have something you want to ask me?"

I made a nervous laugh to cover it up. Did Ryoka know, somehow, that I was following her the other day? No, that sounded unlikely. Sayo might have told on me, after all. But somehow, I got the sense that wasn't the case. So maybe, Ryoka had always been aware that I would be curious after witnessing her conversation with Sayo at the market.

Was she permitting me to ask about Saki?

"Alright," I accepted the challenge and began shuffling. "You will tell me everything I ask, truthfully, right?"

"I swear," Ryoka said, with her hand raised, and a reluctant look. "So, you better not let me win, Rie."

We played again, and the game lasted not many rounds before I won.

"Ask the question," Ryoka said, with a smile that, unlike her usual fox smile, bore an intense feeling.

I opened my mouth, but the question came out sounding like empty air—

Who was Saki?

If I asked that, what then? What would I expect to hear? Though I had wanted to ask her, there existed a part of me that didn't want to. At the sight of Ryoka waiting for me, her eyes unblinking, my instincts kicked in and took hold of my tongue. I felt like I was standing in front of the gate of hell, with my hand over its knob, envisioning what awaited me on the other side.

"About this week, Ryoka." I started again after a swallow.

"This week?" Her head cocked aside with a surprised look.

"You seem—" My gaze lowered as if my head grew heavy. "Ryoka, tell me about your part-time jobs?"

Ryoka finished the tea that had already gone cold before putting it back on the tray. She hung her head to the side, like when she did a warm-up exercise before her gaze met mine again with a disappointed expression. "It's just checkout counter work," she said, "and I have another job at a delivery company. I still help out with morning newspaper delivery when I need extra money. I also used to do traffic research, waiting at a family restaurant, and once, just once, handing out tissue packs."

I nodded in response, allowing a sense of relief to come over me.

Ryoka, however, looked the opposite.

The silence that came a short second later felt like an unspoken agreement. I must never ask a question in which the answer might not give me peace. And Ryoka would never again, indulge me into asking for the reply, if it might end up robbing the peace we had.

There were things better left unspoken.

We stayed up until around nine, and Ryoka suggested we turn in. Because tomorrow we had to wake up early to resume our swimming lessons. Out of habit, I ran through the list of my Sunday house chores. I had finished them all before leaving the house this evening. And I had cooked enough for Aunt Risa tomorrow morning, despite her insisting she could make her own breakfast. Sometimes, I worried that she might get sick for not eating meals at the proper time. Ryoka went for the switch, and I pulled the blanket up to my neck, watching the white neon light snap away. The shadowy shape of Ryoka moved past the window and got in bed, making a slight creaking sound.

The sweet scent of her body caused me to feel like the air grew warmer, suddenly. And I felt an urge, that I could not name.

Ryoka turned her face away, sleeping on her side. I took a deep breath before making a long exhale quietly. Somehow, I was thinking of that girl, now, how she used to embrace me, and how her uniform always smelled like sunflower seeds. But that girl and Ryoka were two different people.

I closed my eyes and gave a long sigh. The strange urges within my body eased.

Ryoka was just Ryoka.

A noise woke me up, and I saw the branch outside swaying in the wind. I blinked until my eyes became adjusted to the dark, and I could distinguish the white tone of the ceiling from the pitch blackness. Something told me that I'd only been sleeping a few hours.

"Are you awake?" Ryoka's voice startled me.

The feeling of her eyes watching me forced my eyes to reopen. "I couldn't sleep," I said.

"Let's stay up and talk. We haven't talked like this for a long time, have we?"

"What do you want to talk about?" I asked, turning myself sideways to face her.

"Say, if I was a boy, Rie. Would you marry me?"

"We are both girls," I said with a small laugh. "It can't be helped."

"Does that matter to you?" Ryoka spoke. "I have never thought it matters, whether you choose to be with a boy or a girl. Words like gays or lesbians mean nothing to me. They're just words, but you and I are human beings. We choose whom we like. So let's say I wanted to make you happy. What would you say?"

At Ryoka's gaze, I felt a familiar emotion long forgotten, warming up inside me like a creature waking up after a long slumber.

"Ryoka, who is Saki?" The words slipped from my mouth. And silence fell between us, so fierce that the air itself sounded like a storm rumbling. Despite the darkness, I could notice the startled expression in Ryoka's eyes. They looked like two beads glowing in the dark.

"Did Sayo talk to you?" Her voice came in a whisper.

"A little," I confessed.

"Saki was my friend," Ryoka answered. "She and I, we used to hang out a lot. And I ended up rubbing Sayo in the wrong way. To her, I was just a pest stuck to her little sister. I can't blame her, though, for the bad things she might have told you about me."

Sayo had said lots of things. Yet, I didn't recall her speaking ill of Ryoka.

"So, what happened?" I asked, "to Saki, I mean."

Ryoka let out a long exhale. The glow disappeared from her eyes. "She died," said Ryoka, "she disappeared into the sea, the exact place where you went."

My lips hung open.

The air felt as if frozen. Words came to my mouth before I swallowed them down. After what had happened last year, I learned that the place held a reputation by the locals, to be the spot where death sometimes washed ashore. Unlike another location on the other side of town, which opened as a tourist spot, the beach we had gone was narrow and dangerous when typhoons came. So there were almost no houses there. And no one would notice if a person drowned themselves in the water.

I had asked about Saki and received the answer.

Saki was dead.

The answer didn't give me peace. A cold feeling, like a large hole, opened in my chest. The cold air rushed inside and filled me up with dread.

"Ryoka," I found my voice again, "how could you ever get over something like that?"

Her eyes disappeared for a second as if blinking. Ryoka let out a soft sigh before lying on her back, with one arm over her forehead. "Ah," her whisper came, "this won't work."

"Ryoka?"

My voice disappeared in the dark. The shape of Ryoka looked close yet felt far away.

"You still haven't answered my question, Rie," she said after a long second. "Say I like you and wanted to make you happy. What's your answer?"

"Ryoka, don't make a joke like that," I said.

"You don't think I am serious?" She said, turning to her side once again. "Rie, I always knew you had feelings for someone else. You have your past, and I understand that. But your past is long over. You may not realize this, but my life has revolved around you for almost a year now. I can't live without you, Rie. And I don't want to live my life, knowing that I could lose you at any time. You and me, we could make it last forever, together. I am not that girl. I am just me. But I am right here, Rie. Choose me."

I felt my heart pound, as if the beast in me was finally awake.

Ryoka's hand moved as if searching for mine. The beast inside me had no name, yet, had many. And one of those names was 'love'. When it spoke its will, I felt like what was happening now had always been destined. Whether I wanted to or not, in the end, I would come to love Ryoka. Fate had decided, and the time for its fulfillment was finally at the door. The wind was stirring up outside the window, causing the branch to make a sharp, screeching noise against the window, like a devil's claw. I reached out to grasp her hand, squeezing as if to confirm that all which began and led up to this point was true.

I didn't want to lose Ryoka, who had become my reason to live. I could bind her to me, like a ribbon tied to my wrist. Only this time, to my soul.

All I must do was say yes.

# SWIMMING LESSON 12

Until that night, I had never known what girls could do for one another when their feelings transformed beyond friendship. Ryoka's hand slipped under my gown, moving up, and squeezing my breast. Her cold body pressed on top of me. Her sweet scent made me sweat under my thin dress. The sheet felt as hot as a pan, and the air felt like summer. I returned her kiss, feeling Ryoka's lips sweet with a slight bitterness, like toothpaste and green tea. My breath grew short as Ryoka's hand began moving lower. My eyes tightened, feeling her fingers breaking in. I squirmed as mixed emotions burst within me.

*"You still don't get it, do you?"*

I pushed Ryoka away suddenly.

Sayo's voice came like a burst, despite being as quiet as a whisper, like a nail hammered down behind my neck. And I turned away from Ryoka, toward the side, clutching myself like a bird without feathers. Intense emotions of joy and bitterness were contrasting one another. I felt sick, and I braced my arms around my stomach. The feeling surged up, until I covered my mouth, forcing myself to swallow down the sour taste saliva.

A thud sounded, as Ryoka fell back into the mattress, followed by her long sigh.

"I'm sorry," I said.

"Don't, Rie." Her voice answered, in a soft tone, yet clear like a water drip amidst the silence. "You just saved me."

My stomach eased at her voice. Though I couldn't comprehend the meaning of her words, at that moment, I sensed she wasn't angry. Instead, she sounded relieved. I turned to lie on my back and forced my face to look at her. Ryoka's eyes met mine, and I felt her grip around my hand.

"We are friends," said she, "let's not ruin that, deal?"

I returned her squeeze. And what had happened just seconds ago felt like smoke blown away by a soft wind. "We are friends," I responded.

Ryoka continued to hold on to my hand. Until I finally closed my eyes.

Some say a sinner can finally be at rest, once they've been forgiven. Because I didn't want to lose Ryoka, I had tried to secure her, using love as the means. But Ryoka was not that girl. I could not love her the same way, so my body had revolted. Ryoka deserved to be angry, after I was about to let her do what she would with me, only to have me reject her.

But she forgave me.

Once the morning arrived, I woke up to the sight of Ryoka still sleeping on her side, next to me. Her face looked peaceful.

I got up.

The clock on Ryoka's desk said half-past five. The sun had yet to come up. I went to the bathroom to fill water in both hands and rinsed my face, feeling awake. Then, I noticed the sunscreen bottle that had been half-full last night. Its contents had been squeezed empty. Ryoka remained in the same position when I returned. I moved my face closer to observe her breathing like a baby fawn. She must have exhausted herself with her work, school, and what happened last night on top of everything.

We had planned to go to the pool today. But I thought of just letting Ryoka sleep.

Maybe, I could invite her to hang out again this Sunday.

At six o'clock, the sky looked deep blue outside the window. I finished changing into a school uniform and left the room, going into the kitchen. Ryoka had many pots and utensils. Most looked unused except for the rice cooker. I could make a dish with rice, cucumbers, and canned fish, but she didn't have miso.

The convenience store I'd passed yesterday had a sign saying it was open twenty-four hours.

But I didn't have enough money.

Ryoka had left her wallet on top of her pile of books. I could borrow some from her and pay her back tomorrow. After what I had seen at the market, I wouldn't take her unusual diet lightly. Returning to the bedroom, I tiptoed past the bed, found the wallet, took out a banknote, and looked inside. Ryoka appeared to have enough to buy meals for herself at a good restaurant for a week. She reminded me of how older people kept money under their mattresses while eating meagerly, and wore the same clothes till they fell apart. Either that or she was just bad at taking care of herself.

I was putting the wallet back when I noticed something sticking out of the pile.

A letter?

I knelt, gripping its corner while holding back the book pile with my other hand. The top stack was tilting sideways.

Ryoka made a stirring sound behind me.

I froze, turning my face aside. But I heard no more noise. Using one hand to hold onto the desk, I stood up and found Ryoka had shifted her position to lay her face up. My hand had crumpled the letter. I moved closer to the window, where the morning light was coming up. Without a noise, I unfolded the letter folded in three parts and found a newspaper clipping inside.

### COUPLE SUICIDE, One Death

*A body was discovered this morning*
*washed up on the local beach. Police have*
*Identified the deceased to be one of*
*the two who had run away from home*
*two weeks prior—*

The article had offered no details regarding the death's identity. I put the paper behind the letter and began to read what was written there in a blue pen. The sun was coming up at the far end of the sky when I finished the letter, from the first sentence until its ending, where a name was signed—*Saki.*

I left her place before Ryoka woke up. My hand clutched the letter as I ran.

~ ~ ~

A week had passed. I had not gone to school and already missed the midterm exam. Aunt Risa bought me dinner last night, which I had not eaten. And this morning, she came to check on me again. I told her I wasn't hungry while sitting in the bed, clutching the blanket, covering me from the head down.

Ryoka had been calling since Monday.

I read the article, then the letter, over and over. Each time, once my eyes came across the signed name, a sharp pain rose in my chest.

Ryoka had lied to me.

The pain cut so sharply that I gasped for breath. Then the pain eased as if the wound inside closed itself. Until the realization once again made another cut. She had lied to me!

The phone rang downstairs. Aunt Risa picked up. She hung up less than five minutes later before I heard her footsteps coming up the stairs. The knocking startled me. She pushed the door halfway. "Your friend called again," she said. "She asked me to tell you that she wants to meet with you. Tomorrow, she will be waiting at the spot you wanted to go?"

Her last sentence came as a question.

I knew the place mentioned.

Aunt Risa had, for the past week, refrained herself from intervening. But I sensed that she would soon reach her limit. Unless I did something, she would snap. And I would have to bear the blame, for failing to explain to her why I had returned home last Monday and had not left my room since.

I told her that I would be fine soon, and in time I would explain to her what was going on. And she retreated from the door.

The next day, I left the house around four, riding my bike through the route I knew well. The salty scent reminded me of what I had long dismissed from my mind. Within fifteen minutes, I found myself arriving at the destination. The strong wind sounded like a devil's howl across the vast blue surface. The surf rushed toward the shore before bursting into white foam.

I felt as if returning home.

Ryoka stood facing the water. The surf swept past her before retreating, leaving her school shoes soaking wet. She turned around the moment I came close, and her blue sailor scarf fluttered in the wind. "Give me back the letter, Rie," she spoke. "That wasn't for you to see."

I stepped toward her, pushing the crumpled letter against her chest. "Read it," I said, as calm as I could, "please Ryoka, read it for me."

Ryoka's grip clung to the letter, as it flapped in the wind. She unfolded it with both hands. Her eyes dropped over the sentences. "Dear Mother. Dear Father. Dear Sayo—"

The sharp air caused her voice to shake.

"First, I would like to say sorry," she continued to read as if reciting a prayer. "Right now, you are probably asking why? Why, after all these years of love and care you gave me, I decided to leave you? It is because I have grown up and found the world a lonely place when Ryoka can't be with me. As you are aware, I have fallen in love with Ryoka. She has offered me a place where my heart belongs. And with her, I no longer fear anything. I no longer fear even death.

"Please—" Ryoka's fingers dug into the paper, "please hear my final request. Please remember me as your daughter and your sister. I have decided to die not because I hate you but because I want to cling on to this happiness that I have found. If I am not allowed to be with her in this world, maybe in another world, I can. Thank you for all you have done for me, Mother, Father, Sayo. Goodbye—"

Ryoka's lips trembled when the word "Saki' came, the smallest sound that got brushed away by the wind.

"Were you trying to kill yourself, Ryoka?" I asked, holding up the article, "with Saki?"

Ryoka's fluttering hair hid her expression as she gazed at the piece of newspaper. She then reached one hand to take it, but the tip of her fingers kept missing its corner. When her fingers finally held onto it, and I let go, the paper flew out of her fingers.

I kept my eyes toward Ryoka.

Her eyes looked like two black holes. Both her hands, now crumpled on the letter, caressed it to her chest.

"All this time, you told me to have hope. Were those lies?" My voice raised as I continued, feeling a tear at the corner of my eye. "I trusted you, Ryoka. You told me things, but what had you been doing? You couldn't even practice what you preached. You pretended to be someone you're not. How could you, Ryoka? How could you!?"

"Shut up, Rie!"

My throat felt as if being cut. Ryoka's face raised. "You were always selfish, Rie," said she, "you have always been nothing but a shackle around my neck. Always, you want things to go the way you want. And when they don't, you cry and whine like a child. I have had enough of you."

"Ryoka—" I called her name, but then my voice died. And I asked myself, who was this girl before me? She bore a face like Ryoka, but not the one I knew.

"Once, long ago, I had Saki with me." Ryoka continued, both arms now hung beside her, the letter in one hand. "Saki was the only warmth in my life, so you're asking me if I tried to die with her?"

I gulped.

"No, Rie, if I tried to die with her, why would I still be here?" Ryoka said, with a smile like two blades. "I just killed her."

The surf pounded the shore somewhere close, and its water rushed past our feet. Ryoka brushed her hair aside, revealing her cold eyes. I felt my feet frozen as if death itself was standing before me. She searched in her pocket before pulling out a familiar green object. "Just take this thing off my hands, Rie," she said, pressing it to my chest. "I don't want it."

I held onto the ribbon with both hands, and felt it flutter.

Ryoka's hand swung across my face. First came the stun, as my foot moved on step back, the surprise was followed by burning pain. "This," she said, "is for hurting me."

I remained standing. My heart felt as if it had turned into an empty vase, broken. And as I struggled to understand what was happening, a single wish filled my heart, wanting to wake up from this nightmare. Until the burning pain over my face continued to cut into my skin. Then I came to acknowledge the blankness inside my chest was real.

Ryoka turned and left the beach, leaving me with my feet sinking into the wet sand.

The green ribbon continued to flutter in my hand as I raised it over my head and threw it away. A stroke of wind picked it up. I watched it fly over the blue surface and disappear.

*"You have only yourself to blame for forcing your ideal onto her, based on your imagination alone."*

Sayo's words felt like a rush of wind against my face. Then, something warm ran down and stopped at the corner of my lip, its taste like the sea.

The next morning, I heard the phone ring while I was still in bed. I had been awake for a few hours now but had no heart to get up. The knocking came before the door opened, and Aunt Risa's face popped in. She told me that I should take this call. So I followed her downstairs, part of my hair stuck to my face, still wearing a sleeping gown. She gave me the receiver before retreating into the kitchen. I pressed the phone to my ear and spoke. The person on the other side responded by telling me to come to school this evening. Once I put back the receiver, I returned to my room and took the green notebook from my desk. I finished the last few pages as best as I could without leaving a single part out. I touched my face where it hurt. The pain remained there as I remembered it.

The school on Sunday looked vacant as if all people had vanished from the world. The security let me in without asking a word. I had arrived late. The clock above the building already said five.

The teacher's office had the radio on, broadcasting a comedy program. I was about to knock at the door when I heard Miss Himura's voice—

"Sayo, it would be better if you don't intervene."

I slid the door open and peeked in. Miss Himura's back sat in her turnable chair. The person on the phone spoke in an American accent in English, loud enough for me to catch a few words of 'you promised' and a string of curse words. Miss Himura turned around suddenly and saw me. So I pushed the door aside and gave her a bow.

"I've got to go." Miss Himura responded in English.

"I'll kill you for harbouring that Bitch! I'll kill you—"

Miss Himura placed the receiver back and heaved a long sigh, closing her eyes as she leaned back against the chair. She wore a black vest over a white top with a long skirt today, the first time in years, I'd seen her in casual clothing. Once her eyes reopened, she took a sip of hot water from a teacup before putting it down next to a book. My eyes caught over its title, the English Version of *Death in Venice*.

"Have you ever read it?" She asked, noticing me looking. "Last year, somebody donated the title to the school library, a Japanese version and this one. I told you, right? That I have been reading an English-translated German classic."

I remained standing before her.

"Why don't you sit down, use any chair you want."

"I can stand, Miss."

Miss Himura paused, her eyes at the notebook, then at me. "Not you too," she said. "The other day, Ryoka was also mad at me. So for the past week, I have been hated by you, Ryoka, and the girl on the phone. Being a teacher is tougher than I thought."

I felt my fingers press around the book's corner.

"You can keep that book for now," she said, joining her hands together over her lap. "I told you to hand it in on graduation day, right? And you're just halfway through it. You shouldn't rush over something that is supposed to be long-term learning."

"You needed to speak to me?" I asked, doing my best to keep my tone from rising.

"Ah, yes." She took a thin stack of papers on her desk and handed them over. "You haven't come to school, so here are the notes from your classmate. Let me know once you recover from your sickness. You still have to take the midterm exam."

"Is that all you wanted to talk about?" I asked.

"Is there something else?"

"Miss, I know you enough to notice whenever you're up to something. Like that time, when you were in school, and you hid the students who ran away from home in the club room. You always had the habit of reading some book over and over whenever you got yourself into something, saying it would give you inspiration to understand the ongoing."

Miss Himura rested one elbow over the table and raised her left cheek on it. "You're as perceptive as always."

"I always sensed that you had something to do with Ryoka. But I haven't pried because I felt it wasn't my business to get in your way, until now." I took a breath to stop myself from trembling. "Maybe, I just didn't want to know. Since last year, I have been ashamed of myself for being a nuisance to my Aunt and you. So I didn't want to admit that you had gone as far as assigning Ryoka to take care of me."

"Rie, now you lost me."

"Ryoka is—" I ignored her, "not in a position to take care of anyone. She has her own troubles. I still don't know in full details. But Miss, if you've assigned the blind to take care of another who is blinded, both of them will fall into a well. So please, help me understand. Why did you do such a thing as sending me to her?"

"Are you implying that I arranged for Ryoka to take care of you?"

"What else could it be?" I asked back, with the tone of something exploding inside me. Before all went silent, and a burst of laughter came from the radio.

"Rie, you misunderstand me," Miss Himura said after a sigh, "think back on the day when you came to me after I signed you up for the Swimming Association. What did I say to you?"

I forced myself to think back.

"I told you to get to know other people, didn't I? Have I said anything to imply that someone has to take care of anybody else?"

My gaze fell at my feet.

Miss Himura was nursing her temple with one finger. The laughter from the radio grew louder. She bent aside to open the top drawer, taking out a light green color notebook and handing it to me. My eyes spotted the name written over its cover in blue pen. "Rie, you couldn't possibly think," said she, "that you are the only one suffering in this world, do you?"

I was reaching out both hands to grasp the book when the office's blue-grey vinyl floor gave me the feeling of being drowned. Memories were flooding back to me, of the sea, the campfire, and the beach.

That night, Ryoka had saved me.

*"Live on, Rie, stubbornly, until you learn what value life is. And once you can do that then,"* her next sentence got enfolded away by the sound of the sea.

But, I could read her lips.

I couldn't place a word back then. Until now, when the second notebook in my hand offered the hint. Her last sentence went something like—

*"Please, save me too."*

"Did you fake it?" She cornered me.

"He forced me," I said, with my eyes staring into hers.

She raised her hand. I gulped, thinking she was going to slap me. But instead, she held my face in both hands. Her eyes exposed a piercing expression. "Tell me the truth," she said, the tips of her fingers pressed under my chin. "Aunt and Uncle are now scorned by everyone. Someone also sent those photos to the University. Takeru has lost his place there. His future is in shambles. So tell me the truth, did you fake everything?"

"I didn't."

"I won't get mad," she said. "And I will side with you no matter what. I won't even tell anyone, so tell me."

"I am telling the truth." I spoke, "he forced me to lie in his bed and said he would make me feel pain if I tried to run or tell anybody. I pleaded with him, said that he should stay true to you. But do you know what he said? He laughed, saying who would want to be with a stupid girl. He called you ugly and said he likes me better. If I did what he said, he would take care of me and buy me the things I want. And again, I cried, asking him not to break your heart. Still, he laughed, and laughed, said he was planning to dump you on graduation day anyway. A girl like you, he told me, there were plenty of idiots like you. He even had sex with heaps of girls beside you. He boasted about it, saying I could be one of his girls, and we would make the best couple. He promised to marry me, and we would move abroad together, never having anything to do with you anymore."

Her fingers continued to press under my chin, and I felt my heartbeat against her fingertips. The steady sound, without rising, confirmed my innocence.

For a moment, I almost believed my own lies.

Her hands grasped around my neck, suddenly, and she forced me down over the bed. My mouth gaped for air. "What are you?" Her voice came in a whisper before it burst, "what the fuck are you!?"

I grasped her hands. And the grip loosened a little.

"Aren't you afraid?" She asked, "aren't you afraid to die?"

I shook my head.

Her grip tightened once more. "I'll kill you, you bitch. I'LL FUCKING KILL YOU!"

I thought I was going to die. But then something warm dripped over my face. I looked and saw that she was crying.

"Do you want me that much?" She said, with a tone like something shattering in the air. "Fine, I give up. From now on, I will be with you. I will cling to you like a collar to your neck. I won't let you be free from me. And if you ever try to build your happiness, I will tear it down. I will inflict anyone who dares get close to you with all kinds of pain. I will make your life feel like taking poison each day, till you want to die ten times over. And no matter how much you try to escape, I will come after you. I will drag you down to the bottom of hell!"

She let go of my neck.

I coughed in an attempt to breathe. Then I saw her face. The face looked familiar yet different. The face that once held a warm expression when calling my name now looked pale as porcelain. Her eyes looked like shards of ice. And I felt the sudden realization that I had hurt her, just like that time when I broke that doll in my father's office. I tried to reach my hands out, to hold her. But she got up and left the room.

The girl I loved, I had broken her.

The prickling sensation felt like a piece of the broken porcelain stuck to my heart.

So, this is feeling.

———◇———

PART 2

# RELATION

## Ryoka Namie

# SWIMMING LESSON 13

_____

As a child, I had learned my name written in kanji as 'Ryo' for cold and 'ka' for evil. Still, I had never disliked the name that my father had given me. Most of the children had fathers, and their fathers loved them. But for a reason that I was too young to understand back then, I was told by Mother never to show myself in front of him.

"You will make your father get mad." She told me.

Every day after school, I walked to a Daycare across the street, run by a Christian Organization. I would wait there, as told, until Mother came to pick me up after eight or nine at night. Father would be going to bed by then, exhausted from his work, according to Mother. I didn't dislike the Daycare. We always had toys, games, and a teacher who loved to tell stories from the Bible.

"So long as you believe in God, you will never suffer." The teacher said, "because God always listens and will answer your prayers."

And so I prayed, day after day, that Father would love me.

One day, instead of going to the Daycare, I took a bus home. I wanted to see my father. It was his birthday, and I wanted to congratulate him. I waited outside our house until after six that he got home, then followed him into the house. Mother looked at me coming through the door like she'd just seen a cockroach. And Father slapped me, so hard I rammed into a porcelain vase by the door, crushing it. By some luck, the shattered pieces didn't hurt me. But my face became numb, and I tasted salty blood at the corner of my lip, followed by a sharp pain.

"Have I not told you," he screamed at my mother, "never to let me see it in my house!"

At that moment, I understood. Though God answered all prayers, his answer to me would always be no.

God hates me.

Since that day, Mother no longer sent me to Daycare. Father had come home even less, and she had never forgiven me. Years passed, and I became like a stranger living in someone's house. So once I got into high school, wanting to make it up to Mother, I decided to stay away from home as much as possible. Then, I came across the school's swimming pool. No one ever came here unless there was a swimming class. Students preferred to go to a beach nearby than this twenty-five-meter pool. So I made this place my sanctuary. I came here two times each school day, during lunch break and after school. Once winter was over, there came many days where the sky had not a single cloud. And I would lie over a pool bench, letting the sun bask over me.

I had been born with an unusually low body temperature. My body was always so cold, that I never broke a sweat.

The sun always warmed me.

The night before I met Saki, I had a nightmare of the world turning white. My house was white up to the roof. The road to my school was white. The walls were white. The birds, the flowers, the sky had all turned white. Even the people and my parents had turned faceless, wearing white clothes. They stopped as I moved past them, turning my way. My feet paused before the paddle. I looked down, then woke up in a startle. The clock by my bedside said three at night. The dream felt like an omen, foretelling misfortune soon to come upon me. I couldn't go back to sleep after, and the following day, I came to school in a dreadful state of mind. I struggled through morning classes, half asleep. Then, once the bell signaled lunchtime, I went to the school's pool. The pale turquoise water looked transparent in the sun as I entered. I lay over my favorite bench and closed my eyes, feeling the sun over me.

The rippling sound of water in the wind deepened the silence, giving me peace.

My eyes opened, sensing an interruption. I saw a girl just entering the pool area from the other side. She searched for something under the bench before pressing her face against the staff office's window.

"Excuse me!" I called out.

She turned.

"Whatever you're doing, could you please hurry?"

"Sorry!" She responded. "I lost something yesterday here. Could you help me?"

Yesterday was Sunday. The janitor usually came to clean the pool in the afternoon, from what I knew. "Why don't you check inside the *Lost and Found Box*?"

The girl turned toward the office before looking back at me. The place had never been locked, but she probably didn't know that, seeing as she wasn't wearing a school uniform. I went over, moving past her into the office. The box sat at the bottom shelf, with 'Lost and Found' written in permanent red ink.

"Found it," she said, picking out a pair of orange swimming goggles. "My big sister bought me these for my birthday. She would get mad if I lost them."

A pair of goggles in such an ugly color for someone's birthday? Her sister sure had poor taste. She seemed interested in the other items in the box—the two ten yen coins, a few accessories, and even a car key. The girl herself, I saw, had blue eyes like a bisque doll. Her dark brown hair looked like gold in the sun. And she bore a strange sweet scent. The shape of her bra strings were showing beneath the light yellow T-Shirt. And her short pants exposed her full legs. She looked Japanese. However, those blue eyes suggested she was one of those halves, with one parent being a foreigner.

"Give me your hand," she said suddenly, with a smile. Her eyes raised to meet mine. "Come on. Any side would do."

I gave her my left hand.

She picked out a faded-looking green ribbon from the box. Tying it around my wrist, she secured its end with a knot.

"What is this for?" I asked, pulling back.

"I return your favor with a gift," she said, "And a thing offered from a maiden's hand will give you good luck by shielding you from misfortune, like a Protective Charm."

"That's if I was a boy," I said. "I am not."

"So you don't like the gift," she cocked her head aside, eyes unblinking. "What then should I give you?"

"I don't want anything. Just take this thing off me."

Her eyes dilated as if I had surprised her somehow. "You were looking at my legs earlier," she said. "Do you think I am pretty? Maybe I should let you kiss me to return the favor?"

I felt warmth over my face.

She put a hand over her mouth, half hiding an amused expression. Then, she extended her hand. "I am Saki Odani, nice to meet you."

I gazed down at her hand until a few seconds had passed, and she finally retreated.

"And your name?" Saki asked.

"Ryoka Namie," I answered.

"You're blushing." Saki's face came closer. I forgot to breathe for a second. And her lips parted so that I could see her perfect line of teeth. "Well, Ryoka, since I have already somehow satisfied you, given how your face turned red like that, consider the favor paid in full."

She turned to leave.

"Wait, take this thing off me." I raised my voice and her face turned. Her eyes narrowed at the ribbon hanging below my wrist.

"Take that as a bonus," Saki said. "And if you should come to hate it one day, pass it on. Who knows, you might give your good luck to someone."

She left through the front gate, and I found my left hand dropping just below my chest. A bell rang, signaling the lunch break was over. I put the box back before hurrying to the pool bench, where I had left my blue sailor scarf. Redoing my uniform as I ran, I returned to the classroom just in time. As I sat down at my desk, however, Saki's voice sounded within me—

*"Do you think I am pretty?"*

That evening when I returned there, I peeked through the entrance first before finding the pool empty.

I had not seen her again, even after a whole week had passed. During this time, I began to notice that something in me had changed. No longer could I close my eyes and feel relaxed. The sun remained where it had been. Yet, often I found myself opening my eyes in disappointment to see the sun so far away.

The sun had felt weak ever since that day.

"Sa—ki," I found myself calling her name one day while laying at my usual spot, like a fragment of a daydream escaped through my lips.

The light vanished. I opened my eyes, startled to find a shadow, like a person was bending over me. "Are you alright?" said a voice, "you've been twitching around like you're having a nightmare. Anything I can do to help?"

"You could help," I said, "move aside. You're blocking the sun."

Saki retreated, and the light revealed her figure, clutched inside a black one-piece swimsuit. The sudden exposure to the sun caused my sight to falter before I could look again at her from a different angle. She was tying her hair back in a ponytail before putting on a swimming cap. I watched as she moved toward the far end of the pool and onto the jumping platform.

Her body leaped through the air, and it felt as if time had stopped. The sound of the impact caused me to awaken fully.

I wasn't dreaming.

Saki swam freestyle toward the other side, then back. She repeated the process, not stopping until after her tenth lap. She was swimming toward the poolside. I lay my head back, listening to the sound of her getting out.

"The water is nice and cool this time of year, isn't it?" She said.

"It's always hot, almost all year here in Nagasaki."

"Aren't you going to swim, too?" Her voice felt close. I heard her footsteps and sensed her sitting on the bench next to mine. "It's a shame to be at a pool and not be swimming."

"Don't want to," I said with my eyes closed. "I hate swimming."

"But if you aren't going to, why are you wearing a swimsuit underneath your clothes?"

I sat up, consciously wrapping my arms around my chest. Saki's expression changed like once again I had done something that amused her. Her breasts looked fully grown, unlike mine. Water formed beads over her shoulders and was dripping down her arms. I turned my eyes away as she crossed her legs, stretching out her toes. My face burnt at the sight of water dripping down her legs.

"Do you always use a swimsuit for underwear?" She asked.

"It's practical, easy to clean, and I got two of them when entering this school," I said. "So, I thought I might make good use of them."

"Nice idea," she spoke the two words in English, with the quick accent that I once heard during a school trip to Okinawa. "But swimsuits are made for swimming. Come on, let's swim. How about a race?"

"Can't you leave me alone?" I said, directing my gaze at hers. "Seriously, who do you think you are, coming here and acting like you own the place. Just leave me, shoo!"

"No," she spoke. "I like it here too, you see. How about we decide this with a game, Ryoka? Whoever wins can order the other person around. If you win, you can command me to leave. Fair?"

I didn't remember letting her call me by the first name.

"What game?" I asked, curious.

"Tell me what kind of person I am, and I will tell you what kind of person you are." Saki said, "whoever gets it most correct, wins."

"But how I am supposed to know you," I said. "I just met you ten days ago."

"Oh, so you've been counting. I am flattered to be missed."

Somehow, the sun was getting stronger over my face. "You're annoying," I said, avoiding her eyes.

"Guilty," she said, "tell me more."

"You like everyone to pay attention to you," I said, "and you often succeed in getting people to cater to your needs. But neither of those lasts because people aren't stupid. The moment they get tired of you, you're left alone once more. And so now you, with nothing else going on, have to spend your time here annoying me to death, like a brat wanting attention."

Her eyes narrowed for a second. "You sure speak your mind, don't you?" she said.

"I was right, wasn't I?"

"You are," she said, resting her face over one hand. "Because you just described what's true about everyone. Who in this world doesn't want to be loved?"

I closed my eyes, feeling pressure from the light.

"My turn," Saki said before stretching both arms past her ears. Then she leaned backward, supporting herself with both arms. "You are a loner. You have tried to get me to leave from the start, and I thought you were just a bully. But that wasn't the case. No, it's the opposite. You are just afraid of people, aren't you?"

I gulped.

"You have an unpleasant home life," she continued, "otherwise you wouldn't spend hours here after school. It's not that you don't have any friends. You just never know how to keep one. You think everyone dislikes you, and so you try to act all intimidating. But I feel you are probably kinder than you look. Say, if you came across a puppy drowning in a river, you would jump in without a second thought to save it, even though you can't swim—"

"You are wrong," I interrupted. "I can swim."

"Ryoka, come on. You can't cheat now."

"I can!" I said. "What kind of person can't swim at this age?"

"Liars get a long nose, you know."

I got up, unbuttoning my uniform to reveal the one-piece blue swimsuit underneath. The heated ground burnt against my feet as I stepped toward the pool. I tested the water first, and my toes clenched upon touching the surface.

My legs froze by the poolside.

"Don't hurt yourself, Ryoka," Saku's voice spoke. "It's not like I am forcing you."

My heart was pounding like a hammer as cold fear gripped me. Saki's stare from behind began to feel heavy. I jumped, feeling my legs crushing down the surface first. Then my whole body submerged down into the icy sensation. Realizing that I wore no goggles, my eyes closed tight. My breath felt as if it had stopped, but then my body remembered the old lessons. I'd had learned to swim before, back in elementary, when learning to swim was mandatory.

My legs began to kick under the water. My body moved upward and resurfaced. I took a deep inhale while stabilizing myself with both arms. My wet hair draped over my surface. I was shivering.

I gripped the poolside to get out when I saw Saki crouch down above me.

"So you can swim." She said.

"Move aside, Saki." My voice shattered.

"Ryoka, are you perhaps afraid of the water?" She said, "what is it, some health issue from birth?"

"Saki, please. I have to get out."

"Ryoka," Saki spoke, her hands parted the hair off my eyes. And she held me by the face, fingers under my chin, so that I felt my heartbeat drum against her fingertips. "You lost the game. So now you will do what I say. I want you to swim."

"Why would I? Let me out!"

Saki sighed. "Alright, take my hands."

I took her hands, thinking she was going to pull me out of the water. But instead, she knelt over the poolside and continued to hold onto me. Her hands felt warm, like tiny hot water bags. "Feeling better?" She said, "now try kicking the water, slowly."

Saki had not blinked once for the past ten seconds.

I did what she said.

"I'm going to let you hold the poolside now. But I'll still be here, ready?"

I nodded, and she placed my hands down. Once the warmth from her hands left mine, my legs subconsciously sped up.

"Now, I want you to listen to me while continuing to kick the water." Saki said, "I am sure there are reasons for you to be afraid of the water. But the water itself is not scary."

"It's cold—"

"Don't stop." Her voice raised a little.

I began to move my legs again and found myself in a rhythm. The water didn't feel as cold as before.

"The only person who decides what's scary is you. The water itself has no power unless you give it one. Tell me, Ryoka, do you want to be under the thumb of your fear forever? You are not weak. And I often find that when people put their mind to something, they can surpass even their worst fear. Are you feeling a bit warmer now? Good. When you are ready, slowly let go of the poolside and swim over to that platform. And from there, swim straight forward to the other side and back. I will meet you next to the first platform. Any questions?"

I shook my head.

"I will never let you drown, so long as I am here. So you must give it your all. I want to see you surpassing your fear."

I took a deep breath, then pushed myself off the poolside. My legs and arms fought their way through the water, toward the nearest platform. And from there, I swam toward the other side and then back. Saki was there when I raised my face over the water.

"One more lap, as you did before. Keep swimming, or it will get cold."

I obeyed her and swam one lap after another. Comparing the cold, Saki somehow felt less scary. The thought of getting out of the water didn't occur to me so long as I could see her within sight. And her presence reassured me.

She would never let me drown.

The sky turned red when she finally signaled for me to stop. The clock above the office said half-past five. There was still almost half an hour left before a teacher came to lock the pool.

"Are you going already?" I asked, grasping the poolside.

Saki finished putting her clothes back on. "My big sister would get mad if she couldn't find me," she said. "I've left my towel over the bench with your clothes. Come back tomorrow morning, and we will resume our lesson. Your class starts at eight, but the school gate opens before six. So we'll start our lesson at six. I don't have school myself, so I am flexible with time—"

"And if I say no?"

"Then this place is mine." She said, "learn to swim until you overcome your fear, or I will take the pool from you."

"What are you? The school owner?"

"No," she said, "but my family donated money to build this pool. Make sure you have plenty of sleep tonight, and bring goggles and a cap tomorrow. See you."

"Wait!"

But Saki had already left while I was struggling to get out of the water. Once exposing myself to the air, the cold struck me. I saw a towel above where I had left my clothes. The front gate sounded shut with a clang. I staggered over to the bench and wrapped myself in the towel, trembling. Water continued to drip down my hair.

I watched the sun setting in the distance.

~ ~ ~

I didn't want to go. I disliked receiving orders, like a slave. But if I didn't go, I would lose my favorite place to that awful girl. So once my alarm clock ran at five, as I had reset it last night, I got myself ready and left the house to catch the bus. I barely made it to the pool by six. And the building already had a light on inside, its gate unlocked.

Saki stood by the poolside, in the same outfit except with a new t-shirt. Upon seeing me approach, she raised one hand.

"Yaa!" She greeted me with a smile, with teeth, like a child seeing Santa Claus. "Are you here because you want to be?"

"No," I said.

"Well, I believe you," said Saki. "Thank you for coming anyway."

I threw the towel at her, already washed and dried before I stomped past her into the changing area. Last night, I found my old kid-sized swimming goggles. Adjusting them, however, I found I could still wear them. And I had a swim cap with me. I finished changing in less than ten minutes and came out. Saki remained at the same spot. The turquoise pool glowed behind her.

"Let's start with a warm-up." She said, "I'll teach you how—"

"Shut up already!" I said before jumping into the water, feeling my senses numb at the touch of cold bursting through my pores. Pushing my feet against the poolside, I swam off with the best speed my arms could make. And by the second lap, my body felt warmer. Saki was sitting at the poolside when I came swimming back and resurfaced.

"Ryoka, no need to be rush," she said. "Come on out of the pool."

I exhaled into the water, pretending not to hear.

"Ryoka, get out of the pool." Her tone changed when my face raised over the surface. I shivered, and not because of the water.

I got out.

Saki moved her legs in the water, causing ripples. "Ryoka," she turned my way, "you haven't had breakfast, have you?"

I had not realized I was hungry until she mentioned it.

"This won't do. I can't have you swimming with your stomach empty. So we will do just half the practice today. Let's wait for a little, till the sun comes up and the water is a little warmer. Then I will have you swim a few laps before calling it a day."

"You called me here this early, just to tell me not to swim?"

"Have a fruit or something ready in your bag for a light breakfast next time," she ignored my pouting. "I recommended tangerine. The sourer, the better. It gives you energy and is good for your teeth."

She spoke the last sentence with a smile.

"If you're not going to let me swim, can I leave now?" I said, "what do you want with me anyway?"

"I want to train you."

I looked her way.

"I meant that in a good way, you know." She returned my gaze. "What have you got to lose, learning to swim from me?"

"I don't have a reason to," I said. "Or is it wrong for someone not to swim? I never asked you to train me or do anything for me. I never even wanted to see you, and so I wouldn't ask for any favors. If, say, in the future, you come across me drowning somewhere, please leave me to my fate and go off on your way."

"Do you want that?" She said, her legs stopped, "to be left to your fate and me off on my way?"

I avoided her eyes by staring down at my knees.

Saki stood up suddenly. She walked toward the office and turned on its light. She returned soon with something in each hand before sitting back down. "Look at this rock," she said, showing a fist-sized stone. I recognized it as being used to hold papers in the office. "And look at this ball."

I had no idea how she found a tennis ball in there.

Saki proceeded in her demonstration, where the rock ended up at the pool bottom while the ball bounced off the water surface, causing tiny ripples within the larger one. "Instead of you becoming like that rock," she said, "I want you to be like that ball. For our lessons to work, first, there must be trust between us. Trust me and my instruction, and from then, we can develop a proper relationship between learner and instructor. Together, we will work until you can swim on your own. Then finally, I will let you go. And you will never have to see me again."

"Still," I said. "I don't have any reason to learn how to swim with you."

"Ryoka, are you afraid of me?"

I took my eyes off the ball and looked her way. Saki's eyes looked like two sapphires in the pool light.

"So I have scared you," Saki made a small sigh. "I am sorry. It was not my intention. But I will say sorry anyway. I won't hold that against you, you know, for not trusting me. After all, the world is a scary place, filled with people and things that can hurt you, fire that can burn you, water that can drown you. But Ryoka, would it help you even a little if you could have one less thing to be scared of? If you need to live strongly, you need to find courage somewhere. Once you surpass your fear of water, that could become your new source of strength, which will lead you to overcome many others. My earnest wish, Ryoka, is that I might be able to do some good for you and that you would learn to trust me."

Somehow, though I had been sitting with my legs in the water all this time, I had not felt cold.

"If you don't have a reason to swim," Saki continued, "Then let me be your reason. Ryoka, won't you swim for me?"

Maybe, Saki was not that bad a person.

"And what do you want in return?" I asked.

"Nothing." She said with a smile. "Except perhaps, a self-satisfaction, for one's deed is by itself a reward. I shall reap what I sow."

"I don't trust people who claim to do something and without expecting anything in return."

"Ryoka, you still have a long way to go, learning to trust me. So we better get started soon."

The sun was coming up. Above the office, the clock said it was only ten minutes from seven. "No matter what I say," I said, "you just want me to swim, don't you?"

"I do," she said. "And you, too, want to swim now, don't you?"

Over the next few weeks, I became used to waking up at five and arriving at the pool for the first lesson. Then, I came again after school for another hour. Saki proved herself capable of teaching me. And by the time July arrived, my body felt accustomed to the water. During this time, I had never asked Saki about herself. After all, she showed no sign of wanting me to know. And because I wished not to feel obligated to tell her about my situation at home, in time, her not revealing anything of herself gave me comfort.

Saki gave her all to teaching me. And I put all my effort into swimming, only so that I could reach the poolside.

I wished for nothing else but to see Saki waiting for me there.

Back then, I didn't know whether what I had with Saki could have led to anything more. My inexperience had been like a rock, where the new seed got planted above. And the roots were unable to grow further. So my feelings remained dormant, as I knew not what they meant. Suppose God had let me be born a boy. Or, should he have sent Saki into this world as one. I might not have found myself as startled, toward the event soon unfolded.

"Swim on your side!" Saki's voice came as I moved through the water. "Relax your stomach and shift your body, left, right. That's it! Go! Go!"

I reached out my arm and touched the finish line. Raising my face, I exhaled into the water. Saki crouched over her feet and lowered the stopwatch for me to see. The thirty-six seconds appeared over the meter.

"Congratulation, Ryoka, you did it."

Saki's smile looked genuine, as I had always seen it for the past month. She offered her hand to help me out of the water. I took it and saw her face moved down. Her lips touched mine. In surprise, I let go of her hand and swam backward.

I touched my lips where her warmth still lingered.

Saki remained at the same spot, now with an arms a distance between us. Her eyes looked as if they were waiting. So I returned to the poolside where her face bent down once more. And this time, I didn't move away.

The world felt warm when Saki kissed me.

# Swimming Lesson 14

I was eating dinner on my own when the phone rang.

"Can we meet tonight?" Saki's voice came through, "seven sharp."

The thought dawned upon me after hanging up that I would get to see Saki on Sunday. A feeling like joy arose, before mixing with nervousness. I still hadn't forgotten the kiss. In my room, I picked out a simple top with a long skirt to match. Then I took scissors to the bathroom to trim the ends of my hair a little, before splashing some water and combing it down. Finally, ready to leave, I came downstairs to find my mother in the living room. I told her that I would be going out.

"You should eat something, Mom," I said. "There's no point waiting. Father hasn't come home for dinner for the past month."

The look on her face made me ashamed of having spoken at all. I left the house as if running away.

Only the thought of seeing Saki soon comforted me.

The pool already had a light on inside. Saki always arrived before me, no matter how early or late our appointment. Going inside, I spotted Saki standing near the wired fence behind the pool benches. The clock above the office said a few minutes before seven. Saki turned around, noticed me, and stepped into the turquoise light.

I paused suddenly, feet stumbling. Saki was wearing a yukata of dark blue, with white waves and a goldfish pattern.

"What do you think?" She asked, then turned herself three-sixty degrees.

"You called me out here, just to show off your yukata?"

"Wrong answer," Saki pouted before stepping closer and making another circle turn. "What do you think?"

"God, you're so cute," I muttered, feeling my face warm.

"What?"

"You're cute," I said.

Saki's face turned pink in the light. I had never seen her in such an expression, where her cheeks showed color. Unlike most girls I knew, Saki had never worn makeup. But she would not need it if she could blush like that.

"Are you hungry?" Saki spoke after a moment, moving away toward the nearby bench.

"Yes," I said. "Have you got something?"

She handed me one of the two paper bags. I took a look inside and felt myself getting hungry. "Come," she called me then as she moved toward the wired fence. "It's about to start."

I followed her and stood at her side, within an arm's length. Our school was on a hill, overlooking high ground. From this spot, I could see a few lights from buildings in the distance. Through the corner of my eyes, I noticed the intensity in Saki's gaze as if she was waiting for something. "Ryoka," she said, turning toward me, "why are you standing so far away?"

My hands tightened on the paper bag.

"Come stand here with me," she said in a soft tone, her expression hidden in the dark. "I won't bite."

My heart was pounding as I took one step toward her. I gripped the wire fence and squeezed. Saki looked beautiful even in the dark.

"You do not hate me, do you?" Saki asked.

I did and didn't.

How could she pretend as if nothing happened after kissing me?

"It's starting!" She looked away suddenly toward the horizon, where lights flashed through the sky and burst into three different colors. Today was the seventh of July, I now remembered. The Tanabata Festival was supposed to be held somewhere in the city. The white and orange color brightened up the sky, followed by purple, yellow, and pink, though we couldn't hear any sounds from here. Saki was making crumbling noises around her paper bag when she took out her taiyaki. She chomped into her fish-shaped sweet, starting from its stomach while focusing toward the lights with an intense look. I was going to start with mine from the tail when I decided to copy her. Somehow, the red bean tasted sweeter in the middle.

Gold fireworks consecutively shot into the air.

They said a wish made on Tanabata could come true. Though I believed neither God nor Buddha would ever answer my desire, I couldn't help but making one at that moment. That Saki would kiss me one more time.

The sky turned bright at its climax before the night fell dark again, with only a few stars.

"Do you like fireworks, Ryoka?" Saki spoke suddenly.

"Not really," I said. "I don't dislike fireworks. But I have no reason to like them either."

"You are so cold, Ryoka."

I wanted to ask her if she liked fireworks. But Saki had already moved away, crumpling her paper bag in a ball and leaving it on a bench. I put mine next to hers while my eyes continued to observe her back. She paused before the pool for a long second before she rolled up the Hakkake that revealed her lower legs. She sat down, her legs in the water. I rolled up my skirt too and sat down next to her. The cold sensation froze up my legs, but I had already gotten used to the feeling during the past few weeks.

"Thank you for coming tonight." Saki said, "even on such short notice."

"Why are you so formal now? As I said, I don't dislike fireworks," I said, swaying my legs in the water, then muttered the following sentence. "So long as I watch them with you."

"Lie down," Saki said, laying herself back over the rough ground. "Do it. Think of this as training."

The ground felt hard against my back. But the moment I rested my head, the feeling of discomfort vanished at the sight of the sky. The few stars above me felt close as I continued to move my legs in the water.

I was swimming in the sky.

"Ryoka, how long have we known each other?" Saki's voice spoke, "a month, and yet you have never asked about me. Why?"

"Because I'm not interested."

"You're not interested in me," said she, "and yet you came when I asked you to?"

"I was looking forward to seeing the fireworks."

"You?" Saki spoke in a laughing tone, "looking forward to seeing fireworks? I saw your mind completely was on something else."

I tried to hold my gaze on her when her face turned my way.

"If you are not a good liar, you should try to make it in life by being honest," Saki said.

I closed my eyes till I felt calm, then I looked at her again. "Wasn't it supposed to be you," I said, "who should tell me about yourself? You came out of nowhere. So you owe me at least an explanation. Why then should it be my fault that I never asked the obvious?"

Saki blinked, then turned away.

"Do you not want me to know about you?"

"You would never believe me," she said, after a second. "Even if I told you."

"Why would I not?"

"My sister," Saki paused, turning toward me. Her eyes looked like a pair of stars. "My big sister is a pathological liar. And they say bad DNA runs in the family, so whenever I opened my mouth, I put people on guard. After all, I had shared the same womb with my sister, so there's no way anyone could tell if I might have gotten the liar gene rubbing off on me. And now that I've told you this. Do you still want to hear my story?"

"Tell me," I said, after a swallow.

"I have an American Father. These eyes and my bits of gold hair came from him." Saki began, "Before we moved here, I lived and went to Elementary in California. I was born in Switzerland, though. My Japanese mother met with my father there while studying art. They called it love at first sight and married within a year. We used to live in Corsier-sur-Vevey, the same neighborhood as Charlie Chaplin. As a child, I was a father's girl, while my sister was closer to my mother. One day, my father took me to feed ducks at Lake Geneva, and that's how we first ran into Mr. Chaplin. I was scared of his fake beard, mistook him for Hitler, so he pretended to fall into the lake to make me laugh. Our families then became close, and his wife often invited us for tea and kidney pie. Then when I was seven, my Grandfather passed away, leaving my father the business. So we moved to the States. My Grandfather used to be in an inner circle with Theodore Roosevelt, until he got sacked for speaking up too much against the war. So after the war was over, he started an exporting company, supplying Japan's black market with buckwheat flour that made us rich. While I was in California, I got scouted to play a minor role in a Soap Opera. And I got an invitation to be a guest star in Hitchcock's film. The man thought that having a Japanese faced little girl in a film would somehow contribute to the film industry's future. But I never got to play that role because my sister got jealous of me, and she slipped glass into my shoes. Then she threatened to make me drink a whole bottle of toilet cleaner if I didn't quit working in the film. As if God also took her side, my father got hired as a business advisor in Japan. So we moved to Nagasaki. I went to a middle school and high school here. I graduated last year and have already applied to a few universities. Until then, I have all the free time in the world."

I realized I had not breathed for many seconds now.

"Well, I lied," Saki continued, "about half of it, do you want to know which half? Be mindful, though, that I might be lying about that too."

"Saki, what color is the sky during the day?"

"Green," she said after some hesitation, "like musk melon."

"I believe you."

Saki's eyes narrowed. "Ryoka," said she. "It would do your future lots of good, learning to distrust people instead of trusting them."

"I believe you because I want to," I said. "Whatever you say, so long as you want me to believe it, I will. Even if you said you were a seal dressed up in human skin, I would still believe you. So when you feel like it, just let me know what you want to believe, ok?"

Saki's smile reappeared, the most beautiful thing I had seen tonight. "Ask me one question," she said, "and I promise to tell the truth."

"Why are you here?"

"Because you are here." She answered immediately.

"What is it about me that you should take the time to bother?" I said after swallowing, tasting the sweet red bean paste in my throat. "I am just me."

"Because you are you," Saki said, her lips parted. "Have you been someone else? I wouldn't have bothered to be here."

I sensed Saki, so close that her warmth made me hold my breath.

"Ryoka," said Saki. "Can I kiss you?"

"You are so weird, Saki. Why ask what you could take?" I said. I closed my eyes and waited. I had heard many stories about kisses in books and movies. Some said a kiss contained a special feeling. One even said a kiss tasted like the morning dew. Neither of those stories, however, was true.

For Saki's kiss tasted like a sweet red bean.

~ ~ ~

The inside of Saki's house was pitch dark as we entered. Her hand guided me by the wrist, upstairs, and into a room. She sat me down in a bed before going to pull the curtain shut. Her body, shaped like a shadow, stood before me.

I gripped the bedsheet, sensing her sweet scent close.

Saki untied her obi, letting her yukata drop. Before she kissed gently, her hands felt for me under my dress. She pinned me down, then guided my hand to touch her warm breasts while using another hand to stroke my stomach. She squeezed around my nipple and

I twitched. An intense feeling woke up within me, like a beast roused by divine force. Her tongue was at my navel and my body arched upward like a bow. Blood rushed through my veins and my breathing turned hot like steam. My eyes rolled back as her finger came inside me. My toes clenched.

What were girls supposed to do with each other? I had asked myself after Saki kissed me.

Tonight, the answer came to light, with pain and pleasure mixed inside me, like two beasts of the same breed. No more. No more. Or I would die. I might have cried, but Saki continued to do as she pleased. When finally, I let out the loudest cry, I felt like skipping five years and bursting into adulthood. Then, I passed out into a dreamless sleep.

When I woke up again, my body felt light. I sat up slowly.

The warmth still burned between my legs. Once my eyes adjusted to the surroundings, I noticed the curtain had been opened. It was still dark outside. My eyes spotted Saki's naked back, sitting near the end of the bed and before a mirror. "Saki?" I called.

"Sorry, did I wake you?" Saki spoke as she turned.

I climbed out of bed. "Aren't you going to sleep too?" I asked, seeing my reflection appear in the mirror behind her.

"There's no way I could sleep," Saki said, her eyes bright like a child. "You made so many noises, like a kitten. And you clung to me like a baby."

"Is that so? Wasn't that partly your fault?"

I wrapped my arm around her, feeling her full breasts, still hot. "You are mean, Saki, with what you have done me." I said, "you better take responsibility."

"And how may I do that?" Saki asked, leaning her head back.

"One, more, time," I whispered.

The memory of what she had done was still fresh within me. And I took it out on her, the desire and all. Saki was panting under me after I finished.

"Are you hungry?" She asked. "I am. Let's get something to eat."

I lay flat over the wet sheet as Saki left the bed. A white light appeared on the ceiling. After a moment, I sat up, looking at my reflection glaring back from the large oval mirror. Saki took two towels out of the closet and threw one my way before wrapping herself with another and leaving the room.

The sound of the shower turned on from the end of the corridor.

The deep grey carpet felt soft under my feet as I stood up. Saki's room looked clean and four times larger than mine. My eyes paused over a writing desk facing the window. A tall teacup stood there, filled with blue pens, and there was a tiny fake beard stuck to its side, just below an autograph that made me swallow hard. I turned, then, toward the books stacked against the wall, all in English. I recognized only the last one at the right end, Thomas Mann's *Death in Venice*, Japanese translated, which I used to read in the abridged version back in middle school.

I opened the book and saw a library card at the back, with my school's name. Flipping through the pages, sentences were written all over the margins.

The shower stopped, and Saki reappeared at the door.

"Oh," she saw me with the book. "I borrowed that from your school's library. Could you return it for me?"

"There's no way they would accept this back," I said, showing her a page filled with blue.

"Then you can keep it." She said, "come on, let's go downstairs."

I put the book down on the desk, then gathered my clothes from the floor, dumping them next to it. I followed Saki, one hand holding onto the towel wrapped around me. The outside remained pitch dark. Only the sound of Saki's footsteps guided me. Then suddenly, the light turned on. I paused halfway and found myself in the middle of the broad stairs. A living room stood to my right, with a green carpet, a set of light brown arm couches, and a coffee table. The walls looked clear as if I could see my reflection in them. Upon reaching the ground level, my feet felt the stone floor, which sent a shiver up my spine.

The living room alone looked as big as my entire house.

The sound of the refrigerator slammed shut. Saki brought out a large ceramic bowl and poured white sugar out of a bag. Taking a cucumber, she tore off the plastic wrap, snapped it in half, and dipped it in. Thick white sugar glossed around its end. She took a bite.

"Is that good?" I asked.

"Delicious," Saki said, covering her mouth. "Do you want half?"

I took my half of the cucumber, pulled down the plastic wrap, and dipped its broken end into the bowl. Chunks of white sugar thickened around its tip when I took out and bit a mouthful. "Delicious," I said after I swallowed.

"Hey, don't take all the sugar," Saki said, pulling the bowl back a little to her side.

Saki seemed on edge. Did I make her angry somehow?

"Where are your family?" I asked, making conversation, "your parents? Your sister?"

Saki froze at the last two words. Her eyes moved around as if to confirm a particular person was not here. Before, she took a breath and made a small bite off the cucumber's tip. "They went to Kyushu yesterday for a funeral," she said. "Our cousin from my mother's side just passed away."

"I am sorry."

"Don't be," she said, rubbing the sugar stuck at the corner of her mouth with her hand. "My sister forbade me from crying. She didn't shed a single tear. Honestly, she scared me."

She muttered the last two sentences.

I was about to dip the cucumber down for the sugar when Saki pulled the bowl more to her side.

"I told you, don't take my sugar," she said.

I sensed irritation in her tone.

"What?" She asked, looking me in the eyes. "Do you have something to say?"

"Saki," I said, "You shouldn't write in a library book."

Saki added more sugar to the bowl. "When I read fiction," she said after swallowing another bite of cucumber, "by its third chapter, I start to feel loathing, and I have to get it out. So I write them down, how it's so obvious what character A got himself into, mingling with character B. Most fictions are, to me, like the foregone conclusion that boiled down to only one genre, the tragedy. And do you know what causes tragedy? Love. Every fictional character looks for love far too much, like kids stuffing candies in their mouth, even though they might get sick. But love hurts them, you see, cruelly, by denying them from having it. And do you know who denied them of love? The author, the God of the story."

Saki had not blinked once as she continued speaking. "The worst antagonist of all stories is not a killer with a knife, but the author with a pen. The author looks at them from above the page, reads the script with glee as the characters weep tears, till the page could turn hole. The author jabbed his pen over their skin, darkening their souls with ink, scripting over their skin till the characters bled oceans. The more the characters suffer, the better the fiction. So I felt like putting down warning messages, to say, hey, watch what you're doing. You're making yourself a fool in a third-rate tragedy, all to satisfy the author who has no love for you, and the dark fate at the end of your script."

I had never thought Saki could speak so much, with such emotion.

"My cousin killed himself," Saki said. "He hung himself on a doorknob. No place in the ceiling would support his weight. So the doorknob, who would think that's possible? He tied a rope around his neck, like this, before swallowing a sleeping pill. And as he dozed off, crack, peaceful death in his sleep."

I took the last bite of my cucumber, then washed down the feeling that came up in my throat upon the sight of Saki's demonstration.

"Ryoka, why are you here tonight?" Saki asked suddenly, after wiping sugar off her hand over the bowl. "When I took you here, you could have resisted, so why?"

I looked into her face. "I love you."

Saki's expression looked painful. "If you love me, will you do anything I ask?"

"Anything."

"Then promise me," she looked troubled getting to the following sentence. "If, one day, I ever become your burden. I want you to leave me."

"What's that supposed to mean?"

"If I ever try to hurt you, or hinder your happiness, save yourself and run. It's a simple request."

"Saki, are you trying to make me leave you?"

"Can't you take me seriously when I am warning you?" Saki said, with genuine anger between her brows. "Don't you have any love for yourself?"

"Saki, for someone to love themselves, they have first to live a life they treasure. But my life up until now has been nothing. There's no need to worry that you would make anything worse. So please don't ask me to leave you, Saki, because I won't. I don't want to. Let's say, hypothetically, you got into some accident and couldn't walk. I would be happy to carry you for the rest of my life."

"Ah," Saki looked away, "that didn't work."

I watched her taking the sugar bowl away in an abrupt manner. She put a plastic wrap over it and placed it in the refrigerator before banging the door shut.

"Ryoka, I am not happy," she said, "with you."

I waited for her to continue.

"You can stay here till morning. Then I want you to leave." She said, before moving away. "I'm going to sleep, alone."

I grasped her arm and pulled, causing her to turn around. "You have taken me in, Saki. But what makes you think that you can make me leave?"

Saki's surprised look came before I kissed her.

"Sorry," I said when I finally let her lips go, "for taking the sugar. Here, I give it back."

Saki trembled all over like a bird getting dumped with water. The anger vanished from her face, replaced with something else. Her eyes sparkled like a child on her birthday. At first, I thought I had made her cry, that I was letting go of her. But then, she grasped my wrist, the side where the green ribbon was and squeezed it.

I saw her lips shake as she struggled to speak.

"I love you," Saki's voice came in a whisper. "I am speaking the truth, so please believe me."

# Swimming Lesson 15

I collapsed next to Saki. And when I woke up, the outside window had already turned evening. The smell of chlorine still stuck in my hair, mixed with the sweet scent of Saki. After school, we had a swimming lesson this afternoon. Then Saki asked me if I would stay over tonight. After all, tomorrow was Sunday.

Saki left the bed.

I lay still for a while before leaving the room for the bathroom. After redoing my hair by splashing some water over it, I noticed a sunscreen bottle in the right corner. Saki always had the same smell. I had never asked her why. Upon reentering the room, I saw her sitting at her dresser.

She looked up as I came to stand behind her. Her naked back was bathed in red-orange light.

"Why are you always looking into the mirror?" I said, embracing her from behind. "Are you in love with yourself more than me?"

"I have been casting a spell," she said, "to make myself ugly."

"What's wrong with the face you have now?"

"I am always scared of my face, thinking that the madness within me is wearing this as its mask. Beauty could make mischief. But if I was born ugly, or at least having a scar, that might help me be content, to live as a good person."

"Are you hating yourself again?" I said, "here, I will help you feel better."

Saki's face relaxed, then aroused, as my fingers squeezed around her nipple. Then I placed my face over her shoulder, next to hers in the mirror.

"Do you know, my name written in Kanji, means cold and evil?" I said, "If you have evil in you, Saki. Then I am a full-fledged devil."

Saki leaned her face against my cheek. "Behold," she said, "the two beasts of doomsday."

I kissed behind her neck till she giggled.

"Ryoka, let me rest."

"Come back to bed, then, and I'll help you rest."

"You are greedy, Ryoka."

I grasped her hair and started running my fingers through it. Her face softened, her eyes close, and her lips broke apart.

"That feels nice," she said. "Can you cut hair, Ryoka?"

"I've cut my own hair since I was little," I said.

Saki turned around, a childish smile beaming across her face. She opened the dresser drawer and took out a pair of scissors. "Cut my hair," said she. "Make my hair short. I always wanted to try short hair."

"Saki, you should go to a hairdresser."

"I want you to do it," she said, leaning her head against my stomach. "Please, Ryoka, I already had two hairdressers give up on me. I get ticklish when someone touches my hair."

"But I have been touching you," I said. "And who in the world gets tickled in the hair?"

"Your hands are fine," Saki said, looking up.

I sighed in surrender, the scissors in my hands. "Fine," I said. "But I like your hair long so I will only trim a little. Promise me that you will always wear your hair long."

"If you like it, then, I will keep it long."

"Swear it."

"With my life," she gave me a peace sign and a line of teeth. Before she closed her eyes, "I will always keep my hair long for you to cut them."

I gave another sigh to calm myself, placing my hands through the scissor handles. Then, I began to work around the ends. Saki's hair felt soft, like a wave of sunlight. Once in a while, I would lower my face down to peer closer at my work. With my fingers, I combed through her hair's length. Saki's shoulders drooped, revealing a peaceful expression.

"Ticklish?" I asked to see if she was still awake.

"No," she answered. "I like your hands, nice and cool."

I ran my fingers through one last time as I finished. In the end, I hadn't done much. Saki turned to the right, examining my work, then to the left before the broadest smile broke across her face.

"Ryoka, you are the best." She embraced my still naked body.

The sky was getting dark outside.

I heard a noise downstairs. At first, I thought I imagined it until I saw Saki's eyes turn wide. She sprang off the chair and looked from side to side, like an animal sensing a predator. She gathered my clothes from the floor and pushed them into my arms.

"You have to leave," she said, looking down at herself as if realizing she had no clothes on.

I wanted to ask what was going on.

"There's a door over the left side of the stairs. It will lead you to the back gate. I will distract them. Please, don't let her see you."

I put on my school uniform, as told. Saki pulled up her short pants but looked as if she'd forgotten how to put on a bra. I zipped up my long pleated skirt, and the slight sound made her glance my way.

"I am sorry, Ryoka," she said, stepping over to help me redo the sailor scarf. "I thought they would be back tomorrow. Just leave now, and we will still see each other on Monday."

"But, Saki, my shoes are at the front."

Saki's hands froze, and she let out a curse in English.

The voice from downstairs had gone quiet. Saki's face turned pale, and her eyes closed in defeat. Her arms shivered as she took my hands and squeezed. Seconds passed until she finally reopened her eyes. The color returned to her face again with a new expression, like she just decided to put up a fight. She took my hand and guided me out of the room, and we went down the stairs. Two people stood at the bottom, waiting for us. I kept my eyes on the back of Saki's head. The warmth of her hand was my only comfort. We finally stopped, and I found myself standing before a woman with short stature. She wore her hair short, with a pair of glasses, and looked to be in the mid-thirties. I guessed her to be Saki's mother.

The other person beside her, however, caused my breath to stop.

I looked at her face, then back at Saki. And from Saki, I looked at her. Saki had told me that she had a sister. But she had never mentioned that they were twins.

"Mother," Saki spoke, pulling me forward to stand next to her. Then, with an expression like a fawn talking to a lion, she muttered toward the other, "Sayo. Here is my friend, Ryoka. I told you before. I have been giving her swim lessons."

Saki's hand felt cold with sweat.

Sayo was looking at Saki, then me. Then, her eyes narrowed. "Saki, our mother, would like to speak to you," she spoke. "Go, I will see your friend out."

I turned to Saki.

"Saki, do as I say," said Sayo.

Saki was shivering, staring down, and her grip loosened. Until finally, I could no longer feel her warmth. She then followed her mother, who glanced my way through the corner of her eyes, like she was looking at an insect and wished to crush it with a tissue.

"Ryoka, isn't it?" Sayo spoke. Her voice was the same as Saki's.

I found myself alone with her.

"So you have been keeping my little sister company," she said, crossing her arms. Her eyes felt like blades. Her face and everything looked the same as Saki's.

No, I reconsidered, not all the same. Unlike Saki, Sayo wore strong perfume. She was wearing a long pair of jeans, with an expensive-looking top. And she wore makeup that, in my opinion, made her looked like a noh actress with lipstick poorly put on. If she and Saki were to stand next to each other, I was confident I could tell them apart.

"So, Ryoka, what do you think of Saki?"

I looked up.

Sayo relaxed the arms by her side. Her eyes looked calm, waiting for the answer.

"I like her," I said.

Her one hand swung across my face, causing a deep sound to echo through the air. Then, I felt the pain.

"Tell me," Sayo's tone remained unchanged. "What do you think of Saki?"

"I lov—"

She slapped me again on the cheek. Then, she sighed. "Tell me, what do you think of Saki?"

"I love her," I said quicker and got another slap.

"Say you hate her," Sayo's tone came as gentle, just like Saki's. "Say it, and I will let you go."

I remained stoic. And Sayo slapped me once, then twice, and another time. I took the hit like a pillar until she rose her hand to strike a fourth time, and I glared at her. "Go on, hit me," I said. "Your hands don't hurt one bit."

Sayo's fourth strike caused my body to tilt over to the side.

I looked up once I could raise my head. And before me, I saw an expression that gave me a shiver.

"Do you think I am a bad person?" Sayo said, "here I am, trying to save you. It's that bitch, isn't it? What lies has she been telling this time? What things has she been spouting about me?"

"Nothing—"

She slapped on the left, then the right. "Tell me, what that bitch has been telling you?"

The pain burned over my face. Yet, I continued to fight by keeping my gaze on Sayo. I saw a rare type of soul in her eyes, like a mirror where my fear reflected upon it in a twisted image. "Saki said," I spoke, "she was afraid of going mad one day. I have never understood that, until now, that I see you. You are the very picture of her worst fear. You are mad."

Sayo slapped me the hardest.

It was not her slap, however, that hurt, but her face. The face of Saki, gone mad, filled with hatred.

"You call me mad?" She said, her hands shot for my neck. And I thought she was going to choke me. But she held my face to look at her. "Look well, at a madwoman, for this would be your future. I am the reflection of what you will become. And so I curse you, Ryoka, to suffer. When your time comes, you will suffer so much that you, too, will curse the day that bitch was born. Now get out."

She let me go before giving me a final slap, as if to make me remember.

~ ~ ~

I arrived at the pool on Monday by six. But for the first time, I found the inside still dark and its gate locked. I waited until the sun came up. The bell rang, signaling the first period was starting.

Saki had not come.

I passed my morning, sitting at my desk while pretending to focus on the opened textbook. The new substitute teacher just walked past me toward the front, reciting a Confucius verse before writing it down on the board. My toes turned numb by the time class was over and the lunch break began. I ran toward the pool and found its gate open. But Saki was still not there.

She didn't come after school either. I sat down on my regular bench and felt the sun on my skin. Lifting my legs, I braced my arms around them, feeling cold.

The sun felt cold today.

She would come tomorrow.

A whole week went by without her. I continued to come to the pool at six in the morning, at lunchtime, and after school. Tomorrow surely she would come, I told myself. Tomorrow, I just had to wait for tomorrow.

Two more weeks passed.

The sun began to set from the sky. The clock above the office already passed six, but no one had come to lock the gate yet. So I stayed, sitting over the pool bench with my arms around my legs until the light disappeared. I finally got up, going to the office, and found the switch control. Once I pushed it, the turquoise light flashed, glowing under the water.

I wondered if the pool had always look this small?

The water's surface looked still as if time had frozen, until I came to a stop by the poolside. My feet caused the water to stir. I crouched down and reached out my hand, feeling the cold through my fingers. Ripples spread toward the middle of the pool. Then silence fell once again. The world without Saki felt cold. "Don't take her away," the sound came through my mouth, "don't take away what's precious to me. Please, God, don't take her away."

I had lived my life, despising God for never letting my parents love me.

But then, when Saki had come into my life, I thought God was finally rewarding me with a consolation that made up for everything. And yet now, after two weeks had passed, the reality finally settled upon me.

Saki had gone, taken away from me, forever.

I knelt over the water's edge. My pleat skirt became soaking wet. "Don't take Saki away. Don't take her away!" My voice raised as I pounded into the water, "don't take away my hope! Don't take away what's mine! It's unfair! Unfair! Don't take Saki from me!"

Cold water splashed over my face. Its chlorine taste mixed with my salty tears. And I saw my reflection in the water.

*"Look well, at a madwoman."* Sayo's voice resounded in laughter.

"I won't let you take her away!" I pounded the surface and screamed to the sky. "Not Sayo! Not you, God! You won't steal my happiness!"

Large ripples spread across the pool.

I wanted to die. The thought came across my mind, the moment I could cry no more. The slight warmth from the daytime was disappearing into the ground. And I felt like the broken porcelain vase that I rammed into in my childhood. My soul, even the feeling of pain, had shattered away. Death itself felt like it was closing in, like the night. I removed my shoes and slipped my legs down before moving myself into the water with my clothes still on. My fingers squeezed around the poolside. Cold fear gripped me.

The fear of death.

But I was more afraid of a world with Saki. I cast one last glance over the wired fence. There, only a few weeks ago, we stood watching fireworks together. Then, I turned to look at the pool entrance.

Tonight, Saki was not here.

I took a last breath and closed my eyes, submerging my head down into the water. The sound of my heart echoed in the dark. The pool bottom felt far away from my feet. I dug my fingers into my arms and felt as if floating amidst the nothingness. My chest began to feel tight, like a balloon about to burst. Sensations of pain cut across my chest, and my legs began to struggle. My teeth grit together, the dried salty taste of saliva filled my tongue. Once I opened my mouth, the water would flood in. And that would be the end.

I saw a flickering image of a person standing above me. My arms let go, and my legs started to kick.

My face resurfaced, and fresh air filled my lungs.

"What are you doing, swimming with clothes on, Ryoka?" Saki asked, crouching by the poolside.

"It's your fault for not training me properly," I said. "It's your fault, Saki, for not showing up. It's all your fault."

"Move back," she said, standing up and kicking away her flip-flops. I swam aside, watching her take a deep breath. Saki came running, then sprang in the air with both arms forward. Water burst where she pierced through the surface.

I wiped the water off my face and saw her resurface.

"I am here, Ryoka." Saki said, her arms open, "come."

I swam toward her. Saki's body felt warm under the soaked wet t-shirt. I buried my face into her neck. Then I kissed her on the lips.

"Ryoka, you're like a baby," Saki whispered.

"Let me be a baby."

Saki shivered when I nipped her ear. "Ryoka, please. Ryoka," her voice raised, and I stopped. "We need to talk."

I didn't let Saki go. Until she held my face in both hands and gave me a long kiss, she swam back, then, and got out of the pool, moving toward the staff office. I got out of the water and waited until she returned with two towels. She placed one over my head, then sat down and began drying my hair. Saki dapped water off my cheek, gently, like she was afraid I would break.

She finished by wrapping the towel around me. Before, she took another towel and began drying herself. I grasped the towel corner, pulling tight against my wet uniform.

Saki had not smiled today.

"I am sorry, Ryoka." She broke the silence suddenly. Her hair was still damp when she put aside the towel.

Why was she saying sorry?"

"I shouldn't have let you meet Sayo," continued Saki. "She's not always like that, you know. I know that because we were born out of the same mother, after all, with only four minutes between us. Long ago, she used to be kind and tolerant toward people. Even toward those who deserved her hate, she never hated them. It's my fault. I made her that way. I have become her burden, and she feels an obligation to protect me. So, she doesn't hate you, Ryoka. Not really. She's just overprotective."

"She's protective of you," I said, "and so she hates me."

"She does that to everybody!" Saki snapped. Though I had seen her anger before, this time, she sounded in pain. "It's not just you, Ryoka. Back in school, I used to have friends. But she started to tap my calls and then called them one by one, pretending to be me. She drove them away. Then a few months back, just before I met you, I used to keep a canary. She drowned it in a bathtub and left it in my bed, because she didn't like it calling my name—"

I felt Saki's hand wrapped around mine, below the green ribbon, as if searching for comfort.

"Just know this, Ryoka," she said. "It's not your fault for what happened. It's my fault, all mine, just mine."

"Saki—"

"Ryoka, listen," she continued before I could speak. "What I am about to say, I want you to accept and agree with simply. Remember when I asked you if I should cause your unhappiness, I wanted you to leave me? Here comes the time that I must ask you again to do so. I am going away, Ryoka. Sayo got accepted into a university back in the States. And she wants me to go with her."

My lips parted.

"I would have gone, even if I had never met you. I am sorry, Ryoka, for never telling you this. You have been my brief moment of peace. But now I must go my way. I am sorry for having been the cause of your pain. If I had never met you, none of this would have happened."

"Saki, why?" My voice finally came out, "why are you crying?"

Saki raised her hand over her left eyes. Her lips parted as if trying to smile. But then something came down her cheek. The turquoise light reflected over her face revealed the glimmering tear.

"Would it make you happy if I let go of you? Speak the truth, and I will live with it."

Her gaze dropped, then her eyes closed as if to hold back her tears before her head shook, slowly, one side to another. "No," she said. "It wouldn't."

"Why?"

"Because," she raised her face, tears in her eyes. "Because you existed in this world. It's so unfair how real you are and not a dream. When I touch you, you don't disappear. I could see you, hear your voice. And I feel for you like I have never felt for anyone before. For the first time in my life, you make me feel like I was born with a purpose, to meet you."

"Then, don't go," I said, gripping her shoulders.

"But Sayo and my parents. What can I do? They would never approve of you and me."

Saki had never looked the way she was now, helpless and needing my guidance. But what can we do? The question was for me to decide. "We could," I said, "run away."

Saki's eyes widened.

"We could run away together," I repeated.

"Where?"

"Anywhere but here," I said.

"Ryoka, you will make yourself miserable just by staying with me. " Saki said, "please, Ryoka, just let me go—"

"That's not an option." I raised my voice. "I will find us a place where there's no one but us."

"Ryoka, you are not making any sense." Saki said with a faint smile, "and you are making me weak in my resolve too. What about your family? Could you leave them?"

"I don't care about them!" I spoke, the intense emotions burning within me like red coal. "I was born in this world alone. My life up until now has been nothing. You are all I have, Saki, and I will fight for you. I will fight whoever is trying to take you away.

I won't let your sister, or anyone, not even God take you from me. I won't, Saki, I am not weak. And I could be strong enough for both of us. I have decided to go away. Saki, will you come with me?"

Saki's face softened when she looked at me again. "Ryoka," she called my name.

I won't let her go.

A smile broke across Saki's face. Joy expressed through her tears when she said, "Ok."

# Swimming Lesson 16

---

I woke up one evening to the sound of a shattered roof, moving in the wind, and realized I had missed the midterm exam. Four days ago started the first week of August. Two weeks had already passed since we left home.

What now? The question sounded in my mind.

We couldn't stay in a hotel, because police were out there looking for us. Saki's family had put her picture in newspapers as a missing person. So no place was safe. To my surprise, however, my photo had never been in the papers. My parents had never kept my photo. But there should be a photo of me in the middle school yearbook or high school registration. So I supposed I wasn't as important as my companion. After two days of sleeping under a bridge, we came across this abandoned house. Its construction looked bent toward one side from the outside like it would crumble at the first gust of wind. The moldy tatami gave a musty smell, and we had no way of fixing the large hole above the living room. At least we could have rooms, now, and more than half the roof over our head. The bathroom's smell was intolerable, however. After the first time we had opened its door, we agreed never to open it again.

The beach was just fifteen minutes away, walking. We could smell the sea first thing in the morning.

We found canned food in the kitchen. All had passed the expiration date. But surprisingly, they tasted good after being heated up. The discovery allowed us a chance to rest and take leisure. Part of me was hoping something would happen. Something that would inspire us or give us resolve on what to do next. Nothing happened, however.

It felt as if we were living in an hourglass, apart from the world. And in time, the sand would bury us.

I would disappear, forgotten, and drag Saki down with me.

The shoji door made a creaking sound as Saki slid it aside. I sensed her eyes above me. "There you go, stressing out again," she said.

I kept my eyes on the candle over the low table, flickering.

"Let's fight," Saki's voice spoke. "Ryoka, have I not told you to keep the shoji open? It will fall off. I have to keep closing and opening it."

"But, it's cold," I said, bracing myself.

"It's still August. Bare with it a little." Saki gave me a little scold before coming to embrace me, "there, better?"

Did people who fought usually comfort each other? I sensed Saki's eyes moving toward the candle, half already gone. We had neither water nor electricity. Next to it, a half donut was on the plate.

"You haven't eaten it?" Saki scolded me, for real this time, "ants are going to come."

"I am not hungry. You eat it."

"Ryoka, I told you that I have money," she said. "My savings are plenty to keep us on for years. So you don't have to worry. You have eaten so little, what if you get sick? Medicine will be more expensive, you know."

I always kept in mind how her family could freeze her bank account at any time. Either Saki didn't know or knew it but pretended not to. My parents had already done it. I had not told her. Though we had run away, our lives still depended on our parents' whim. At least, her parents loved her more than mine did, and they probably didn't want her to starve. But even that could change at any time. So I couldn't let myself be at ease and let her feed me. I owed her too much already. And I had some pride.

Saki took the donut and put it in front of my face. I grasped it with my teeth.

"Good?"

"I would rather have beef stew," I said, referring to the stew can we had on our first night here. We hadn't been able to go to convenience stores, with police cars seemingly everywhere we went. So we had no choice.

The thing had expired ten years ago but was still edible when heated up with a candle.

"It was delicious beef stew," Saki said, then cracked a small laugh at our favorite joke. "The best I ever had."

We laughed, like two little kids reminiscing over the first time eating an insect. And that meal had almost tasted like one.

"Saki, let's go to Tokyo," I said. "We can't just stay here. I want to get a job or two, to support both of us."

Saki braced her legs and hid her face between her knees. "No," she said, shaking her head slowly. "You don't know cities, Ryoka. I have heard stories of how girls get tricked into doing awful things in awful places. I am afraid, so no."

Once again, we reached a dead end.

Saki moved over and put her arms around me. "Ryoka, I won our fight," said she. "Come sleep with me."

"No," I said. "Sorry, Saki, but I don't want to use your body to solve my problem. It's not your fault. I am—".

I was regretting it, having brought her with me. Though, I couldn't say this out loud. I wanted to make her happy. But all I had to show for it was this shattered house, where we kept the light at night with candles, washing dishes with bottled water, and using the backyard as a toilet. Unlike me, Saki had a home and a family. But now, all she had was me. I had stolen her future.

"Fine, I'll let you win the fight," Saki said. "Now tell me what you want? I hate to see you sad on my account."

"Saki, isn't there anything you want?" I said. "I want the same thing you do."

Her arms paused for a moment around me. "I want to go to the beach," she finally said.

"Ok, tomorrow."

"No, tonight," she said with a renewed energetic tone.

"But, it's late."

"The beach is so close, and we have never gone there," said Saki. "Come on, let's go for a night walk. I haven't had any real exercise for days. And we could have a bath too, finally. No one would see us at night. It's the only good time."

I sighed, admitting the soundness of her reasoning, and got up. We began packing what we needed and were ready to set out in twenty minutes. Saki went ahead of me, running like a child over the empty street. I shouted a warning that there might be a car. And she teased me for sounding like such a grandfather. Saki had not looked this happy for a long time, so I no longer spoke.

Saki was calling me to hurry up.

Strange coldness overwhelmed me as if something whispered a premonition in my ears. I looked up and saw more stars had come out tonight. Beautiful, though they were, I felt like seeing a pattern that warned me of an omen. Saki paused in the distance, waiting for me to catch up. And my heart drummed with fear. As if by the Providence that I received this forwarning, tonight would be the last night I ever saw her smile.

I heard the waves and saw our destination come into view. The mass of black water lay beyond the narrowed beach, stretching past my eyes.

The tide crashed against the shore. Its sound felt close, like the roar of thunder.

Saki climbed down the slope before kicking her slippers away and running toward the sea. I dropped a bag over the high ground and began taking out the firewood we'd obtained from a partly demolished house. Using a lighter, I made fire with a piece of paper before placing it under the wood. Once the fire grew, I added more paper and watched. The firewood turned to charcoal, gleaming with red embers. I rubbed my hands over the fire before looking up. Saki was chasing after a retreating wave. Then she ran when another wave rolled towards her.

I sat down on the hard sand and watched. Finally, Saki came running back, her clothes soaked wet. "Aren't you going to swim too?" She asked, dropping at my side, "the water is so nice."

"Maybe later," I said.

"You better take a bath before we head back." Saki nudged her head against my arm. "If you smell, I won't sleep with you."

"I will. I will."

Saki's blue eyes were staring into the fire. I observed her through the corner of my eye. For a long time, I had hated God, though I refused to believe in heaven. After I met Saki, I realized that heaven existed here on the earth. Me with Saki, sitting together by the fire like this. How I wished it could last forever.

"Ryoka, talk to me."

"About what?" I whispered.

"Anything, I want to hear your voice."

I took a deep breath, felt the warm scent of Saki sitting close to the fire. The black tide crashed against the shore in the distance before retreating. "Did you know," I began, "two hundred forty-eight thousand and five hundred fifty species were living in the sea? One thousand years ago, the humans were just one of the species coming out of the water. I used to think it was a miracle how creatures like elephants and us were once as small as planktons. We built ourselves from scratch, growing arms and legs and eventually making tools. And yet, one teacher in my elementary tried to tell us that the world was made in seven days by some old man. Because God loves us, so he created us, she said. I told the teacher that this God must be selfish, creating us in his image, and wanting us to love him only. I ended up making her cry. She called me blasphemous and a devil child. All I said was the truth."

"Can you blame the teacher?" Saki said, "you were mean."

"Well, sorry for speaking my mind."

"But Ryoka, " Saki said, "I must say that from your way of acting like God is your enemy, you probably are more of a believer than many."

I paused, before responding. "Do you think God is good, Saki?"

"Who knows?" She said, "maybe, maybe not. But if God is supposed to be the contrasting term to the devil. Would that mean God is whatever is the opposite of evil? I have seen a devil, Ryoka. And you too have seen her, even though you might not have recognized her as one. So much sadness a real devil can cause. I often think the world has fared much better because there's a God in this world."

I thought of Sayo.

"Do you have a dream, Ryoka?" Saki asked.

"Dream?"

"What you wanted to be when you grew up," she said. "All children get asked that at least once. Tell me yours."

"No way."

"What? Is it something embarrassing? Did you want to be a famous idol or something?"

"It's not like that," I said.

"So tell me."

"Why would you want to know?" I said, picking up a piece of firewood and throwing it in.

"Because," Saki said, with seriousness in her eyes. "I want to know about you."

I sighed, gazing into the fire, then toward the sea. "A marine biologist," I said, looking at Saki again. "I used to like collecting seashells. And science was my favorite subject in elementary. I used to spend most of my lunchtime in the library, reading books with pictures of fossils and creatures under the sea."

"That explains why you were so knowledgeable earlier," Saki said, looking disappointed. "And here I thought you had some strange prospect for the future. Although, you probably were the only kid in class with a realistic dream."

We laughed.

"What about you?" I asked, "what do you answer when you get asked?"

"Nothing."

A crackling sound came from the fire. I looked at Saki through the corner of my eyes. Though light reflected in her eyes, her expression looked empty. "Saki," I said, "are you the one with an embarrassing dream and not wanting me to know?"

"Really, nothing." She said, "the idea that every person born, would naturally come to know their own purpose in life, is a fantasy cooked up by adults with wishful thinking. It's like when a factory mass-produces cars, it's a known and accepted fact that one out of every ten cars is bound to be defective. I am one of those defective humans, born and unable to perceive the purpose of my existence."

"Saki, you hate yourself too often, and I always think it's unfair."

"Do you want to see the proof, then?" Saki said, laying down, her head in my lap. "Give me words, any words, and I will quickly answer with the first thing that comes to mind."

I looked into her blue eyes, gazing at me as she waited. Her clothes had already dried and stuck to her skin. The shape of her bra was revealed in the flickering light. A word, I thought, "night," I spoke the first thing that came to me.

"Light," she answered at once.

"Sky?"

"Grey."

I blinked. "Mirror—."

"Truth."

"God."

"Forgiveness." Saki's eyes remained unblinking.

"Swimming pool?" I said, after hesitating.

"You."

I bit my lip to contain the happiness. "Sunscreen."

"Love."

"Fiction."

"Tragedy."

"Life?" I wanted to know.

"A real tragedy."

"The sea," as I spoke, a roaring sound came from the distance.

"Salty, like a tear," Saki answered. "See? I am a defective product of God, who never would recognize the beauty of anything created."

"It's not a sin to be pessimistic, Saki."

"Tell me the truth, Ryoka," Saki said, still in my lap. "Are you regretting running away with me? Now, that you know, I am an existence without a good soul."

"Never," I answered immediately.

Saki frowned. "Why? Even though I have caused you to suffer?"

"You haven't," I said.

"I have never done anything good toward you," she said. "Because of me, you are where you are now."

"You have saved me, Saki."

"I—" Saki paused, "saved you?"

"I had nothing until I met you," I said.

"That can't be true, Ryoka. Anyone who says they have nothing, has more than they claim."

"I don't."

"What about your family?" She asked.

"They wouldn't care if I was gone."

"Ryoka, don't ever say that," Saki said. "It may be easy to say you hate your family. But trust me when I say this. Family can be the only thing you have when everything else falls apart. If you take them for granted, you will regret it one day when it's already too late. You have abandoned them just to come with me, Ryoka. I am sure that they have been worried sick about you—"

"They don't care if I die!" I snapped.

Saki's startled look brought me back to my senses.

"I am sorry," I said, "I didn't mean to yell at you."

Saki brushed her hand over my face. "Tell me," she said.

"My parents," I began, "my father never wanted me. My mother had been dating him for six years when he tried to leave her. So out of desperation, she got herself pregnant with me. My grandparents were old-fashioned types, with lots of pride. So my father failed at getting her to abort me. And that's how I was born. Ever since I was little, he has never tried to hide how much he hates me. I never got a birthday present. Neither of my parents ever came to a parents' meeting. We have never had a single meal together as a family—"

I wiped a tear away.

"Why don't you let yourself cry, Ryoka?" Saki asked.

"I won't," I said, despite feeling warmth linger at the corner of my eye. "I have sworn to never cry for them again. My mother blamed me for everything. She said, 'can't you try a little harder?'. 'Because of you, he hates me.' 'The neighbors are talking behind my back. Do you know how that feels?' I love my mother, and I believe I still love my father. But I won't give them my tears. If it's my fault for being alive, then they shouldn't have had me in the first place. Don't have a child for your gain. I am not a tool. People keep saying that parents have children out of love. What a farce! Children are born for the parents' gain. And if a child grows up useless, she's treated like trash. Parental love? Warm family? Happiness? They don't exist! And I have learned that my whole life. My parents wish I had never been born, so what? Fine, I don't want them either. I don't want—"

Saki got up and held me. "I am sorry, Ryoka." She said, "there, there. It's ok now. You can cry. I won't watch."

I tried to stop myself but failed.

Saki continued to hold me for as long as I needed. Till I could cry no more.

How could I ever live until now without her?

"I am here, Ryoka." She said after my tears finally stopped. "I will always be here. So tell me what you need me to do."

I wanted her.

"Ryoka?"

Without realizing it, my arms had tightened around her. "Come with me, Saki," I said, "to the sea."

Saki moved back, and I loosed my arms around her. Her blue eyes that looked empty before now held the flickering light of the dying campfire. I knew what I had said, and I could not take back the words. I wanted her and her alone. Though I still had her now with me, there was no telling what would happen. When tomorrow came, we might get caught. Either police would find us, or Sayo would. Or by some act of God, an accident might occur that one of us became injured, and our time together ended. So while I still could, I must secure her to myself, using any means, even death.

I would not let God say no to the only thing I wanted, ever again.

"Ok," Saki answered, with both hands squeezing around mine.

I heard her voice, clear, like a word of kindness spoken to me in the darkest hour.

"Did you think I would refuse?" Saki spoke with a smile. "Ryoka, if you ever want to know how much a person is worth. Just imagine her or him vanished, then, ask yourself if it would make any difference. And I know this for the truth, Ryoka, that the world will go on even if I no longer exist. But Ryoka, you are saying just now that you want me to come with you. I am so happy. I feel the same. If you were to disappear, then I would have no reason to live on. So I will go with you, no matter where you want to go. Be it heaven or hell, I will go with you."

The waves crashed against the shore, sounding like the devil's roar.

The green ribbon fluttered in the wind. I let my hand squeeze around Saki. Together we walked down toward the beach. A tide was rushing toward us, breaking. The water stopped only an inch away from my feet before retreating. Despite it being summer. The world felt cold.

But Saki's hand alone felt warm.

"You won't change your mind?" I asked and felt her hand relax.

Saki was looking at me. And she smiled a faint smile, different from the childish one I used to see. "I will never let you go, Ryoka."

My fear melted away. "Shall we go, then?"

"Let's go together." She said.

I took the first step, guiding Saki forward. My eyes fixed toward the thin line between the water and the sky. Cold water washed over my feet. As I sensed the world I was about to leave behind, a moment of regret came over me. I had lived my entire life, just for these last few weeks when Saki had been in my life. How could my happiness have been so brief that the end was already here?

The water reached my face.

The black wall came rushing toward us, and I closed my eyes in surrender. The force threw me backward. My feet were no longer held to the ground. The sky had disappeared as the water jerked me forth, then back. I continued to hold my breath until a sharp pain cut through my chest. My body gave a final struggle before giving in.

My mouth opened to call out her name. But I no longer heard the sound as the dark water swallowed me down.

# Swimming Lesson 17

I blinked till my eyes adjusted to the light. Then, I saw the white ceiling and white curtains surrounding me. Looking down, I was wearing a white gown and covered up to my chest by a thin white blanket. Startling, I sat up and felt struck with nausea.

Where am I?

My vision turned blurry. I felt a rough, thick bandage around my head. I moved and touched my arm, pulling on something, a plastic tube inserted in my vein, connecting me to an IV bag dangling on a pole. Then a curtain parted suddenly. A nurse in glasses wearing a white uniform paused upon seeing me. She let out a small cry before running off. And soon, she returned with a doctor wearing a white gown. My nausea worsened. My body was struggling to remember something important.

Saki!

"Where is she? Where is Saki?" I cried, grasping the doctor's gown. "Saki, Saki, that's her name. She's a little older and pretty. Where is she? Where is she!?"

The nurse in glasses stepped back. Another nurse with long hair looked at me, then at the doctor, who gave her a nod. The two nurses held me by the arms on each side. I kicked and cried before feeling a pricking sensation. The doctor held firm at the injection, its needle sunk into my vein.

My eyes felt heavy, and my struggle ended.

I remembered no dreams when I woke up again.

It looked like evening on the other side of the curtain. Then, it parted, and the long haired nurse without glasses was standing next to me. Her stern look gave me a fear that I might get injected again if I caused her any trouble. So I kept my mouth shut while she helped me sit up, then pulled out the table attached to the bedside and placed a tray of food down without the slightest sound. The bowl of porridge looked steaming hot, with boiled vegetables for a side dish, a glass of water, and a container with a few pieces of tangerine.

Before she left, I noticed the look in her eyes, cold, as if accusing me of a crime.

It could be the medicine's effect that my mind felt clearer now, upon waking from what felt like a long sleep. And with food in my stomach, I found the energy to gather my thoughts and assess my current situation. The two nurses I had met so far. Let me call them 'Glasses' and 'No Glasses,' as both seemed to refrain from speaking to me. Thus, I felt no obligation to use their names. Glasses had a bad haircut and looked like a grasshopper with a poorly made wig glued to her head. When she came to take my finished plate, she dropped a metal container that caused the sound to echo across the hallway. I guessed her to be either new to the task, or simply bad at her job. At the sound, No Glasses appeared. She, on the other hand, had an efficient look in her manner. And with her face and that hair, she looked like a soap opera character, whose script title said 'a perfect nurse'. After she finally calmed the other down, No Glasses saw that I had finished eating and soon brought back the doctor. I answered the questions when asked. He told me that my head had scraped into a stone. Luckily, I wouldn't have a scar after it healed.

I waited to see if he might mention anything about Saki. In my wishful thinking, I had made myself believe that she must be near. But the doctor left as soon as he had finished with the questions.

The following day, No Glasses came to take out my IV. Then, after I ate, came another check-up. Glasses and No Glasses stood behind the doctor, on each side. They looked like two lovely assistants, which would make any charlatan sit between them seem like the best doctor in the world. I succeed in creating a satisfied look on the doctor's face, and before he left, he encouraged me to try walking on my own. And so, once being left alone, I hung my legs off the bed. The cold floor caused my toes to hunch. I finally stood up, holding onto the rail at the end of the bed.

It felt as if I had not walked in years.

Glasses returned just before I got through the door. She stutteringly told me to wait, then went and returned soon with a pair of indoor shoes. After she gave me the warning to walk carefully and avoid the stairs, she left me be.

Later that day, I heard the patients talking, that Glasses had tripped and fell down the stairs.

So long as I must stay in this hospital, my utmost wish was that Glasses would never get to do anything such as injecting me. For I was afraid that she might trip and ended up injecting herself. By the second day, I learned that this place was an old hospital, twenty minutes away by car from the beach. Despite the rundown look from the outside, the inside had been kept clean. I was put in a mixed room with ten beds, five on each row. Aside from myself, the only other patient was an old lady whose bed next to the window. My bed was the second from the door, far from her, yet she always complained about me making noise at night. Once, in the afternoon of the first day, when I returned to the room after searching for Saki, I saw that she had her whole family come to visit.

No one had come for me.

A week passed by. Saki was nowhere to be found. And I was too afraid to ask, fearing the look the doctors and nurses continued to give me.

Why was I here? I started to ask myself. Or, to be precise, why was I still here? The nurses hadn't objected to me walking around. The doctor had taken the bandage off my head the other day. He shone the light into my eyes and told me to follow his hand movements before he declared that my sight remained in perfect condition. And I no longer felt nauseous these days. Yet, there had been no sign that I'd be allowed to leave this place. Something told me they were keeping me here, waiting for something.

The answer came one day, like the sky crumbling down.

On the ninth day came Glasses' turn to bring me a meal tray. Her glasses bent to one side, and she held an expression of a child scolded after doing a poor job. I felt bad enough for her that for once, I let myself say "thank you" when she successfully placed the tray down, spilling only a bit of miso. I could have a bowl of rice now instead of porridge. She watched as I took medicine with a glass of water before she left.

I lifted the rice bowl and saw an old newspaper, used as a tray cover. It was dated from last week, with giant letters for a headline,

### COUPLE SUICIDE, One Death

*A body was discovered this morning washed up on the local beach. Police have Identified the deceased to be—*

I continued reading. The rice bowl fell out of my hand. Though the article had omitted the name, the fact had been stated. One death, it said. If I was here, alive, then Saki. No, this couldn't be.

Saki!

I swiped the tray off the table and ran out the door. The two nurses came running, and I knocked the closest one aside. Another grasped me by the shoulder as I was reaching for the stairs. A doctor hurried over with an injection in his hand. I won't believe it. I won't believe it! There must be a mistake! SAKI!

Both my arms got restrained by the two nurses. I cried and kicked the air. And I screamed till my head felt like it would split apart.

The prick of the needle didn't even hurt.

But the doctor and the disgust in their eyes, that hurt. I had killed Saki.

Why should I live when Saki had died? God, I beg you, turn back time and give Saki back to me. Please, don't leave me alone in this world.

I found myself strapped to a bed when I woke up. The IV tube had been reconnected to my arm. Once finding my voice, I screamed. Over and over, I struggled. Two times, I tried to bite my tongue. I wanted to die. No Glasses grasped me by the jaws and stuck a spoon in my mouth. I attempted in vain to bite her hand. But then the doctor came and put me down. In my sleep, I dreamed no dreams. And when I woke up again, the world was my nightmare.

Two more days, or longer, I didn't know. I became too exhausted to kill myself. I stared up at the white ceiling, watching day coming and night passing. I left the soil and pissed on the linens. The old lady by the window cried out one night, mistaking the smell for my death.

I started laughing at one point. I laughed, and I cried. I cried till I could no longer cry. My voice had gone.

But I still breathed.

Once again, God took it away. My reason to live, Saki, he took her away.

God, I hate you.

I woke up and found the sunlight on my ceiling. I must have slept a whole day. Looking down, I found the straps had been removed. My head felt clear as I attempted to get up. The air smelled like morning. Once my feet got used to the cold floor, I pulled the curtain aside and began to walk, dragging the IV pole with me.

In the end, I had failed even to go insane.

At the door, Glasses saw me and looked like she was going to faint.

"Please let me use the phone," I gave my all to squeeze the best tone out and succeeded in calming her down.

Glasses ended up accompanying me to the payphone located on the same floor. She lent me more coins than I needed, before stepping back, continuing to keep her eyes on me. I inserted the coins and dialed the numbers. Ringing sounded on the other side.

I waited until I heard the phone pick up. "Father," I said.

"Is that you?" The crude voice came after a silence.

"So you are home. Mother would be happy."

"What do you want?" he said.

"I just wanted to hear your v—"

"Don't bother coming back," his voice cut mine. "Do you have any idea what shame you have brought upon your mother and me? I talked with her, and we no longer want anything to do with you. We will pay for the hospital bill. But once you get out of there, come and get your things. Then you can go wherever, do whatever you damn please."

I squeezed the receiver. Then a laugh came through my mouth.

"What's funny!?"

"Father, I am sorry," I said, still laughing. "To Mother, too, I am sorry. To everyone, my birth has ever offended. I am sorry. I am sorry for having lived this long. I am sorry for ever being born. I am sorry for fucking up. And I am sorry that I couldn't even die. I am sorry. I am sorry."

"Are you trying to make me feel guilty?" His voice shook as if he'd just been betrayed. "Don't you dare try to pin the blame on me, who do you think you a—"

I hung up, feeling a long silence that followed.

Glasses was looking the other way, bracing herself, pretending to have heard nothing. I noticed then that

I had been holding my breath all this time. So I made a long exhale and counted my breaths. One, two, three, four, just like Saki taught me during our breathing exercise. It felt ironic that I should feel happy now, having just heard my own father's voice speaking to me for the last time.

I no longer held any attachments. For my parents had just set me free, to go where Saki was waiting for me.

I had no memory of falling asleep, nor of me returning to the bed. But when I woke up, the ceiling looked gold with evening light above me. And I felt sore around the shoulder like I had fallen down on my side. The light-headed sensation suggested that I had passed out without knowing it. And Glasses must have helped me back here, I guessed, feeling gratitude in her making an effort to help me, someone who had just lost everything.

An approaching sound came from the other side of the curtain.

"This way Ma'am."

I saw No Glasses' shadow, her long hair, and the composed manner as she gestured to another person next to her. The curtain parted. My eyes narrowed consciously before taking a good look at the person wearing a suit. And I immediately recognized our substitute teacher, Miss Tae Himura.

"Miss Namie," she greeted me. "Sorry, it has taken me so long. I have come to see how you're doing."

Someone had come for me.

"Miss," I spoke, feeling my tears gather. I embraced her, like someone drowning, who had finally found something to hold onto. Her body tensed up, but she didn't push me away.

Somebody had come for me. This thought alone filled me. She let me cry.

No Glasses had already left when I finished. Miss Himura brushed aside my hair to see where the bandage used to be. "Does it still hurt?" She asked.

I shook my head.

"I convinced them to take the strap out, so you can eat on your own." She continued, "have you eaten?"

I shook my head again.

"Have you had enough sleep, at least?"

I nodded, then wiped tears away with my arm. Miss Himura searched her pocket and took out a tissue pack, using one to dab under my eyes. I let her, while taking this chance to observe my teacher up close. She wore a black blazer and office skirt that, with her hair short in a bob style, looked like a Kokeshi doll dressed up in business attire. Her eyes gave out an aura of intimidation, yet, I saw the tenderness in them when she let me have the whole pack of tissues and told me to blow my nose with it.

"I have come in place of your parents." Miss Himura said, after I finally calmed down, "to check on you. And also, to give you this."

She took out a piece of folded paper. "Saki left this on her desk," she continued, "it would cause an unnecessary commotion if newspapers were to see this. So, her family asked me to dispose of it. If you want, you can keep it."

I stared at the letter before accepting it, lifting its folds, and reading it quietly.

Dear Father. Dear Mother. Dear Sayo.

First, I would like to say sorry. Right now, you are probably asking why.

Why, after all these years of love and care you gave me, I decided to leave you. It is because I have grown up and found the world a lonely place when Ryoka can't be with me. As you are aware, I have fallen in love with Ryoka. She has offered me a place where my heart belongs. And with her, I no longer fear anything.

I no longer fear even death.

Please hear my final request. Please remember me as your daughter and your sister. I have decided to die not because I hate you but because I want to cling on to this happiness that I have found. If I am

not allowed to be with her in this world,
maybe in another world, I can.

Thank you for all you have done for me,
Mother, Father, Sayo.

Goodbye

Saki

"When?" I asked, to Miss Himura and myself, "when
did she write this?"

"I have known Saki and her family for a long time."
Miss Himura said, "she was an intelligent girl who
understood her actions and their effects. So she wrote
the letter before she left home, I believe."

Saki always knew it would end up this way, that in
time, either our parents would have us cornered. Or,
we would corner ourselves. She came with me because
I had asked her.

I killed Saki.

More tears scattered over the letter. Saki's final word
of 'goodbye' left behind a long blue smudge. "Why?"
I asked her, "why would you give me this?"

"You have the right to at least hear her last words,"
Miss Himura said. "This favor, please know that I will
call upon it soon."

I looked up upon hearing her changed tone of voice.
But I cared no more if Miss Himura too would judge

me to be a murderer. "It's all my fault," I said, holding each end of the letter. "It should have been obvious how we would never get away. We are just kids whose lives depended on our parents. What could we do? Where could we go? Finding a place we could be together was just a pipe dream. I knew this, yet, I wanted to believe in my own delusion. It's my fault, mine."

"Miss Namie."

"Please, Miss, call me by my first name."

"I heard you called your family this morning," Miss Himura spoke after a brief pause. "As a matter of fact, I have just come from your house. I talked with your parents. It has all been arranged."

Arranged?

"Saki's family finally dropped the charge," she said. "Newspapers have been after them. It's pointless to deny what you two were trying to do. At least, they have succeeded so far in omitting both of your names from going into print. So I convinced Saki's family to let bygones be bygones. They have already got enough problems, and punishing you would do nothing but add oil to flames. They have their own reputation to protect, after all. No one aside from the involved parties knew about you, so you are clear for a clean start. Your mother agreed to support you with the full amount of high school tuition for the next two years. I will arrange for you to take the midterm exam you have missed. You need to return for the next term as soon as possible. As long as you achieve a passing grade, you won't have to repeat. I had the Principal agree on this. The only problem would be your living expenses. You would need a job and a place to live, which I could help with. Your parents consented to have me take full responsibility as your guardian until your graduation."

I could understand only half of what she said.

"Ryoka, I realize that after all that happened to you, it must be hard to take this in." Miss Himura said, "but I promise I will do everything in my power to help you. According to your doctor, you can be discharged in two days. I will come to pick you up then. So rest now because the moment you get out of here, there is much to do."

~ ~ ~

That night, I reread Saki's letter, to commit it to my memory, until it hurt. I wanted to feel the pain. I lay on my side across the bed, bracing the letter on my chest. The green ribbon was a faint shadow in the dark, like a chain around my wrist.

How I wished I could die, simply by wishing alone.

No Glasses gave me a guarded look whenever I got close to where the pills were. And Glasses always came with me when I went for a walk in the hallway. They wouldn't let me get close to the stairs, and I found all the windows locked. Once, I thought of stabbing myself through the eyes with the chopsticks.

But then, on my last night, No Glasses brought me an extra portion of nikujaga that her little sister had made. She said that eating well might lift my spirits. And then, after dinner, Glasses apologized to me for mistakenly letting me see the paper in the first place.

My gratitude toward them caused me delay my plans. And before I went to sleep, I had resolved to call the two by their first names.

Miss Himura came as promised on the day I got released. She was waiting for me by the front gate when I walked out of the hospital. Today too, she wore the same signature suit, which made me wonder if she wore that thing seven days a week. She opened the door of her Honda, gesturing me to get in. And I asked her to wait for a moment.

Both the nurses came to see me off. I bowed toward each of them. "Thank you," I said to No Glasses first, then Glasses, "Miss Asami, Miss Kaede."

It was strange to think that I was going to miss them.

Within less than five minutes, we'd left the hospital area. When the car drove past the beach, I sat up straight, trying to look through the driver's side window. Miss Himura continued to keep her eyes forward, hands at the wheel, her eyes trying to appear like she hadn't noticed my tension. The beach disappeared, and I sunk into my seat again. The light of mid-August felt warm through the window. We entered the town area. Miss Himura turned into an alley, where I saw a convenience store on the corner. She then spoke for the first time, asking if I was hungry. But I told her I had already eaten at the hospital, so she continued without stopping.

The car turned once again into an empty parking lot. I saw the five-storied buildings before me.

Once the engine turned off, Miss Himura got out of the car first to open the back trunk. She pulled out a familiar-looking travel bag. I recognized it as one that belonged to my father. "Your mother packed your clothes and necessities," she said, put the bag down before me. "You can check later if anything is missing."

I tried lifting the bag and felt its weight. My life up until now felt so light.

Miss Himura took the lead. I noticed only one door on the first floor, with a line of bonsai pots before it. The post box had been emptied. The other doors were choked with mail and advertisements. Trash and empty cans lay on the floor. The elevator didn't work. She let me know. So we walked up the stairs on the side of the building. The second floor looked neither worse nor better than the first. We finally arrived on the third floor. And from the look of it, no one lived on this floor.

"Come in." She said once she unlocked the room at the end of the corridor.

I removed my shoes and stepped inside. A considerable living space lay before me, with a kitchen behind a wooden bar. Miss Himura opened the door that led to a bathroom before going into the room next to it. I followed her, pausing to look inside first. The room had a queen-sized bed frame, which looked permanently sealed to the floor. She got the window open and was struggling to push back a large tree branch outside. "Make yourself at home," she said, turning around. "Sorry if it still smells like paint. I had the work done quickly last week, so you should keep this window open, letting in the air. My uncle gave me this place as my inheritance, said I could fix it up. Once the economy improves, I might be able to sell it. But I can't afford the corporate fee on my own unless I rent it to someone."

My hands relaxed, and I felt the weight of my bag. Behind Miss Himura, the light was coming through the window. This room was facing East. It would be warm in the morning.

"It's not rent-free," she continued. "You need to get a job or two to pay rent regularly. I could give you my old mattress that will fit the frame. A desk and a chair, perhaps, some utensils and cooking tools, I can bring them by this evening. The water and electricity are ready to go. I will loan you some money, enough for you to get by a week or two. But I expect you to pay that back too, with what you earn. I also need you to attend school regularly and take exams on time. No special treatment, no delays, and don't be late on paying rent. Any questions?"

"Why?" I finally asked. "You have no reason to go through all this trouble."

"Do you think this is a good time to prioritize your pride, Ryoka?" Miss Himura spoke, her eyes darting across the room. "Instead of an unnecessary question, how about you take advantage of my offer and try to survive?"

"I don't trust people who do something, claiming it's for nothing."

"Then I am calling on a favor," said she. "You owe me for letting you have Saki's last word. And you can repay what you owe by staying alive. You will not do anything like what happened on that beach again. I have taken you into this new life, and it would be my pleasure to watch you living in it."

"I will disappoint you," I said, taking one step back and feeling the wall behind me. "Does this make you feel good about yourself, at the thought of feeding and clothing me? I can't be saved, Miss."

Miss Himura continued to gaze at me. "Ryoka, do you even know what it means to be alive?" She said, "there is no one in this world who has never lost something, or someone important to them. If you thought your life and only yours was a tragedy, please think again. There are people who choose to live on, despite the losses they face. Even if it hurts you to continue, you must never give up."

"So, what if I never pay you back?" I said with a mocking smile. "Are you going to feed me for the rest of your life?"

Miss Himura stepped across the room, one hand raised in the air. She swung it across my face. The slap was only light and did not inflict me with physical pain.

But it hurt inside.

"If you can still feel, that means you are alive." Miss Himura said, "I am giving you a chance, Ryoka. What you decide to do next is up to you. Those who only whine and blame the world have no future. If you don't lift a finger to save yourself, then you are not worth saving."

I was no longer able to hold my head up.

"If you dislike being indebted to me, then work hard and pay me back," she said. "Then you must live, live, and live. Live on until you could see your future again. Live until one day you can look back to this day and say to yourself that it was all worth it. You are still alive, Ryoka. Stop hating yourself, and live with your eyes fixed toward the future. Is that too much to ask?"

I stood like a child taking her teacher's scolding. Until my legs loosed the feeling as if my whole body was turning into stone.

Miss Himura responded to my stubbornness with a sigh. And I could see sympathy in her eyes when I looked up. Her genuine way of expressing kindness succeeded in causing enough guilt that even after she left the room, I found myself sitting down, leaning against the bed frame. I became so exhausted that the thought of running away came, then disappeared. The tree branch was making a rustling noise in the wind. The green ribbon felt warm around my wrist.

I held its tip, pulled, and felt the knot loosen a little.

To me, my life began when Saki took me by the hand and taught me that there was such a thing as love in the world. If my life started with Saki, it only made sense that it should end, now without her.

The new term had already started, a week before I returned to school. I endured, all this time out of my sense of pride, thinking that I must pay the debt to my teacher. Miss Himura made me memorize all the notes, and I got passing grades for the midterm. Math formulas and chemistry codes still crammed my head when I arrived at class for the first time in weeks. Some of my classmates asked how I had been doing. They thought I had been out sick. No one talked about the incident in the newspaper, and no one knew I was involved. It felt as if nothing had happened.

Could it all have been a dream? If I went after school today, would Saki be waiting by the pool?

But the pool gate was locked when I arrived that afternoon. The turquoise water looked as if it were made of glass. My hands squeezed the wire fence till it hurt.

Saki was no longer in this world.

On the second day, Miss Himura summoned me to the teachers' office during the lunch break. And she briefed me on a part-time job she had found for me.

"I'm not feeling well, Miss," I said.

"Would you like the school nurse to give you a check-up?" Miss Himura asked.

"I don't feel up to it, the job."

"Why? Is there somewhere else you'd rather be?" She asked, with a look that pierced through me. "You are now both a student and in the workforce. Don't you think it's time to stop laying back?"

My life now lay in my teacher's hand. I reported for the job that evening at the grocery store, half an hour away by bus. The work took hours to finish, and my body was sore when I returned home at eight. I lay on the bed, feeling this to be Miss Himura's idea of filling up my schedule. She wouldn't let me have time for anything but work. She wanted to destroy my will to die. As if to express my defiance, I quit the job two days later and found myself a new job at a stationary where I bought a box of razors with what I earned. Once I returned home, I got into the bathroom and took a blade with me. I turned on the water, the steaming shower rained on me, and the razor was cold at my wrist. A quick cut and all would end.

My hand shivered. And the blade slipped out of my hand, into the open drain.

Back on that night at the beach, I had been able to hold the courage of walking into the sea because Saki had been with me. Could it be that because she had disappeared, that now I possessed the will but not the strength? Or, did I have the strength but without the will? Could something Miss Himura had said make me hesitate? That awful teacher and her awful compassion stood in my way. I felt gratitude that she'd given me a new life. But I also hated her, as much as I hated myself.

I would make her regret saving me.

The next day, I came to school with a razor in my pencil box. Miss Himura taught the first period. She was moving through the desk toward the back, reading from her book. I listened to her steady pitch, spoken as if she had been the writer of those philosophies herself. Her voice grew distant. And I took out the blade, pressing it under the green ribbon—one cut. The sweat wet my fingertips. The sharp edge paused where my skin sensed its sharpness. My muscles felt as if they stopped functioning altogether.

"Miss Namie, if you could read the next sentence." Miss Himura spoke, standing next to me. Her hand squeezed around mine.

The blade fell over the textbook page. She swiped it away and continued moving toward the front. I stood up with the book in my hands. And I noticed the classmate next to me, staring as if I had just grown a horn.

The whole class was gazing my way.

"To know our inner thought." I read, "is to accept ourselves, both good and bad."

"Thank you, Miss Namie." Miss Himura said, after dropping the blade into a bin behind the teacher's desk. "Can anyone give an example of this saying by Mozi?"

By the end of the day, the rumor spread about what my classmate had seen. The girls on cleaning duty took out the trash bin before the first-morning break. And after school, everyone left the classes in a hurry, as if avoiding me. I sat at my desk, instructed by Miss Himura to wait for her. She arrived after four and sat down behind the teacher's desk without a word. I went to her.

"I am sorry," I said, with my head bowed.

"No, you aren't, not one bit." Miss Himura said, half her face hidden behind her folded hands.

I raised my eyes from the floor.

Miss Himura took something from her blazer, a light green notebook, and handed it my way.

"What is this?" I asked.

"Your new assignment," she said. "Write down, what you feel, what's too painful to speak."

"I was always bad at report assignments, Miss."

"Write down your story." Miss Himura said, ignoring my words. "Write from the beginning, how it turned out, and what continued after. Write until you can no longer bear the pain and then turn this into me."

"Why?"

"Because I want to understand." Miss Himura said, "I can't help if I don't understand."

I refused to move closer to the desk, where the notebook lay waiting. "I never asked you to understand," I said, "or to help me."

Miss Himura leaned back. She held the expression of a teacher with patience toward a slow student. "Imagine, Ryoka, a person drowning in the sea," she said. "She saw another swimming her way. Together, they began swimming for the shore. What is strange about this picture?"

"Please, Miss, I have no head for riddles either."

"Try," she said, her face bore a calmness. "When one let her mind run amok, one got lost and did what she regrets. Try instead, just for the next two minutes, to search for the meaning of this story."

"Sorry, I am too stupid for the task."

"Then picture the two girls in the story as yourself and Saki, if that would help."

The pain that I knew was not what caused my head to feel heavy. I felt suffocated with fear, like I was drowning. I feared to think of Saki. I feared not to think of Saki.

I feared thinking itself.

"Ryoka, have you ever regretted meeting Saki?" Miss Himura asked.

"No," I said, touching the ribbon.

"Can't you, then, let the memories with her be a source of your strength?" Miss Himura said. "Memories can hurt, but they can also be a cure. You lost the person you love, but you are still alive. That must mean something."

"Please, Miss, don't ask for what's impossible for me."

"What's impossible?" She asked, "to live?"

"To live," I said, "in this world where God will never let me be happy."

She took a deep breath as if the word was a boulder placed over her head.

"Let's say there was a child," I said, "she got raised never to get embraced. Then one day, someone embraced her. Can you still expect that child to be the same, once that someone has disappeared? The world would be torture, until death frees her."

Miss Himura closed her eyes. Her composure remained unshattered.

"My life has been a 'no' from day one, and it will be till the end. I am unloved, and I have become too cowardly to hope that it will ever change. So please, Miss, have mercy, have mercy, and do not judge me for wanting to exit this shitty life. Better I was burned in hell, than to live in this cold world where God had taken Saki from me."

Miss Himur's eyes opened. "Ryoka," said she. "Do I have to be on my knees and beg you, that you might find living a better choice than death?"

"Please, Miss, I believe you have more pride than that."

"I won't mind doing it, you know," said she, "if it helped, I would even apologize for God. Since I doubt that if this God existed, he would do it for you."

"No joking, please," I said, feeling my lips twist in a painful laugh.

"If you could promise to never again take your own life lightly, then I would be on my knees. After all, my pride would be cheap if I couldn't let it go for the sake of better outcome. Here, Ryoka, watch carefully—"

I looked as she got up, coming around the desk, and lowered herself before me.

"Here, my knees on the ground," she said.

"Please, stop."

"And here my hands on the floor," she said, putting one hand over another. "Now my head."

"Why are you doing this? You are not even a believer."

"But you are, aren't you?" Miss Himura said, "You believe in God enough that you blame him. So Ryoka, in place of God, I am on my knees, with my hands before me. And I say I am sorry for everything. I offer you this sincere apology for the pain you must endure, the love you were denied. I am sorry. And here comes my head—"

"If your head touches the ground, I will jump out of this window right now!" My voice burst and I felt something shatter inside me. A dark feeling flooded in and I gasped for breath.

The sight of Miss Himura before me, now, made me want to vomit.

I ran out of the classroom after taking the notebook. I ran just to get far from there. The sky looked pure white outside the building. The sun felt distant. Onlookers turned. Their faces looked blank as if wearing plain white masks. The notebook crumbled in my hand.

I threw up.

I couldn't do it, to live, even if I wanted to. I had wanted to, and I had tried, to live a decent life. But no one would teach me how. And now, it was too late. Saki had already gone.

Since that day, Miss Himura treated me no more than a school student and a tenant at home. She no longer summoned me, and we acted like strangers when passing each other in the hallway. I found more jobs to help pay the rent. My guardian continued to make it hard, though not too hard, for me to survive. She never gave anything for free. Instead, she made me go through an amount of hardship to keep a roof over my head and three meals a day. And yet, despite that her methods should have been a success, the failure continued to be mine, for I saw no point in living. I woke up each morning, ate, went to the toilet, took a bus to school, reported myself to work, then returned home to sleep. Then the next day, everything repeated. Eventually, the last of my strength crumbled like a house built on sand.

I wanted to see Saki.

One afternoon, I took a different bus instead of my regular one. I called my workplace to change for the night shift, though I probably wouldn't make it to that shift either. Arriving at my destination, I watched the bus disappear. And I began to walk down the road where I had walked with Saki on our last night. The nostalgic salty scent in the air and the sound of the sea. Finally, I returned to the narrow beach, stretching before my eyes.

I saw the figure of a person in the distance, standing where the tides reached her. And she began to walk into the sea.

# SWIMMING LESSON 18

T he girl had already gone into the sea by the time I reached the spot on the beach. Removing my clothes, I ran into the water.

I dove downward, forcing against the current. My eyes squinted to look through the blue water, and my heart gave an echoing tone amidst the world without sound. My breath ran out after less than two minutes, and I kicked the water to resurface. The incoming wave threw me back before I could take a breath. My arms struggled, and my legs fought against the water. The surface became smooth again, and I inhaled a mouthful of air before submerging. The water density felt as if I was swimming up a waterfall.

I resurfaced the seventh time, looking left, then right. But I saw no one within sight.

Could I just be seeing things?

The shore looked far behind. If I continued, I might never return. I let out a long exhale before breathing to the limit of my lung capacity and submerging again. The surface looked transparent above me, though, below the darkness felt like a grave. Finally,

I saw the girl in the distance. She was drifting through the light blue water, like a religious image of an angel falling from heaven. My stamina had already reached the limit. The pain cut through my chest. In my stubbornness, I ignored the pain and pushed further until I got the girl from behind and slipped my hands beneath her arms. A force gripped me, and I felt like my lungs were going to burst. Then came a strange sensation, like I was held by an invisible hand that raised me into the light. Once my face was above the water, my mouth opened wide. The sun felt warm over my face—the fresh air flowed through me. I felt the weight of the girl who had gone unconscious in my arms.

Her body felt cold when we returned to the shore. I dragged her away from where the tide could reach. And I finally noticed that she was wearing the same school swimsuit as mine.

She was from my school.

I pressed my ear over her chest and heard the faint sound of beating under her ribs. I didn't remember what I did, exactly, except that I managed to save her. By the time she sat up, coughing out the water, I'd already moved away from her. My mouth tasted like salt. The girl had long black hair extending across her back, and her dark brown eyes looked like two mud pools. She was glancing right and left like a lost child.

"What a show you put on out there," I said. "Were you trying to long-distance swim to Korea?"

She looked my way before she answered. "No."

"Then, what were you doing?"

"Swimming."

What a liar. They said anyone with experience at something could always tell apart the genuine from fake. After my previous failed attempt, death became like a half-skill that I had mastered. And like a sixth sense, I could perceive what she was trying to do.

She was trying to die. I had stopped her.

"You shouldn't have bothered," she said. "Or do you always go pulling everyone out of the water?"

I didn't even know her name yet. And already, I wanted to slap her. How could I mistake her for Saki when their resemblances were as a rock and the sun? "This is not a good place to swim," I said. "Others have tried to do the thing you just did. Not everyone survived. You did, though, so good job."

That was meant to be sarcasm.

I gazed down, by accident, and my eyes came to pause on the green ribbon, hung loosely around my wrist. Its knot felt soft when I touched it.

*"Pass it on."* Saki had said, *"who knows, you might give your good luck to someone."*

I couldn't tell if it was good luck or comedy caused by God, making it impossible for me to die today. But since I did not know this girl before me, I had no reason to wish her to succeed in the same thing I had come here to do. So, as if receiving a suggestion, for a second, I became hypnotized by Saki's words from the long past. I gripped the ribbon's end between my thumb and forefinger and pulled. The knot came undone, easily, as if it had been with me all this time, waiting for this moment when it left me. A warm tear rolled down my cheek. My face was still covered in seawater, and the girl next to me noticed nothing. I shivered, at the sense of longing, like being naked in a cold wind.

For the first time, since Saki had gone, I felt close to her again, doing her bidding.

"Put out your hand," I said. "Come on. Any side would do."

Either this ribbon would be good luck, or a curse I passed on to the girl.

"What is this?" The girl asked.

"Protective Charm," I spoke, like a puppet acting out an old script. Then, I offered her a handshake, the way I remembered Saki did. "I am Ryoka Namie. Nice to meet you."

Two days passed when I received a summons during the lunch break. Miss Himura needed to see me after school, my classmate said. And a fright came over me, at the possibility of her learning what I had almost tried to do. I didn't have to work in the evening. But I had cleaning duty. So I couldn't get to the teachers' office until four.

Miss Himura had already left.

Someone came to see her suddenly, the teachers said. And she took the guest to the counseling room.

The counseling room, I remembered, was on the same floor, close to the stairs. I heard voices coming through the door at the end of the narrow pathway. "I have been worrying about her," a woman's voice spoke, likely a parent of some student. "Ever since she returned home suddenly, she won't talk about what happened in Tokyo. I used to think as long as she came to school, she would open up a little. But she's just getting worse. I can tell that she's been keeping something from me, and it hurts her. I am already at my wit's end, Miss. You have known her since she was little. Isn't there anything you can do to help?"

I heard Miss Himura's voice, answering the woman.

The two continued to talk for about ten minutes more before I heard them getting up. The door opened. When the woman appeared around the corner, she saw me and smiled. The creases around her eyes deepened. Despite her hair, which had already turned white, I could tell she used to be a pretty girl in her youth.

She left.

"Ryoka," Miss Himura's voice startled me. "Sorry for keeping you waiting. Come in."

Miss Himura held the door for me as I entered. The square-shaped room had only one window opened.

A large table stood before me, with a folding chair still left on each side. A thick folder that looked like students' records sat on the table. A cold shiver ran up my back, despite the room's humidity. Based on the rumors, once, a girl with an inappropriate part-time job had been summoned here. And upon her confession, she was expelled on the spot.

The door closed behind me. Miss Himura came around the table and sat down opposite. "Have a seat," she said.

"Miss, if I have done something wrong, I am sorry." I remained standing and bowed ninety degrees forward. "I know I didn't do well on the test last week. I have been busy with a new job."

"New job?" Miss Himura said, "what happened to the job at the Stationary?"

"I've quit that," I said. "That place doesn't offer a night shift, and I needed one, so I could do extra hours."

"May I ask what the job is?" She asked.

"Just the checkout counter at a supermarket," I said.

"No alcohol selling?"

"No." I said, "just usual necessities, like rice, miso, cucumbers."

"That's good to hear." Miss Himura said, bending forward as if to examine me closer. "I heard about your test last week from the teacher in charge. He said the average score was pretty low, and yours was considered well-done."

She still kept her eyes on me, despite pretending not to.

"If anything comes up, you know I will help you, right?" Miss Himura continued. "Are you doing alright financially? I won't mind if you pay the rent a little late during exam season. Say, within a week overdue, would be alright."

"I will manage, Miss," I said.

"You don't need to be so tense," said Miss Himura. "I am not calling you here to scold you. Now sit down already."

I let in a sense of relief upon sitting down. Though it had been some time, I would never forget what happened the last time we talked. Even now, it felt awkward, despite Miss Himura acting as if nothing had happened.

"I do need to talk to you, however," she said. Opening the folder, she took out a piece of paper, "about this Swimming Association, that has your name and Saki's on it."

I stared down at the paper, not recognizing it, except my full name spelled out in Saki's handwriting.

"The Principal asked me if this was still active," she said.

"But," I said. "Saki and I were just using the pool."

"I made Saki filled out this form." Miss Himura said, "when she requested permission to use the pool. After all, it's school property you two were using."

I always wondered how Saki could come and go around the pool, despite her not being a student. So she had Miss Himura help her get permission by passing off our activities as an Association. There were countless of those in our school, when a student or outside guest wanted to borrow a room. It would make sense, also, how Miss Himura had come to involve herself in the matter after what had happened. Saki's family must have been using her to clean up the mess we caused. "So," I said, "what do you need me to do?"

"Ryoka, do you want me to give you access to the pool?" Miss Himura spoke.

I raised my head. The pool was the only place that preserved my memory of Saki. Ever since that night, I had never had a chance to mourn. Since no one ever told me what happened to her body, and I had no courage to ask. Miss Himura took my reaction as confirmation that I wanted what she just offered.

"You could go there, to say farewell, if you like." She continued, "on two conditions. First, don't cause trouble—"

I looked away, understanding what she meant.

"Second," she said, "if you don't want to return there again after you've had enough of looking around, that's fine. But in case you want to hang around there, you have to get a member or two and organize practices. You could even offer lessons or anything that would give me a solid reason for letting you use the pool."

I worked to understand what she meant when Miss Himura pulled out another piece of paper. There was a two-inch color photo of a girl attached to the right corner of a student registration.

"I believe you two have met," she said.

I recognized the girl from the beach.

"How?" I asked. Did she know about the other day after all?

"I saw Saki's ribbon around her wrist yesterday," said she. "She recently transferred here during the summer holiday. She was a swimming club member in her old school, too. A perfect candidate, don't you think—"

"Are you kidding me?" I felt something within me snap.

Miss Himura paused. Her expression of calmness, now, acted as a piece of fuel to a flame.

"Miss, sometimes, I think you are cruel." I said, breathing hard, "Is this your way of punishing me, that you are going to send me to her? So you hate me after all, I see."

I swallowed, feeling the saltiness, just like that taste over my tongue when I brought that girl back to life.

I rubbed my mouth till it hurt, feeling the hatred forming within me.

"Ryoka, I'm introducing you to a person. Why are you acting as if I've showed you a devil?"

I got up, and the chair creaked across the room. And I slammed the table. Miss Himura remained undeterred in her seat. I raised my hand and swung down. Miss Himura's face remained unflinching as my hand stopped an inch away from her cheek. Her eyes continued to gaze at me. My breathing felt hot like fire. I grasped the folder and threw it against the wall, creating a giant burst as it exploded mid-air. Pain rose within my chest, and I had to hold onto the table. Pieces of paper swayed left to right as they rained down around me. Then, the room returned to silence. "You hate me, don't you?" I said, "that's why you torment me."

"Ryoka, what have I done to earn your distrust?"

"Stop pretending you don't know!" I cried, slamming the table with both hands, again, and again, and again. "Always, you always pretend not to know something while working some trick. You took me from that hospital, forced me to live a life I never wanted. You have toyed me with your kindness. It makes me sick every time, like you were force-feeding me living worms glossed over with honey. And now, you finally show your true intentions. Instead of a quick death, you're going to make me suffer a slow death, fit for my crime of killing Saki, aren't you!?"

"Ryoka," as Miss Himura spoke my name, her eyes turned cold. "Sit down."

My fist clenched, my stomach turned, and my strength failed. I dropped to my seat, half angry and half afraid. Miss Himura got up and was coming around the table. My head dropped.

I felt her hand on my back.

"Ryoka, I too share the fault of what happened," she said. "I was supposed to take care of Saki as her teacher. Her parents hired me to give her homeschooling. After her sister had caused trouble to the point that Saki could no longer go to school. You met her, didn't you? Sayo had been unstable for a while at that point. And so, when the two of you became close, Saki asked me not to let her sister know. She was afraid, for your sake. Thinking back, now, I should have intervened then. If I could get you two and her family to sit down and let everyone calm down. Maybe, things wouldn't have turned out the way they had. Saki's parents are reasonable people, and I had earned their trust. But then, you two ran away. If only I could have found you earlier. I could still prevent the worst from happening. But I failed. And I have regretted it, even now."

"You have done more than you should have, Miss." I said, with my head feeling heavy, "you have helped me more than my parents ever had. And I know you must have some good intention, in what you are doing, trying to get me involved with this girl. But I can't. I just can't. There's no way I could bear getting close to someone like her."

Miss Himura continued to caress my back, which calmed me a little.

So I glanced over the registration, still on the table. "Rie Mitzusada." The name that the girl herself had introduced to me the other day. Now, I was attempting to sound it, "Rie," the sound felt heavy over my tongue, like an invocation to a devil. By the third time I recited her name, I felt like seeing the image taking form in thin air, of a girl with a pathetic look, hair stuck to her face. She was, as my experience would judge her, a person without redeeming merits. And the thought of me getting close to her felt like seeing my own shadow without a head. I had not the quality to judge her. But I had the right, at least, to be afraid of her who stood as the image of my worst self, the death itself.

"I am sorry, Miss." I said, shaking my head. "There's no way I could meet her."

"Why can't you?"

Miss Himura continued to act clueless, to force me into accepting the task. How crafty could she be? "Because—" I paused, "because I don't know how to talk to her."

"Ryoka, she's a human being just like you, speaking the same language."

"She won't listen to me." I continued.

"I don't care, Ryoka, just go recruit her!" Miss Himura snapped, startling me. "If you don't know how to speak to someone in Japanese, then try English! Ryoka, if you ever thought your life ended with Saki, you were wrong. This world is full of people. All you have to do is go out there, talk to them, meet them, and learn about another person. Make a friend, Ryoka."

My shoulders drooped. Miss Himura returned to the other side of the table. She took a key out of her pocket to let me see it.

"Come get this, after you've successfully recruited her," she said, then put the key away.

"Why don't you talk to the girl yourself?" I asked.

"This is still officially a school-activity related. The responsibility rests upon you to recruit a member, not me."

"At least," I said, "could you write me some kind of note?"

"A note?"

"Something with your name signed on it," I said. "It would make my job easier, with some stamp of approval, I think."

The tension eased in Miss Himura's eyes, replaced with an amused look. She took out a pen, then took out a pack of tissues from her pocket, already half used. Its cover had an advertisement for a newly opened flower shop. She folded the inward part of the opening and wrote on the white surface with a blue pen. After she gave her signature at the bottom, she handed it to me.

"What is this?" I asked, accepting the tissue pack.

"She will know it's from me," said she. "This way, even if you fail, she won't reject you outright."

I looked at the tissue pack, then at her, too exhausted to argue.

"Any questions?"

"You are cruel, Miss." I said, "you are kind, but you are also cruel."

"That's fine to hear," Miss Himura said, folding hands before her face. "Because that's what teachers are. We occasionally act cruelly to our students because we have high expectations of them. We force them to take the paths they wouldn't have done otherwise. We could go as far as tormenting you till you cry blood. You can weep, you can complain, you can even hate us. That's alright, so long as you still do what you must. You are not wrong, Ryoka. Teachers are cruel because we have the right to be cruel. Otherwise, we wouldn't be teachers."

~ ~ ~

I put one and two together to guess Miss Himura's expectation of me. She wanted me to save the girl, Rie Mitzusada. And I accepted the task, despite having no confidence in the success. It had been more than an hour since school was over by the time I left the counseling room. But I went anyway to see if the girl was still in her classroom.

The class one-three was located just two doors away from mine.

I hid by the door and looked in. I saw Rie, with her head in her arms, at her desk. Three of her classmates hung around another desk nearby. Their eyes were saying, what do you want? And I had less than ten seconds, maybe less, before one of them approached me. So I called out her name.

Rie startled. And she hid under the desk, like a cockroach running to hide behind furniture.

I admitted to having overdone it. But at least, I got Rie to come out into the hallway. After I relayed Miss Himura's message, Rie made a face like a Japanese doll with an angry look before she grasped the tissue pack and ran off toward the teacher's office. I sighed, partly in relief. It had been an impossible expectation for someone like me to help anybody. I tried, and Rie still rejected me. Thus, I'd freed myself of the matter.

So, I hoped.

Miss Himura summoned me again the next day to see her in the office during lunchtime. "I talked with Rie," she said, "now you can follow up."

"Miss, she doesn't want to," I said. "And I can't say I am suitable for whatever you're trying to do."

"Call this number if you want to reach her house," she said, giving me a piece of paper this time, with a phone number. Then, she told me the place where Rie was likely to be. "She's been there a lot lately, from what I heard from her guardian. If you go there, you will likely find her."

The beach where Saki had gone to, Rie, too, had been going there.

I didn't have work today and had wanted to sleep the whole evening off. Once I returned home, I poured half a sack of white sugar into a bowl, took a cucumber from the fridge, and broke it in half. I put on the cantaloupe-scented sunscreen while eating. Then I changed into the short pants that I had bought from the flea market the other day. I returned to the kitchen, resting against the kitchen bar. I smelled my arm while crunching on the sugar and cold cucumber. Had I put on enough, did this smell like Saki? The taste, was it sweet enough? And these pants, this feeling, was this enough to feel Saki on my skin? I stuck the end of the cucumber down into the sugar pile, swirled, and a chunk of white sugar came thick around its bottom. I bit a mouthful.

Rie came to my mind.

What happened to Rie was none of my business. But I couldn't simply discard her either, not when I knew what she wanted to do, going to that beach. So, if something like the other day was to happen, would it be my fault, if I didn't stop her?

It took more than half an hour to get there by bus. I then walked a few minutes more and arrived at the beach. The sight of a narrowed sand area stretched across my eyes, plastic bags and empty cans scattered around. Rie was not there. So I began to walk back to the bus station. Then, I continued to walk up the same path I had once walked with Saki. Twenty minutes passed when I arrived at our house, where it had been. Nothing was left but a plot of land. A giant *For Sale* sign had been put up.

Gone, the place where I had once been with Saki.

I made my way back down the road, closed my eyes, trying to remember that night. Saki's smile, her moving through this street, still alive. I wanted her. I wanted her to touch me, to make me feel warm once again.

A car's honking made me jump aside. It rushed past me, the driver yelling some curse.

Rie, too, would disappear, like Saki. The sound of water crashing against the shore caused my eyes to rise. I had returned to the beach without knowing. And I saw her there, facing the sea. The tide reached her feet. The evening light cast down toward her, causing a long shadow. The setting sun reflected over the water, looking like the fires of hell. From a distance, I saw Rie and the green ribbon around her wrist. She turned and began walking the other way.

I ran after her.

The sun had set when I returned to school. I had called from the payphone on the way, asking Miss Himura to wait for me. And when I arrived at the teacher's office, I found her in her seat at the table, a book in her hand, the same title Saki had given me.

Miss Himura put the book away. Her face looked like someone who had just read a funeral eulogy.

I struggled to catch my breath before reporting everything to her. And Miss Himura handed me the key. "Is the book good?" I asked.

"It's an interesting read when you put perspective into it," she said, resting her hand over the cover. "And unique experience offers such perspective, for one to see what most do not."

"Any moral from the story?"

"When you get lost into a frenzy of passion, it can be a lonely thing." Miss Himura answered, "that's my impression of the book anyway. I recommended you get a copy and give it a good read yourself."

My hand hurt, squeezing around the key.

"How did you do it?" Miss Himura asked, "recruiting Rie, I mean."

"I just did what you told me," I said. "I spoke to her in English."

Miss Himura blinked. "You went and did that?" She said, "I said that as a joke."

I rushed to the school's pool, and with the key, unlocked the gate. The sun had already set. I found my way through the dark, into the staff office, and turned on the light. The pool water glowed with turquoise light, as I had remembered. I came out, reached the water's edge to feel the cold sensation at my feet. I sat at the poolside, dipping my legs in, causing ripples to spread across the surface. And I gazed over the direction of the entrance.

A part of me still hoped, what had happened until now had been a nightmare.

Fifteen minutes already past seven. And I sighed with relief that Rie had not come. But then, I heard a creaking noise that caused my heartbeat to sound. The light footsteps made me look into the dark, hoping and wishing that Saki would appear by the next second.

I felt disappointed at the sight of Rie.

What was that first thing that Saki had said when I came for the first-morning practice? Oh, I remembered now.

"Yaa—" I said to Rie, with one hand up.

Rie didn't look happy.

I got her to change and get into the pool. After some swimming, Rie challenged me for a race. And to my own surprise, I beat her.

*"You have become a strong swimmer,"* Saki had once said. But I never realized until tonight. Although the world remained a cold place, my fear of water had already dissipated. And Rie, I could tell from a glance that she was a strong swimmer. Yet, I beat her. Rie sulked and continued to challenge me. And she lost one round after another.

Then, she nearly drowned.

To my eyes, Rie was a shell of a human being, with death possessing her, like a mischief master handling a marionette. Miss Himura's placing her into my hands felt like God had given me two choices. I could either leave her be, and watch as she walked into the sea. Or, I could save her.

"Save you or let you drown," I said, after taking her back from death the second time. "Are those my only choices?"

I might not be a good person. But I had no heart to push down someone who had already sunk to their lowest. After saving her twice, I couldn't hate her as before. So I ended up passing the night, talking to her. It felt like forever since I got to talk to someone and listen without judging. Both of us wanted to die. This thing we had in common caused a sympathy to grow in me. But why her? My sympathy developed into curiosity. Even though I had tried to die with Saki, I would never treat life like nothing. I had become a coward in life because I never had anything worth protecting. Even Saki, the littlest I had, was taken away. Until now, after meeting Rie, I felt the last bit of pride rekindle within me, like fire receiving its fuel. Miss Himura had expected me to do something for her. So, if I could save her, then maybe my life up until now had been for something.

The night after my first meeting with Rie, I returned home, took the razor blades, dumped them in the toilet, and flushed. Upon showing myself this resolve, I found the courage to go after her. I visited her class, and I called her home. Until the following Sunday, I finally succeeded in getting her to return to the pool.

But then she drowned again. And the third time, I saved her.

"Sorry, your God didn't save you. So I did."

"I didn't ask you to save me!" She screamed and tried to tear off Saki's ribbon.

"Please, don't do that," I said.

She tried to run, and I gripped her arm. "I am not bound to you!" She cried and pushed me away. I couldn't make sense of what happened until the water exploded around me. The cold felt like a thousand shards of glass shredding through my soul.

God, you hate me, don't you? Whether I tried to do good or evil, you would never let me have my wish.

Rie was escaping.

I got out of the water and caught her. "Why won't you swim!?" I snapped. "Do you want to die that much!? DO YOU!?"

"Why?" Rie asked me.

Why couldn't I let you die? The answer, I felt shame to admit, was that despite feeling no happiness in her company, Rie was the only piece of straw I found while drowning in my misery. Her existence had become the new core of my life, a chance of atonement for causing Saki to die, a redemption that I might regain my status from nothing into a human being.

Rie was my new reason to live.

# Swimming Lesson 19

"Please, save me too," I said to Rie that night.

But she didn't hear me. Or, she didn't want to listen, so subconsciously she wouldn't let my words reach her. I saved Rie. And I had enjoyed the success, in my heart, until the accomplishment soon turned sour, when Rie made herself a shackle around me.

I had saved her. And I must continue saving her.

The fault lay with me, who had created a persona that passed me off as a too-good individual. And I had lived ever since the life, like a criminal frightened of her own reflection. Rie didn't know how every time I met her at the pool, I felt like walking into an execution chamber, knowing I could get exposed any time. But even though I wished to confess, I was too afraid of the outcome.

Suppose Rie learned my true self. Would she accept me as I was?

Something told me that she would reject me. A girl who tried to die herself could never be fit to save another. Rie stayed alive at the expense of my pain. I suffered for carrying this burden, which far exceeded my natural strength. The truth would threaten my accomplishment with the prospect of her death. And I, too, would lose my reason to live. I could do nothing but feigning to be strong while perfecting my role further as a fake friend, whom she relied on as a fake saint. Things continued to worsen when Rie started inviting me to hang out outside the pool. And every time she did it, I felt like jumping at my own shadow. I managed to decline her as best as possible.

If I had to spend even one more day with her, I believed I would end up strangling her. In time, I came to regret ever saving her at all. My experience with Rie had taught me one thing, that any soul capable of saving another required no goodness of heart, but the talent of a con artist. For the real challenge of saving one's soul, the rescuer had to hoodwink another into believing black was white. Life was suffering, but one could always fool another into thinking that life, after all, was not that bad. With a fake smile and forced positive expression, Rie came to trust me. So I supposed, if my lies could save Rie as good as any priest, then all saints, who excelled at saving souls, must be the best of charlatans.

In November, Miss Himura asked me about the Swimming Association's progress, and I reported everything to her.

I let it slip how I had met Rie the first day when she tried walking into the sea. Up to that point, I had thought that Miss Himura already knew. Until I saw the surprised look on her face, and Miss Himura asked me to tell her everything. Once I finished, her expression looked as if she had hit someone with a car, and didn't know it until now.

"What do you intend to do now, Ryoka?" She finally asked.

"Shouldn't you tell me that?" I asked back, "I saved her. So what do I do next?"

"I am thankful, Ryoka," said Miss Himura. "But I have underestimated the situation. I knew that she had a problem. Her guardian told me that she always went out to the beach and didn't return till late. But I never thought that Rie, too, would do something to harm herself."

"But, if you didn't know," I said. "Why did you send me to Rie?"

"Ryoka, I told you to get to know another person, to make a friend." She said, "But I would never expect you to do anything beyond your power. So what now? You must first ask yourself, what do you want?"

What did I want from Rie? At one point, I realized that I just wished myself to be saved. By performing a good deed expected of me, I mistook that it would only be natural, that I should receive salvation for a reward. But to find out, now, that all this time, I had been overthinking things. There had been no expectation entrusted upon me. I felt like laughing and crying at the same time.

Rie invited me to hang out again.

I was about to refuse, when she mentioned the movie tickets based on the novel Saki gave me. So I agreed to meet with her.

The night before our appointment, I dreamed of that white world again. This time, I found myself on a white street. White walls stood on both sides, thick with white trees. And I could sense, somehow, that if I followed this white path, it would lead me to hell. My head felt heavy as if my skull got filled with lead. And it hurt so much, that I fell to my knees and smashed my head into the paved stone. Red color burst like squished tomato and left before me a giant red puddle. I watched as the red liquid formed into two shapes, of my father and mother, rising over me. My mother was looking down, like seeing a cockroach. And my father screamed—

"Don't let me see it in my house!"

I smashed my head, causing the forms to shatter. But then, from the puddle came another shape of Miss Himura all in red—

"If you won't save yourself, then you are not worth saving."

I cried and smashed my head a third time. The whole world shook. White walls transformed into an ugly tone, not red and not black, but a color like red bean paste. From it came hundreds if not thousands of Saki's faces, like grapes on a vine. "Ryoka," they all spoke at once, "can I kiss you?"

I screamed.

The faces burst away. The color then turned pale as if being washed away by an invisible force until the world became without color once again. And amidst the whiteness, the light formed together. Rie appeared, with her face white, even her pupils. She was dressing in a monastic white robe, whiter than her skin.

"Who are you?" Rie asked.

I woke up. The last sentence continued to resound in my head through the night, so that I could not return to sleep.

Once the first light came to the sky, I left the house to catch the first bus to the seafood market, where I was supposed to meet with Rie. I arrived one hour too early. And I made my way through the path I had gotten used to for the past months. Finally, I arrived at the yukata shop. The dark blue yukata with white waves and goldfish pattern that Saki once wore, was now being worn by a faceless white mannequin behind the glass. I leaned over, kissed the glass, and felt Saki's ghost still warm.

*"Look well at the madwoman."* Sayo's voice came in laughter, as my eyes opened and I saw the reflection of myself with hair and eyes like a starving beast.

I ran. How far, I didn't know. I ran until the slight warmth of the rising sun offered me a soothing comfort. Exhaustion caught up, and I fell on my knees. Please, Saki, save me.

Anyone, please save me.

"Ryoka, are you alright? You look as pale as a ghost."

I looked up and saw how much Rie had changed from when I first met her. Could she be the same girl who once drowned last year? Now, she looked more lively than before.

Rie took me to a place where I could sit down. And I observed her through the corner of my eyes while she was putting beansprouts onto a small plate. The two of us were a bad combination, like an angel and a devil descended on earth into human form, unable to recognize one another. By a cruel comedy that only God understood, we crossed paths, and tragedy was set into play. If Rie was good, then I was a sham, a quack doctor whose remedies worked accidentally. Sitting next to her, I felt like a poorly written fiction character, fated to die or go mad at the end.

*"Who are you?"* The question had chased me from the dream of hell.

Rie, when are you going to open your eyes? I was a liar, a wolf, who got mistaken for a sheep. I was afraid that you would hate me upon revealing myself as a wolf. I had deceived you and sought your forgiveness. To you, I confessed these in my heart.

"Rie," I asked, "have you been happy?"

You couldn't have been happy with me deceiving you. You shouldn't.

"You're always helping me," Rie said.

I almost coughed a laugh. Even though I hinted, wishing Rie to see through me, and save herself, freeing us both. Her genius at trusting me, made me sick.

"Ah, this won't work." Before knowing it, I let out the sentence, then felt a strange vagueness like I had heard this before. The green ribbon resting over Rie's wrist now looked like a chain that bound the two of us together. Suppose one of us was to fall out of this charade of friendship. The other would drown too.

Was all relation this way? I wondered, two people bound to one another by some promise, never free, till death do they part.

Either she died, or I did. Either way would result in two deaths, from losing the anchor of life. Rie would never let me go. She had no strength to do so. And I couldn't let go of her, for the same reason.

Only death, now, might set us free.

~ ~ ~

I thought I finally had gone mad upon seeing her, whose appearance resembled Saki, her face and even the voice, all except the clothes and eyes. Then, that Sunday night, after I returned home, she called me.

"Can we meet?" The familiar voice spoke, "come see me first thing tomorrow morning."

I arrived the next day at the location she told me, a high-end café with a fancy door. Once inside, I heard light jazz in the background. All the tables had white sheets, and I spotted her sitting at the last table, next to the window, leaning over a couch in a deep red color, like blood. A waitress had just served her a drink. I saw no other customers and wondered if she booked this entire place.

She raised her eyes from the drink.

"Sayo, is it?" I asked, sitting down opposite her and feeling the chill of the air-conditioner above me.

"Are you sure?" She said.

"Don't you know yourself?" I said, "tell me one thing, and I would believe it."

"Do you want me to pretend to be Saki?"

I swallowed, observing her cream-colored top that matched her long jeans. She wore makeup that made her look like she was wearing a mask, and she reeked of perfume. If I had known Saki well, then I couldn't see her in the person before me.

"Anything to drink?" She asked, "something to eat?"

A waitress came over for my order.

"Nothing for me," I said.

"Try lemon tea," she said. "That's Saki's favorite."

I had never known that.

She turned to the waitress. "A lemon tea, please."

"Nothing for me, thank you!" My voice frightened the waitress. So another waved her away. I braced my thin school uniform as the air conditioning made my hair stand on end. She drank from a straw without a sound. And I took a deep inhale to calm down. "Sayo, it is, then."

"Did you enjoy the movie?" She said, putting down the glass.

"I didn't know you had such poor taste, playing pranks." I responded, "did you slip those tickets to Rie? You weren't stalking her, were you?"

"You didn't enjoy it?"

"Answer the question," I said. "Have you been stalking Rie?"

"Ryoka, so long as you have your head, you could always guess, either I did something or did not. But I have neither the reason nor obligation to answer your questions. So you can think and wonder all you like, and you will never know. Which answers you should have, or not have, I alone will decide."

"What do you want?" I asked.

She leaned back, and her blue eyes looked as if they were studying me. The ice melted inside the glass of brown tea. "It's almost the anniversary of Saki's death," she said. "You didn't happen to forget, did you?"

I swallowed.

"It will be a private gathering," she continued. "Father and all our relatives have been distancing us since the incident. So I have come to stay with Mother, just for a while, to get through this."

"And you've called me here to complain?"

"I just thought of reminding you," her voice turned cold. "But apparently, you have already found a replacement for my sister. Ryoka, what were you thinking, involving someone in your trouble. What's her name, Rie?"

"If only you didn't have Saki's face, I would slap you," I said, "in return for you slapping me that first day."

"Now under what delusion, are you threatening me?" She sat back, "hey, whom you sleep with is none of my business. You can do it with girls, boys, or dogs. I don't care. But acting clueless about what you did to my sister, that gets on my nerves. How long before you end up killing this one, too?"

"Rie has nothing to do with Saki," I said. "And I don't look at her the same way. So you can leave her alone."

"You don't look at Rie the same way as Saki?" She bent closer. "Ryoka, first adjust your attitude a little. I am no villainess here if that's how you see me. I am just a third person who sees the ongoings, like an observer behind a play's curtain. Think, Ryoka, think back to what happened from the first day you met Saki. You found yourself fancying her, that she was the warmth coming to your life. You clung to her like a leech, wanting her to keep taking care of you, understand you. And then, when the situation turned upside down, you got desperate. You walked my sister into the sea."

"What would you know?" I said, crossed my arms against the cold. "You haven't got one or more detectives watching me from every street corner, have you?"

"Maybe, maybe not."

I felt my strength shatter. Sayo had a way of attacking me like a child who caught a firefly, and then, she shook the bottle to observe the flickering light, with amusement.

"And now with Rie," she continued, with eyes fixing at me. "You despise her for burdening you, but you weren't serious about getting rid of her. Why is that? Because to you, Rie had become your new reason to stay alive. You want Rie to understand you, don't you? You want her to sympathize with your past. You want to be the one who plays the tragic heroine, with her as the new purpose of your life. So now you tell me, Ryoka, how is what you're doing anything different from before?"

I had to get out of here, or she would make me go insane. Maybe that was her intention, to turn me into a madwoman.

"You are pathetic, Ryoka," She said. "You have been nothing, and you still are nothing. You have never tried to live with your own strength. You're like someone who's drowning and would grasp on anyone who happened to swim close to you. You killed my sister and are not even going to reflect upon your guilt. And now you are going to kill Rie too."

My eyes felt hard, as if I was going blind. Until the ice clinked inside the glass, then the sound acted as a trigger, and I sensed something that took over from inside, making me laugh.

"What's so funny?" Sayo's voice turned cold.

"Just now, I remember what Saki used to tell me," I said, still laughing, "that her sister is a pathological liar. Now I see. Finally, I see the truth. So this is how it is. There has never been a reason I should be scared of you, because everything that spills out of your mouth are lies. There is no truth in you."

Her dark expression glared across the table, like a blade aimed for my throat.

"Who the hell do you think you are, judging me?" I said, "I am not blameless, but neither are you. It's all your fault that I got hurt. You, and everyone, and God in heaven always trying to rob my happiness, then act like so damn righteous. So I clung to Saki, so what? Can you blame a starving person for stealing bread? I would sell my soul to the Devil, to have an ounce of Saki's love, so what? And if I was to let myself sink so low that I would do wrong against Rie, so what? I saved her. I can do whatever I want with her. If she's stupid enough to trust me, I can even kill her if I want to!"

She swallowed, and a disgusted look came over her face, like she was about to spit blood.

I got up, grasping my school bag.

"Are you going to run away?" She called after me.

I made a sound of laughter that ended up hurting my chest. "I never could run away," I said. "The only thing I knew how to do, was to drown and take someone with me."

"Rie won't fall for you," she spoke as I was about to move away. "Ryoka, your acts aren't that perfect. Any fool would learn in time to look closer."

"Rie might eventually see through me," I said. "Maybe I'll end up killing her before that, as I did Saki. Or, she would learn the truth, lose confidence in living, and croak all on her own. Or, if I should desire, I could talk her into coming with me. Whatever scenario turns out, however, is none of your concern."

I turned my back on her.

"Saki likes Asagao flowers and white chamomiles." Her voice stopped me before taking another step, "bring the flowers tomorrow, and I will place them before Saki's grave."

"Is that another lie?" I turned, feeling my legs tremble.

Sayo drank from the glass, till it was empty, causing sound through the straw. "If you do not believe it, then don't come," she said. "Ryoka, I could always say this again and again, that I am not your enemy. The real villain here is in you, not yourself, but you who have let your desire run out of control. Before it's too late for both you and Rie, Ryoka, one of you must let the other person go."

I squeezed my school bag handle until it hurt. "Another lie." I said, "you are sick, Sayo."

"Sometimes lies are the best tool for telling the truth," said she. "But since you're turning a deaf ear on my warning, maybe I should tell Rie to stay away from you."

My lips twisted, and I could only imagine what my face must look like when I bent over next to her face.

She swallowed, upon my words reaching her ear.

"If you say one word about me to Rie," I said. "I will kill her myself."

I left, feeling like I was walking out of hell and the Devil himself residing within me. I was what God had made me, a human, made inhuman, through his saying no to my worth. The clock above the school building said it was already past ten when I arrived. The second period had long since started. The thought of going to my classroom now gave me no motivation. I found myself paused amidst the empty hallway, knowing not where to go. Rie, I wanted to see her. Being with her offered me no happiness, but neither unhappiness. With Rie, I could endure living in this world until anytime I wished to call it to quits. Then I would take her with me. God would never again take her from me.

My feet stopped at the back door of Rie's classroom. Miss Himura's voice was reciting the textbook inside.

I grasped the door and slid it open as quietly as I could. And I peeked through the small opening. I saw Rie by the window seat, with her face in one hand, gazing out the window. I took out one of the textbooks from my bag, tore out a small piece of paper, wrote a message before folding it into four parts. Then I passed the note to the students sitting in the back. It finally reached her.

Rie turned my way.

I had broken her, the girl I loved. My father eventually realized his mistake for believing me, and he buried himself into work. My mother, too, came to treat me with disdain. And that girl had made her sworn vengeance a reality by devoting her life into becoming my prison. Instead of hurting me directly, she inflicted pain on those who got close to me. She drove them away.

"You faked it," she said. "A faker like you can never love. I will protect everyone from you until your death."

Around November last year, the situation developed for the worse. I returned one day to a room I shared with her to find her scrubbing the floor.

"There was a spot," she said, "and it wouldn't come out. "

Not long after that, I came home one day to find a cat drowned to death inside a bathtub.

"You've done it again," she said. "You fool the whole world into loving you. That cat looked at you when you went out the other day."

It looked as if something inside her was coming loose. I began to wake up at night to find her sitting by my bed, in the dark, looking at me. Her refusing to sleep continued on many nights. She could no longer concentrate on daily activities. So I took her out one day, hoping the air would do her good. And she maintained her usual self for a time, until we came across a church, that she went inside. She knelt before the altar and began to pray the Hail Mary in a loud voice.

People gathered to look.

"HOLY MARY! MOTHER OF GOD! PRAY FOR US—"

I tried to make her leave the spot. And she looked at me with dark eyes.

"Faker," she said, then spat at me. "Faker! FAKER! FAKER!"

My father, who had been keeping distance until then, finally put her in a mental institution. The doctor had given her a tranquilizer when I went to visit her one last time. And in her sleep, her face regained the beauty she once had. With my head bowed, I spoke through my tears—

"Please forgive me," I said. "I was the one who ruined you. I am sorry. I am sorry."

At long last, I set her free. I couldn't rebuild what I had broken. I could only pray. May she find happiness once again, now that I was leaving her.

———◈———

PART 3

# LETTING GO

RIE MITZUSADA

# Swimming Lesson 20

Ryoka's diary stopped there. The last few pages had been torn off. White neon light lit up above me.

"Studying?" Aunt Risa asked at the door.

"Yes," I answered.

"I will keep your meal in the fridge," she said. "Come eat when you're hungry."

She closed the door quietly. The air felt cold, despite the warm season. I got out of my bed to close the window, sensing the salty scent from the sea. The sun was setting outside, and the clock on my desk said six. So Aunt Risa had finally finished preparing lunch. My hands tensed around Ryoka's notebook. I inhaled, then counted to four while exhaling, as Ryoka had taught me. My room felt quiet, like a sanctuary. Then, as I raised my head once more, my eyes faced the cross on the wall.

*"Ryoka is no saint. If you keep relying on her, she will break,"* Sayo had said. *"And you will have only yourself to blame for forcing your ideal onto her, based on your imagination alone."*

What had I done to Ryoka?

The following day, I made a call. Miss Himura agreed to see me on the coming Sunday evening. Both teachers and students had their hands full after the midterm. Miss Himura arranged for me to retake the exam. I had not seen Ryoka throughout this time. She was avoiding me, as I was avoiding her, I believed. Then, on Sunday evening, I arrived at school fifteen minutes earlier than the appointed time. Miss Himura sat at her desk by herself in the teacher's office. She wore her signature suit, and looked to have finished grading—a hot water cup in her hand, reading a Bible. Upon seeing me, she placed a piece of tissue over the page as a bookmark and put the book aside.

I returned Ryoka's notebook with both hands.

After taking the notebook, Miss Himura took a chair from another teacher's desk, gesturing for me to sit down. "Did you read the notebook?" She asked, "to the end?"

"I didn't know her at all."

"Are you angry?" She asked.

Somehow, I wasn't. "No," I answered.

"Why?" Miss Himura'voice expressed no surprise, only curiosity.

"If I shouldn't judge anyone for being loud when they scream in pain. Then, I shouldn't judge Ryoka, who has gone through so much. I always thought my life was a tragedy, but hers has been worse than mine."

"Do you know what strength and weakness you and Ryoka have in common?" Miss Himura said. "Both of you are forgiving toward others, but never to yourself. I met Ryoka's father, and I found it hard not to dislike him. But Ryoka has never hated her father. She directed all the hate toward her own self, making herself carry a burden that no child should bear."

"And I added myself on top of her burden, with her family and her losing Saki." I said, "If only —"

I continued, "if only I didn't act selfishly and take her for granted, I wouldn't have been so blind as not to notice her suffering. If only I could have become strong myself and not had to rely on her. Then, I could have helped her. It's my fault. Should she hate me, then I deserve it all."

Miss Himura's eyes fixed toward me as if determining something.

I felt like a certain weight lifted off my chest, having just confessed my sin for the first time in months. Not to a priest, but a friend I trusted.

"Rie, do you remember the riddle I once told you?" Miss Himura said, "have you found the answer yet?"

"I didn't understand it before," I said. "Until last night, I figured it out. Both the drowning girls already knew how to swim all along. Otherwise, they wouldn't have come so far, as to meet one another."

A slight smile appeared on Miss Himura's lips. "A friend of mine once told me that story," she said, "after she lost someone. She said she had been a burden to another, that she caused both of them to suffer. And so, in the end, she decided to leave the one she loved. So that both herself and the other would live on."

"There is one thing I still don't understand, Miss." I said, "why me and Ryoka? If it was just for us to make friends, it could have been anyone. So, why us to each other?"

An exasperated look appeared on Miss Himura's face. "Because you were my only hope," she said. "I tried everything I could to help Ryoka restore her confidence in living. I kept her busy with school works and part-time jobs to keep her mind away from dying. Still, it did little to help her. I was ready to give up when I saw you wearing Ryoka's ribbon."

So, that's why on that day, she suddenly wanted to walk with me.

"It gave me hope, Rie," she continued. "I thought that finally, Ryoka was starting to rebuild her life by trying to build relations with other people, you. Also, because I have known you, so I had no trouble trusting you—"

I sensed, as she paused, what she was about to say next.

"I had never imagined that you, too, suffered a past almost similar to Ryoka's. She didn't tell me until much later. And by that time, both of you had already become close. To Ryoka, the pride in saving your life served like a bandage that stopped her from bleeding. And you needed Ryoka as your new confidence to restore your faith in living. Suppose I tried anything reckless, such as separating you two. I was afraid to hurt both of you. So, even if it was a lie, I decided it better that you struggled to be each other's reason to live, rather than giving up on each other and walking into the sea."

"We ended up weighing each other down, Miss." My voice hurt me as I continued, "I said before that Ryoka didn't seem fit to help me. But I, too, was not fit to help her. Can't you ask anyone else to help?"

"Who?" Miss Himura said.

"Someone who could."

"And who could help?" She said, "doctors? Do you know that Saki's family was a patron of that hospital Ryoka was staying in? They could have had Ryoka strapped to a bed for life. I talked them out of it. Then, a certain person in Saki's family suggested a mental institution. I talked them out of that, too. Have you ever seen inside a mental institution Rie? There, they treat people like Ryoka by locking her away, at best. And at worst, they use electric shocks treatment. Can you imagine Ryoka lasting in a place like that? Her parents had abandoned her. Her father would sign her away for anything to get rid of her. She's all alone in the world. So you ask me if anyone could help, Rie, who was that supposed to be?"

I swallowed, feeling my dry throat.

"I'm sorry, Rie. I didn't mean to take this out on you."

"You didn't, Miss." I said, "you have done more than anyone could have. And I could have been more helpful, as Ryoka's friend."

"Rie, one could only do as much as one's strength allows."

"I need to ask," I said, "Miss if you had known about my attempt, to do what Ryoka did. Would you still have introduced us to each other?"

Miss Himura had a gentle expression that I had known since my younger days. "I would," she answered, "right after I gave you a good scolding, never to do something like that again. Then, if you were still willing to help, I would let both of you meet."

"You would still trust me to help Ryoka, even after that?"

"Yes, I could see the two of you had enough in common to help one another."

"Because we both tried to kill ourselves?"

"Because you two were trying to understand life," said Miss Himura. "Despite her not finding the answer until now, Ryoka has been searching for that answer. She has struggled to come as far as forgiving her father and even made herself eager to stop you from death. And you, Rie, I have always known you to be stubborn, which often came as a good thing. When you chose death, you chased for it stubbornly. But once you choose life, Rie, I know you would never give up on it. You and Ryoka, in desperation, may drown one another. But I believe that with time and learning, you could become the strength that supports each other. I have faith in both of you."

I went onto my knees, bending over till my head touched the ground with my hands before me. And I prostrated before her. "Is it too late now?" I asked, with tears coming out through both eyes, "to help Ryoka."

"Raise your head, Rie." Miss Himura's voice said.

"Please tell me that it's still not too late."

"Rie, first get up." She said, "there's something I must show you."

I did as told and wiped my tears with the back of my hands. Miss Himura offered me her tissue pack, which I took, and blew my nose. She then opened her desk drawer and took something out.

"I got these last night," Miss Himura said. "It has taken me the whole morning to decide if you should read this."

I recognized in her hand the final sheets from the notebook. Ryoka's handwriting filled the pages in blue ink, blotted with tears.

"I would do something about Ryoka," said Miss Himura. "Rie, you have already helped so much. Ryoka has not done the worst to herself, I believe, because you have stayed alive. However, if you still want to help her more, I would ask only one thing, that you look over Ryoka's poor choice of action. And instead, let what good she has done for you make up for her faults. What you have in your hands, I have read it and must warn you that after you finish it, should you come to hate her, I won't judge you. But if you could, only if you could, please Rie, forgive her."

~ ~ ~

Ryoka wrote the following—

Rie called to tell me that she had confessed everything to her aunt. And then she retold me her story, how she had run away with her lover, the other girl. I listened to the parts that resembled mine. Until, when she confessed—

"Could it be that the dream was just my creation, to leave that girl and justify it as an act of God?"

Something within me snapped.

So, she could have always obtained happiness. Instead, she cast it away.

"What will you do now, Rie?" I asked.

"Ryoka, you were the one who pulled me out from where I fell in. You helped me believe in life again. And now, I have finally reached the point where I can live on with my own strength. I am ready to move on, making my way forward into the world. No longer shall I let the past hold me back. For all your help, Ryoka, thank you, thank you for everything."

Rie's thanks came like acid to my wound.

I had let my guard down, and Rie had come close to slipping out of my fingers. The knowledge that despite both of us losing our love, she alone was forgiven and ready to move on. Her resounding joy upon being set free came like a slap to my face, showing how worthless I was. And I felt, not hatred, but something worse, a confusion that soon sprouts into fear. Rie was going to leave me. She might have left me already. Without her pain toward the past, I had nothing else to hold onto her. The thought of myself returning to the old days, before I met Rie, before I met Saki, caused me such extreme fear that words came off my lips—

"Rie, would you like to hang out?" I kept my tone natural, as one would voice it in absence of ill thoughts, "if you like, you could come to stay over at my place for a night."

She agreed.

After hanging up, I went to my room and picked up a book from my desk. The *Death in Venice*, I had read it many times, as well as Saki's blue pen comments, until I began to understand the tragedy that excruciatingly reflected my own.

*Aschenbach had made Tadzio his saint,* Saki had written, *Now he would die if the saint left him.*

I had made Saki my joy of life, and once God took her from me, the pleasure had turned into pain. Real pain came not when being stabbed or slapped, but to have once loved, and that love became unattainable. Once, I only hated God for taking away Saki. But at some point, I had come to hate Saki, too, for dying and leaving me alone.

Saki, I would never forgive you for not stopping yourself that night when you took me the first time.

Was that your intent, to give me pleasure, then deny me from more? Your love, as great as it had created my happiness, had also been my destruction. Now I thought such vile feelings they called 'love' should be made a crime. Love caused men and women to inflict upon innocents a pleasure that turned free souls into slaves. Had Saki not taught me pleasure, I would never have had to endure its lack. Like God who had said no to me, Saki had sent me to hell.

"*I curse you, Ryoka,*" Sayo's words resounded as loud as being spoken down from heaven, "*to suffer so much that you, too, will curse the day that bitch was born.*"

The curse had become a reality.

I could catch Rie, secure her under my thumb, using the very same trick and trap. And if in her stupidity, should she not find me out by the end of the night, I would have no reason at all to feel the guilt, nor the will to spare her.

Sunday, Rie arrived at my place.

I watched as Rie came in, her in the kitchen, then her in my room, sitting down on my bed. The sickness arose in my stomach, like being forced to watch a fish about to be slaughtered. I must calm down, I told myself, then I excused myself to go outside where the warm evening air soothed me enough that I could swallow down the sour taste. Be it my conscience, or the little good still left in me, that I took more time than necessary to do the shopping, and the sun had already set when I returned. Coming through the front door, I saw no light turned on, except behind the closed bathroom door. The shower sounded inside. I put down two plastic bags on the bed, then turned on the switch. White light flickered twice before the bedroom lit up.

After ten minutes, the shower's steady sound began to give me a cold feeling, so I decided to knock on the bathroom door. "Rie?" I called. "Are you in there?"

The sound of water continued.

"I'm coming in," I said, turning the knob. My face felt the hot steam once I opened the door. I squinted my eyes to see through the white fog. And I saw Rie sitting with her arms around her knees on the shower floor. I bent over to turn the water off. "Rie, what's going on?"

"It's gone," Rie said, in a whisper, then she shivered.

"What's gone?"

"The ribbon you gave me," she said. "I'm sorry, Ryoka."

The sound of water sucked down the drain. "What?" I said. "Don't worry about it, Rie. That thing wasn't really important."

"I'm sorry, Ryoka. I'm sorry." Rie seemed not to hear my last word.

"Rie, it's no big deal," I said, crouching over her. Her shoulders felt cold in my hands. "It's just a piece of ribbon."

She raised her head, then her face twisted like a child who just committed a wrong, and she began to cry.

Meanwhile, I was suppressing myself of a particular emotion, about to burst. I forced myself to stand up. "I will go downstairs to check around the drain," I told Rie after turning my face away. "If we're lucky, it will get stuck around the end of the pipe. Just dry yourself off, Rie. I will be back soon."

I took a torch and left the apartment, rushing to the first floor through the stairs. Once I arrived on the first floor and found a spot behind the building. I burst out laughing.

Why?

Even after she had freed herself from her past, yet, she asked for another shackle? All that crying for one stupid ribbon, like a brat losing her favorite blanket. To think someone like that existed in this world, such a pathetic individual, how hilarious. I laughed, then felt my tears running down. The pain sharpened in my ribs.

I cried, and I cried.

Saki's ribbon was gone. I was relieved, and I was sad. So I laughed, and I cried. The sound of my laughter felt like blades shredding through my soul. My tears held a nostalgic taste, like the cold sea. I must get back before Rie notices something is wrong. But first, I must look for it. After a short walk around the building, I found the waterway and the end of a pipe. I forced the loose stone block out of the way, crouched over, and shone the torchlight down. The streaming brown water gave off a smell that made my stomach worsen. The pipe made a croaking sound then spilled a batch of water.

I looked and waited.

More water plopped out, followed by a gurgling noise, and I saw something hanging under the torchlight. I pulled out a long string-like item with the tips of my fingers, soaked in light brown water, exposing the pale faded green color. The shackle that was once mine, and I had given away, now returned to me.

God in heaven, I sensed him laughing, having sent me this mockery.

I returned to the apartment. Rie stood up from the bed the moment I entered the room. And then tension hardened between my brows. The ribbon, I could return it to her. But then I saw Rie's expression, so innocent like a child expecting a present, the very trait of a clean soul, free from heresy in the world. My hand was frozen, next to my pocket.

Rie's lips opened. I shook my head. Her look of disappointment strangely made me relieved.

No, not yet. My worst could wait.

I turned away and moved toward the bathroom. Once I closed the door, my breath gave out. And I turned on the shower to the fullest before throwing up in the toilet. The pain squeezed around my lungs, and it hurt as if a wound had opened deep in my soul. I took off my clothes, took the ribbon, and got inside the shower. Hot water poured over me, yet I could feel no warmth. So I touched myself, where Saki had touched, my breasts, my navels, legs, and between them while holding the ribbon to my skin. Until my legs squeezed together around my hand, and a hot sensation shot up my head, and my body shook. I had never felt so much pleasure, even when Saki still had flesh and blood. Her ghost could arouse me better. The sense of life, however, soon became like air leaked through a torn balloon. And I felt empty, with despair only for a company.

A warm feeling ran down my legs. I looked down and saw the water turned red.

I left the bathroom after squeezing empty the sunscreen bottle over myself. Rie suspected nothing. We spent time together until the clock said past nine. I suggested we turn in. We would resume our swimming lessons the next day, and things would return to the way they had been. I switched off the light, came to my side of the bed, pulled a blanket over me, and slept on my left side, facing the window.

The tree branch outside swayed, making screeching noises against the window.

I closed my eyes, intending to forget everything, and slept.

But the realization of Rie's sleeping next to me prevented me from falling asleep. So after what felt like an hour or twice longer, I finally shifted and lay on my back. The shadow over the ceiling looking like the claws of a beast out of a nightmare. My face turned toward Rie's side. The shape of her body looked like a peaceful existence, resting under the white nightgown.

"Are you awake?" I asked in a whisper.

The shape remained unstirred. And I almost gave up.

"I couldn't sleep," Rie said.

"Let's stay up and talk," I said. "We haven't talked like this for a long time, have we?"

"What do you want to talk about?"

Words flew through my mouth as if Saki's ghost had possessed me, so that my deception came out naturally. Until Rie mentioned the name Saki, which made me startle. Could she have found out? How? Did a certain someone tell her? Who betrayed me? That bitch, or Miss Himura? Or, did God get into her dream to reveal all to her? I answered her the best I could, choosing my words while adjusting my tone to hide my fear.

"So, what happened?" Rie asked, "to Saki, I mean."

"She died," I answered.

"Ryoka," Rie said, after a while pause, "how could you ever get over something like that?"

I found myself letting out a soft sigh of self-pity. Then I turned away from Rie to lay on my back, resting one arm over my forehead. Rie's question came out innocent but also with an unintended evil. Her cluelessness about what actual suffering could be, made her a fearsome existence, like a pure soul looking down upon sinners, smiling as others suffered.

"Ah," I let out the words, "this won't work."

If she had spoken with better consideration, then, I might find it in me to spare her. But now, all I wanted in the world was to destroy her.

"Ryoka?"

"You still haven't answered my question, Rie," my voice became serious, though my heart was blank. "Say I like you and want to make you happy. What's your answer?"

I had discovered a talent within myself, having lived through disappointments, madness gathered in me. God's tragedy had completed me into a devil with much lies that spilled out of my mouth, getting Rie up in passion through my sweet words. Without shame, I applied myself to deceiving her, for the glory of dragging her good soul down with me, to hell.

Rie didn't love me, not in that way. I knew that.

But anyone with evil intentions could cause fear of being alone upon another person. The fear then made the targeted think that the only offered choice was a genuine emotion of love. Rie had a stupid look when I successfully placed my hand upon her, the uncorrupted body that felt almost holy. Even if it were not me who defiled her, I wouldn't imagine Rie would live long in the future without becoming victim to a rapist. Her genuine trust toward others, such as myself, brought upon herself this sad reality. Rie moaned as I began to inflict upon her with a dreadful passion, the savage way that only the vilest soul could perform. I supposed such a low act suited me best, to destroy the good without much care. My fingers crept up her legs, then went up, up.

Rie pushed me away.

Did she finally realize it? My lies. I lay back over the sheet, arm over my forehead. Fear, I sensed in me, but not regret. Instead, I felt like having been invited to a devil's feast. But then the feast ended abruptly, and the suddenness caused me to regain some sense. Through the corner of my eyes, I saw Rie's back in the dark.

"I'm sorry," Rie said.

"Don't, Rie," I said. "You just saved me."

*"What do you want?"* Miss Himura had asked me.

The feeling of Rie's hands still lingered on my shoulders, causing memories to flood into me. I thought of the first day I met Rie, us at the pool, the campfire, the market. Those were painful memories, but also with happy elements that should have sprouted into a certain feeling. But by the falseness of my passion, I had never let that feeling grow. My heart had been confused with the love I had for Saki, and I had failed to decide my feelings for Rie. Until now.

I wanted to be Rie's friend.

So much suffering had I endured in life, that I had forgotten this genuine wish, a friendship toward another living being. A love that's without overdoing passion, but proportionate energy, free from inflicting pain to the body, yet comforting to the soul.

But was it too late, now?

"We are friends. Let's not ruin that, deal?" I said.

Please, Rie, tell me that we are still friends.

"We are friends," she answered.

Upon her words, my suffering melted away like ice to the sun. And I felt like, for once, after many mistakes and regrets in life, I finally arrived at a new path. A better course, with Rie by my side, accepting me, her existence alone gave me much peace, that I found myself offering a prayer.

God in heaven, I shall admit to all my trespass. If only I could have this only one wish—

Please, I ask you, do not take Rie away.

I pressed the doorbell and waited until I heard footsteps. The door opened, and Ryoka stood before me.

"What do you want?" She said.

"To talk," I said. "Let me in."

"Sorry, I'm tired."

I put my hand between the door before Ryoka closed it. A look of surrender came across her face as she stepped back, and I let myself inside. Her place looked bare, without a single piece of furniture in the living area. And a reeking smell came from the kitchen, like rotten vegetables. Ryoka was retreating toward the bedroom, and I followed her. She sat down on the bed. Her long hair fell, covering her face. She was wearing a shirt too big for her size and short pants loose around her waist. She had grown thin and looked like a moving corpse.

"You didn't go to school for the exam," I said.

"I've called in sick," said she. "Please let me rest, Sayo."

Her last sentence sounded as if she'd accepted defeat. "Do you know why I hate you, Ryoka?" I said, "it's because your existence is the embodiment of everything wrong in the world, the less than human, always relying on someone to feed you. You were like a kitten that no one wanted. You remained in your corner, shivering in the cold, saying with those eyes, please love me, please love me, nobody loves me, nobody loves me. And finally, when someone happened to come along and take pity on you. You bit the hand that fed you and dragged its owner down to hell. How long, Ryoka, do you intend to live this way?"

"Are you having fun?" Ryoka said, cocking her head.

"It's quite boring, like kicking around trash."

"Oh," Ryoka made a sound, followed by a mocking tone of laughter. "I never knew you were so hard to please."

"Aren't you angry to get called trash?"

"What are you expecting? Since you say it, it must be true."

"How about having some dignity?" I said, "if you want to be a human being, then carry your weight instead of involving someone else."

Ryoka's lips trembled, like she was going to cry. But she had no tears. Instead, her eyes hardened with a cold expression, like ice.

"Right now, Rie has found her new life. Her honesty helped her reconcile with her family. Honestly, she gave me a scare when she told me that you invited her to your home. I knew immediately what kind of act someone with your maturity had cooked up. But then, she overturned your scheme. She has succeeded in putting the pieces of her life back together. In time, I could sense that she would discover new happiness, a true one, without you. And yet, what have you been doing with your life? You are a shame to yourself, an oxygen thief, an extra weight to the world. Die, Ryoka, if you won't get out of that bed and say you will live like a human, then die. Die somewhere no one can find you, keep your body hidden so it won't stink, and make sure no one ever discovers your body. Just die, alone—"

Ryoka sprang up, grasping my neck before I could move. She threw me over the bed and sat on top of me, eyes wild.

I saw it coming, only for a split second, before her hand struck down, slapping my face to the left, then right. "How dare you!?" She screamed. "How dare you show up and speak like some damned saint. Look at yourself in the mirror. You are as evil as I am. It's you who dragged me into this hell! You BITCH! BITCH! BITCH!"

She slapped me again, to the left.

Right.

The thought of resisting her crossed my mind, but I let myself suffer. This pain that I had never experienced, such pain as existed in the world.

So, this is feeling.

Ryoka raised her hand once again, but the blow never came. She collapsed over me. Her tears felt cold and numbed my pain. Her weight felt as light as paper, now that she had run out of strength. So I pushed her aside and got up before turning around to take a long look at her. And the image of the porcelain doll lay broken, as clear as if it were happening before me, manifested in Ryoka's form. She was sobbing with the sound of her very soul being shattered.

In the end, I had broken another.

Ryoka struggled to hold herself up from the bed.

"Ryoka," I said, "can't you look into the future? Saki is death, and you have been chasing a ghost. Where would that lead you, but death itself?"

"SHUT UP!" Ryoka screamed, "just shut up, please."

I watched as she let herself lay back over the bed, turning the other way. The pain on my face now burned as if failure had been branded into my very soul. The first time when I had learned about Ryoka's involvement with Rie, I had the hope of her finding happiness. But after I had looked into Rie's past, what I found caused me alarm. So I brought the concern to Miss Himura. And she warned me not to intervene.

But I had not listened.

First, I called Ryoka, attempting to warn her away from repeating another tragedy. Then, I encouraged Rie to confront her past so that Ryoka would not have the leverage to control her. And I had come here today, hoping that losing Rie might encourage Ryoka to do better at living. But at the sight of Ryoka deteriorating, the anger had made me react and take things too far.

Miss Himura had predicted that careless intervention could result in, at best, only one death, rather than two. Rie lived. Ryoka, however, took a turn for the worst.

I could no longer help Ryoka. Maybe I never could help her from the beginning. A girl who knows only how to break things can't possibly know how to fix them. So I turned around, about to walk out, when my eyes caught the pages on the desk with handwriting filled out in blue ink. From a glance over the first and last sentence, I could tell what it was.

There was still one last hope.

# Swimming Lesson 21

After I finished reading Ryoka's last pages, emotions came over me. Ryoka's words told my story in an alternate version, in a perspective that didn't show my best self, but the truth.

Miss Himura made me a cup of hot water that calmed me down.

"Miss, if last year I confided in you about what happened in Tokyo," I said, "what would you have said to me?"

"Do you want me to give you a long overdue scolding?" She said.

"Please, do."

"Rie, there is a type of love that can help someone," said Miss Himura. "And there's another type, where you bind someone to you for your own sake. That latter type will always result in harming either one or both. And from the perspective of a human, with commonsense, love that harms deserves to be told 'no'."

I couldn't, ever since leaving the teacher's office that evening, stop myself from thinking over the possibility. They said God decided fate, though humans designed their own course. If what had happened until now, God had decided, then my meeting with Ryoka should have been without tragedy. Suppose I had confided with Miss Himura, or my aunt, instead of acting stubborn. By the time I met Ryoka, I might have done better at supporting her. If the thing they call alternate worlds existed. Somewhere out there, I might still be Ryoka's friend, hanging out with her, going shopping, eating at a café, and visiting each other's home. If this version of our fate had been God's plan, then I had failed to let it come to be. Instead, now that my ignorance had driven Ryoka to the edge, she had tried to destroy me. I must confront myself with the question. Could I forgive, really forgive her?

If our positions were swapped, I asked myself, wouldn't I resent Ryoka?

I was no saint, just a human. And I knew myself capable of selfishness, as much as her.

Ryoka had put on an act, faking her smile, her words. Did she think I wouldn't want to be her friend unless she did that?

Maybe I wouldn't.

Both of us had been the hope for each other to live. What then would become of Ryoka now? I could see it in my own heart. In the version that Ryoka walked out on me, I would have lost the will to live.

I had condemned Ryoka to death.

Miss Himura had said that she would do something about Ryoka. But I had known her long enough to notice the downhearted look on her face. I watched the sunset from my window. Cold fear gripped me, the feeling as if an invisible force was whispering in my ear, that time was running out. I went downstairs, ate my dinner, then helped Aunt Risa clear the table. She was in an uplifted mood tonight, having just redecorated the living room with a purple curtain. Once I returned to my room, finding myself alone, the silence caused my desperation to deepen as if the air had been squeezed out of me.

Ryoka would soon disappear from the world.

What could I do? I was alive, but what now? What do I do next? Should I wait? Or, should I give up on Ryoka?

Back when Ryoka had followed me to the church, she had tried to make me believe that God didn't exist. I could understand her intention, now that I knew her better. As much I had been her salvation, I had also been her vengeance. She had turned me against my faith as her revenge against God. I took out a Bible from the desk drawer, skimmed through the pages, searching for a sign. And I read the first sentence that my eyes came across—

"One who has unreliable friends soon comes to ruin," my voice came out a whisper.

*Proverbs 18:24.*

I fell over my knees, eyes raised toward the cross above my desk. And for the first time in a year, I prayed. "Please help," I said. "Help me. Help Ryoka, please, please, help me help Ryoka."

The answer came in silence, mixed with the salty scent in the air.

In my way, I had always known the answer. I could, within my power, go after Ryoka, and we could back the way it was before. Or, I could let her die.

Were these my only choices?

The clock on my desk said ten minutes past eight. I put the book away and went downstairs for the phone. I dialed the number and waited for what felt like the longest time in my life.

Her voice answered.

"I want to see you." I said, my breath quickening with relief. "Meet me where you're planning to go. I will be there."

I returned to my room to change into a white one-piece dress and tiptoed downstairs. Aunt Risa was watching television in the living area. I left the house, quietly closing the door behind me, took my bike, and rode off. I had told her to meet me there, though I had not told her when. She might not come tonight. But I knew she would come, eventually, and I intended to wait as many nights as it took to see her again.

But what if she decided to kill herself somewhere else?

Somehow, it felt unlikely.

The scent in the air, I sensed upon arriving at the place. The sea beneath the night, though a year had passed, felt as if I had never left. I took off my shoes, inhaled, and the cold pleasant feeling filled me with emotion. I closed my eyes. Then, when they reopened, I felt as if I'd just come home. The sight of the narrow beach stretched on the horizon, facing the endless black water. Another tide crashed toward the shore, and water burst into white foam. The sand still had the warmth of daylight beneath my feet. And there were stars in the sky. Once, for a short period, I had doubted if God truly existed. But now I knew the answer. If a place to die could be this beautiful, of course, there was God in this world.

I heard footsteps and turned around. Ryoka stood before me, wearing a long skirt falling to her ankles.

"Yaa, Ryoka," I said the first thing that came to mind.

Ryoka was not wearing her sunscreen tonight for some reason.

"I am sorry for not talking to you until now," I said.

"You read my notebook, right?" She said, "I asked Miss Himura to pass it on to you. So you might come to your senses, and set me free. Have you come to hate me finally?"

"No," I answered immediately.

A surprised expression spread across her face. "Are you going to—" she scoffed a laugh, "forgive and forget, then?"

"Should I not?" I responded, then breathed in. "Because I, too, have been doing the same thing. You've tried to use me to keep your confidence in living afloat, and I, too, was using you. Now that I finally understand, please, Ryoka, let me make it up to you. I want us to be friends again."

Ryoka blinked when I finished. And her lips curled up into a smile. "I have always known you to be strong, Rie." She said, "so you are going to forgive me, even after you finally know the truth. And you even say that we should try to be friends again."

I looked as she approached me and held me by the face in both hands.

"Here's the problem, Rie," she said, "I don't want to be your friend."

I swallowed.

"We never were friends, Rie," Ryoka continued, her eyes dilated like a beast. "Always, always, I hated your guts. You left someone for your own damned selfish reasons and acted like some tragic heroine, begging to be saved. Every time I had to spend with you at that damned pool, I felt like I was swallowing something rotten. After, I went into the bathroom to throw up. And now, I'm tired, Rie. Please spare me your sentiment, like asking us to be friends again, because I don't want to. I hate you, Rie, I hate you!"

"I'm sorry, Ryoka. " I said, swallowing my tears. "It's my fault for never noticing how you felt."

"It's too late, Rie." Ryoka let my face go, with a bit of a smile and a mocking expression. "Finally, I am free from you to go where I should always have gone."

"So you are going to die, for what?" I kept my voice steady after wiping a tear away. "Going to see Saki?"

Ryoka turned toward the sea. "No," she said. "once, I might have thought that way. But recently, I realized that I just wanted to disappear. Even if I had never met Saki, I would have come to this wish eventually."

"Why?"

"Rie, even now, you still don't understand." She said, after a sigh.

"Help me understand, then."

Ryoka's face turned my way again, a smile of pity on her lips. "Someone like you will never understand. Rie," she said, "because you always had someone to care for you, a family, the comfort you could always fall back on. I have never had that, not once in my whole life. Do you want to understand why I want to die? Rie, if you had lived your life till adolescence kicked in and still couldn't make peace with your life, then you would know that no matter how much you try, you'll always be nothing but trash. So all I wanted was a merciful way out of this damned life. So please, Rie, don't make it hard for me. You have my thanks, though, for calling me here. I had no strength to get up until you gave me a call. And now, I am finally here where it all started. I will end it, at last, tonight."

The sea roared, another tide crashed against the shore. My feet deepened into the sand.

"Do me a favor, Rie," she continued. "Don't look, walk away, I won't get mad. If you stay and see it, somehow, I would leave you with a bad impression. Even though it was a fluke that I saved your life, I suppose success is a success. With your life, I finally paid my debt to Miss Himura. Live on, Rie, and never do anything to become like me. Now, let us say goodbye. Or no, let's not. Just turn around, Rie, and keep walking. And tomorrow, don't read a newspaper or watch the news, for two weeks or so. Then, you will forget about me. Rie. I wish you all the luck in the world."

"Ryoka, could you shut up for a moment?"

She blinked. "Rie, if you still think you can talk me out of death, forget it." She said, scratching her head. "Seriously, dying shouldn't be this hard, right?"

"I have been thinking a lot, you know, about what you wrote, that God always says no to you."

"Please, spare me the religious talk." Ryoka raised on hand.

"I won't accept it." My voice raised. "I am a believer, but I will never accept it!"

"You are a believer but won't accept the decision of your God? Are you going to be alright, living with this contradiction?"

"I don't always understand why something should or should not be. Why God agrees or says no. There is no way I could perceive something like fate or heaven's will. After all, I am just a common human being. All I can do is pray, to express my wish, that I want you to live Ryoka. I want you to live stubbornly, despite all the disappointments and sufferings. I want you to live!"

The sound like thunder came from far away. Water reached our feet, then retreated.

"And if," I continued, "if, after I pray this, God still refuses to let you live. Then I will go and complain to him myself, in the afterlife. Ryoka, since you insist on going to walk into the sea. Then, I can't let you go alone."

"What are you talking about, Rie?"

"Ryoka, I—" My mouth opened, "I want to quit the Swimming Association."

She looked at me with her eyes wide. Then she burst into laughter. "Rie, really," she said, continuing to laugh. "And here I was wondering, what nice words you would try to pull. But to ask this just now, you sure are funny."

"Ryoka, I want to leave the Swimming Association."

"Go then," said Ryoka. "You could have done that anytime. It sure took you long enough to get it. Alright, fine, I accept your resignation. The Association has disbanded tonight."

"That's not what we promised," I said. "I must beat you first."

"There's no need to take that seriously," Ryoka said, shrugging.

"I am challenging you to a race, Ryoka." I said, "a long-distance race into the open water. Whoever lasts the longest, wins."

"No, thanks."

"Ryoka!"

"Rie, explain why I should do this or forget it."

"No matter how far you go, I will catch up to you," I said. "You can swim after Saki's ghost or after death itself. But I will be right behind you. Then, when you reach your limit and are about to drown, I will save you. I will save you as many times as it takes."

Ryoka's lips moved as if trying to smile.

"Ryoka, I believe there is always a reason for a person to meet another." I said, "even the briefest time they spend together has meaning. I can't speak about you and Saki. But you and me, us meeting each other, I don't believe it happened without good reason. Ryoka, you saved me. But you can't just save me and then run off to your death. I would hate you for real, then. From now on, I will fulfill this role that I perceive as God's will, to swim after you and to save you. If God lets both of us survive, then so be it. But if I am to die with you, then let this also be. This is my decision."

~ ~ ~

Ryoka had finished her preparation. I folded my clothes and placed them together where the water couldn't reach. She was doing a warm-up routine, and I, too, stretched my arms backward before standing up straight and pulling each leg back as far as I could. I had neither goggles nor cap with me since I figured she wouldn't bring one.

"This is your last chance to walk away," she said.

I looked toward Ryoka, who stood six feet to my side.

"Between you and me," she continued. "No one would be sad with me gone. But you, you have your family, friends, and future. Aren't you selfish to toss them aside like this?"

"I owe you, Ryoka," I said, finishing the warm-up. "After you saved me, I always felt undeserving of this new life."

Ryoka's gaze turned from the sea toward me.

"Tonight," I said. "I will earn the life you have given me, by saving you."

"I had lived my life, long dead before I met Saki." She said, "how arrogant of you to say that you're going to save me. Rie, you can only save the drowning, not the dead."

She sprinted off.

I chased after her. Ryoka sprang forward and into the water while I stumbled upon a bad start, with my feet in the sand. Once in the water, I moved my arms and put strength to my legs, kicking to catch up. But the moment I came closer to her, Ryoka's speed increased, and she left me behind.

Even at sea, Ryoka remained a strong swimmer.

No, she had become stronger than I remembered. Her determination to go away had added a difference to our skill. I breathed to the side while pulling through the water. Another wave came crashing down, and its force threw me backward. The sea sounded like a legion of demons. I raised my face and saw a tide forming in a large black wall rushing toward me. Its impact threw me back and down into the black world. I swallowed a gulp and felt like I was going to throw up. My adrenaline turned on at full flow, erasing my fear. I moved once again, with my arms and legs, and resurfaced.

Ryoka had disappeared.

I dove, squinting my eyes to see under the water. And I pulled the water to my side, forcing my way down further through the darkness until I could no longer tell which direction was above and which below. The water resistance squeezed in, forcing me to resurface again. And I finally saw Ryoka a distance ahead. She was still swimming against the current, toward the dark horizon. I breathed, and felt my stamina replenish before continuing to swim in her direction. Miss Himura had said once that in long-distance, I had an advantage over Ryoka. No matter how large the gap, so long as I didn't give up, I would win this race in the end.

Once Ryoka's strength ran out, and she could swim no longer. I would return to the shore with her.

A sudden pain gripped my legs, and I opened my mouth. The water pulled me downward. In a panic, I swallowed water. The cramping took over my leg, and my body became paralyzed with fear.

Why? Why now?

My arms struggled, feeling like I was fighting against the darkness. I was drowning. The warmth within my body was disappearing in the cold water that tasted like tears.

# SWIMMING LESSON 22

D own, down, I continued to drown—the torturous sensation increasing each second. My body ready to give way. But as I came face to face with death, something within my consciousness woke up, and my body moved for the last struggle. I couldn't die. I couldn't die.

I wanted to live.

Forty seconds, I had, maybe less, according to what Ryoka once told me. I'd done the research myself and learned that most deaths by water were caused by panic. The moment one felt death closing in, they opened their mouths. Water flooded their lungs, leading to shock and loss of consciousness. So I resisted the urge to open my mouth, despite my lungs feeling like they were going to pop. I reached for my foot, grasped my toes, and pulled until the cramping pain eased. The water continued to press at me, like an invisible hand squeezing me in its palm. I gave a kick and felt my body resurfacing, slowly as if being lifted. My head, my chest, was at their limit.

A cold sensation blew over my face. I inhaled a lungful of air.

An incoming tide threw me back into the water. But I resurfaced again. I evaded the next one by diving down and swimming under the water. Then, once my face was above the water again, I looked left and right. But Ryoka was nowhere to be found.

"Ryoka!" I cried. My voice disappeared amidst the roaring sea. "Ryoka! Ryoka!"

Another wave came. I ducked under it before resurfacing.

"Ryoka! Answer me! RYOKA!"

The sea shook as if the world was trembling. I continued swimming toward where the tide formed its giant waves. I dodged some, while others threw back. But I continued looking, searching, for Ryoka.

Finally, I saw her.

"Ryoka, Ryoka!" I swam toward her. Ryoka was still swimming forward. She might have heard my voice and tried to swim away. But she no longer had as much speed as before.

I reached her just as a black wall of water came upon us. It pulled us both underneath the surface. Ryoka slipped away from my hand. My eyes squinted until I saw Ryoka being dragged downward. I followed her, pulling water to my sides. She no longer resisted when I reached her from behind, inserting my arm under her shoulders. I kicked against the water, resurfacing with her secured in my grip.

Ryoka made a sharp noise, gasping for air.

"Can you swim back? Ryoka, let's go back."

For a moment, time felt as if it had stopped. The sea turned calm, and the water became still. Ryoka's face moved, and a glimpse of light showed in her eyes. I knew then that she had heard me. So I let her go, and she swam away from me, toward the direction of the shore. Then time moved again. The sea expelled its final cry.

I left behind the black horizon.

Once my feet could feel the bottom, I walked through the water toward the beach. Its long narrow stretch of land gave me warm emotions of gladness. Never in my life had I felt so alive as in this moment. The sea sounded like it was moaning from a distance. My legs felt like two sticks. I collapsed on my knees. So I lay over the compact wet sand, feeling its softness against my back. My heart pounded. I was alive. A coughing sound made my face turn, Ryoka, too, collapsed at my side. The water reached my lower legs, then retreated. A few stars could be seen in the sky.

"I saw the light," Ryoka's voice said. "It was brighter than the sun. And in that light, someone was coming toward me. She was calling my name, with a voice like yours."

I listened.

"I was scared, Rie." Ryoka continued, "to live, to be around people. I always felt this part of me would keep me insignificant from the rest, preventing me from truly belonging to the world. I don't know how to be anyone's friend. Because no one ever showed me how. I am sorry, Rie. I am sorry."

"You and I have done bad things, Ryoka." I said, "not because we liked the people we liked. But because we bound them to ourselves, and used them as a reason to give up on living."

Ryoka turned my way.

"You know, Ryoka, I haven't come to regret getting off that train. Because if I insisted on going with that girl, in the end, we might have ended up doing the same thing as you and Saki. When I heard that she was doing well, alive. I found myself wishing with all my heart that she would continue to live on, finding someone else better than me that she could fall in love with. And you, Ryoka, though I still don't know why God allowed many disappointments to fall upon your life. I believe there's a good intention in God to let you meet Saki. Had Saki not taught you to swim, you wouldn't have survived tonight. And had you died with Saki back then, you wouldn't have lived to save my life. So I think, Ryoka, when God says no to us, it's for a reason. All the suffering that I received upon God's saying no to my wish has led me to this conclusion, where you and I are still alive. And I could only feel thankful. So Ryoka, let both of us live from now on, without ever again giving up, till the end."

Ryoka's hand squeezed against mine. The soft squeeze felt like the warmest thing in the world. "Why?" said she, her eyes turned toward the sky. "Why is it that back then, no one told me any of the words you're saying? If I would have known, maybe—"

I knew. It took us so long to learn.

"Strange for me to say this," Ryoka said once her voice turned calm. "I'm starting to like your God a little, having met you."

"I could have said the same."

"Do you think," Ryoka paused, "if I died today? Would I go to heaven?"

"You saved my life, Ryoka. Isn't that enough of an answer?"

"And you, too, saved mine. I see, so that's it. We both have reserved our place in heaven."

A silence fell before we burst out laughing. I turned toward Ryoka and saw a slight smile there, a genuine smile. Our swimming lessons had come a long way. We had suffered and learned, feeling pain and joy. We hurt another, and we got hurt. I thought back and realized that our lessons had been a long time of suffering, for the sake of this one moment full of hope.

We would be fine now. I knew we would.

~ ~ ~

Miss Himura gave me a long scolding once she knew what I had done. Then, she thanked me while holding back the tear. Soon after that, she informed me that the Swimming Association had been abolished at Ryoka's own request.

I let myself feel grief over the fact that I would never have another swimming lesson. Now that I no longer need one.

Ryoka and I still saw one another when we ran into each other in the school hallway. But we no longer met. In a way, I understood her intention. So long as we could still see each other alive from a distance, that alone was enough. So we gave one another the space to not be each other's burden. Miss Himura began to visit my home at Aunt Risa's invitation for late dinner. And she let me know when I asked about Ryoka. She had been doing well. And so I, too, had thrown myself into my studies.

From time to time, when I felt lonely, I let Miss Himura know. And she assigned me a list of books to read. I ended buying for myself Thomas Mann's *Death in Venice* and read it many times over.

"When you let yourself fall into passion, and you couldn't tell apart true happiness from suffering." Miss Himura often warned me, "that's the loneliest thing."

Another year passed.

A week before my last day of high school, I checked out Shikibu Murasaki's *The Tale of Genji*, which I had not read since returning from Tokyo. In the appendix, I read a particular poem written by the author and found myself rereading it till I memorized the lines.

Graduation arrived, finally.

I sat with the others from my class in the ceremony hall. I passed the three and a half hours resisting the urge to turn around, hoping I might see Ryoka sitting somewhere close. Her class, after all, was right behind me. When we were led back to the classroom, our homeroom teacher presented each of us with the certificate, followed by a farewell speech. Then the class was finally declared dismissed.

My hands squeezed around the tube containing my diploma. My high school career was over.

Almost.

Aunt Risa had already left after the ceremony. She said she would go to the local shrine to light incense and tell my parents the news. We planned to meet later at home this evening. She had intended to make dinner, but I talked her into going to a restaurant instead. Most of my classmates still hung around their desks, saying their farewells. Some would take graduation trips. Some would go to the same university. Some had chosen to work, and one even had a prospect of marriage. I said farewell and took photos with my friends before leaving my classroom.

I, too, had my own future before me. And so, I could only move forward.

Miss Himura was at her table, taking photos with two of my classmates. And there was a queue that extended outside the teacher's office. Starting this year, she had passed the entrance exam and become a full-time teacher. Despite having been here only a few years, Miss Himura had earned considerable popularity among the students. The last group of students finally left the office. I approached Miss Himura and presented her with my notebook. She accepted it and placed it on top of Ryoka's.

"Thank you, Miss, for never giving up on me."

"Rie, you were always a person whose gift is to inspire others," she said. "You inspired me into becoming a teacher. And I will always be grateful, to you, for allowing me to be yours."

My head lowered to hide my blush.

"Today is my last day to act as your teacher. So let me say this one last thing, Rie, never forget what has happened. Let your past continue to teach you its lessons as you continue toward the future. In life, there will be a time when you find yourself facing a predicament. You may lose heart, you may feel fear, or want to run away. But always remember that you have come so far already. Remember what you have accomplished as you make your way in the world."

I bowed. No words could be enough to express my thanks to my teacher and old friend.

More students arrived, asking if Miss Himura was still here. I took the opportunity to excuse myself and made my way to the door.

"Rie," Miss Himura called after me. "Congratulations on your graduation."

# Swimming Lesson 23

I rushed toward Ryoka's classroom. A group of three who could be her classmates still hung around. I approached and asked if they'd seen her. They looked at each other. One said she didn't know. Another said she had seen Ryoka when they were returning from the ceremony. Then the last girl made a sound, like having just remembered something, and said she'd seen Ryoka leave immediately after the class was dismissed.

Neither answer gave me a clue.

I arrived at the pool but found its gate locked, as usual. The twenty-five-meter pool looked small, without Ryoka here. Where could she be? I tried to figure out the possibilities.

Did she have a part-time job? Or did she go home?

I was making my way toward the school gate when I saw a tall figure with long brown hair, like gold under the late afternoon light. Her blue eyes noticed me, and she stopped. My feet paused, too, some distance away from her.

"You're not looking for Ryoka, are you?" Sayo said.

My silence gave away the answer.

"I could tell you where she is," she said. "I have still been watching, you know, the two of you."

"Please, Sayo, I have to see her."

"Why now?" She asked, "first, tell me, Rie, what you intend to do with Ryoka?"

I saw no reason to hide from her. So I told her.

Sayo's cold face softened, like a mask of ice melting away, and revealed a gentle expression I had never seen before. "You finally get it," she said. "Letting you read Ryoka's last pages turned out to be my winning gamble."

"Were you testing me back then?" I asked, "if I would forgive Ryoka or not?"

"If you could forgive her. I knew you would do anything to help her, something that I couldn't."

"Sayo, I have always wanted to ask you this," I said. "Why do you care so much for Ryoka? Was it because you felt a responsibility to save her after losing Saki?"

Sayo closed her eyes for a moment before she looked at me again. "You are an intelligent girl, Rie," said she. "So I will let you think about it. Keep thinking, Rie, and you might be able to figure it out in ten years."

I looked at her face in the light. Yet, I felt like staring into a shadow that prevented me from seeing through. Somehow, I sensed that if I was to think about this rationally, my pursuit of the truth would always lead me to a dead-end. If, however, I reexamined what I had learned and replaced one factor with another possibility. Then, all pieces of this mystery would fall into place.

Sayo walked closer, about to pass me by.

"A chance encounter," I spoke—

"Seeing a vanished friend

"Or was it?

"The clouded-covered

"Midnight Moon."

Sayo stopped next to me. "What was that?"

"It's a poem about two friends," I said. "Shikibu Murasaki, the composer of this poem, had a childhood friend. And the two of them promised to always be together. But when they grew up, her friend got married and lost the old passion in youth. Then, one day, years later, she ran into her friend in the street and called out to her. But her friend, probably in shame, would not answer her call."

I looked through the corner of my eyes at Sayo's face, hoping to see some gesture or expression, that might confirm my suspicions.

I saw her lips part.

She placed her hand over my shoulder. "Ryoka is at the beach. You better hurry before it's too late."

My tongue felt dry upon hearing the words.

"Rie," she said. "Thank you."

I took a bus home, then left with my bike, without going inside. Another had told me that it might be too late. Fear ran through me, and the warm breeze of the evening felt cold over my face. I finally arrived at the sea and left my bike at the parking area before rushing toward the fence, where I could look down over the narrow beach. There, at the very spot where Ryoka and I once made a campfire, she was sitting, looking in the direction where the sea met the sky.

Sand got into my shoes, walking down the slope. So I took them off, and my socks, too.

Ryoka turned around, saw me, and smiled the same smile I had missed so much since that night.

"Do you mind if I stay here, too?"

"Please," said she. "Call it a sixth sense. I had a feeling that by some chance, I would get to see you today."

I tugged my pleat skirt in before sitting down on the sand. Ryoka was gazing toward the horizon where the water looked peacefully still, as if uninterrupted by the continuous waves and tides. The sight of the sun setting from the sky, turning the water gold, made my chest filled with warmth. I leaned my head over her shoulder. And Ryoka let me.

"I just couldn't bring myself to leave here," she said. "To me, this is the place where all the parts of my life connect, the bad and the good."

I said, after a moment. "Ryoka, I still owe you an apology."

"What for?"

"For throwing away the ribbon."

"Oh, so that's what became of it," she said. "So you finally threw it away, the one action I didn't dare to do myself."

I raised my face toward her. Ryoka's face looked thoughtful as she watched the tide retreating from the shore.

"Do you still feel sad when looking at the sea, Rie?"

"They say that the world never changes, only our perceptions." I said, "and I like to think that mine has changed for the better. You know, Ryoka, when my mother met with my father, she was already pregnant with me. I overheard Aunt Risa talking to my mother when I was eight. My mother was raped and found herself carrying me. Despite knowing this, Father married her, cherished her, and loved me as his own. He saved her life and mine. Without him, I think, I might never get to be born."

"You've never told me much about yourself, Rie. So why now?"

"I know more about you, since reading your diary. So it's only fair that you should know, too, about the past I have been too ashamed to let anyone know. The reason my mother always said the sea made her feel sad, I never truly understood it, until I tried to walk into it myself."

Ryoka's eyes were stormy, like stirred water.

"You ask if I still feel sad at the sight of the sea." I continued, "maybe a little. But at the same time, I feel courage when I remember that you and I have survived the worst. And we're still alive."

"Are you saying that we all can redesign our past by replacing the worst parts with the better?"

"Maybe." I said, "I think it's important to move on. But since you can't change what happened, the memory would always serve as our trauma. And it always comes back to haunt us. So it became necessary for you to face your own past. We have to somehow, eventually, bring ourselves to look back at our own passion. Only then can we truly know if we are ready to move on. If we can finally make peace with our old trauma, then, only then, we can finally replace what once hurt us, with what would make us strong."

Her face turned my way. "Rie, did something happen to you?"

"Lately, since last month, I have been having this dream," I said, "of riding on a train alone. I arrived at the destination, in a remote countryside with a narrow road. And I knew that if I followed it, I would arrive where that girl lives."

Ryoka's face leaned over my shoulder. "You want to see her, don't you?" She said, "that girl, you never told me her name."

"Hisae," I said. "Hisae Sasada, that was her name."

"She sounds like someone who would steal a heart."

"Do you think, Ryoka, should I go and see her?"

"Are you asking me for advice?" Her voice came out soft, though with intense feeling.

"Sorry, should I not?" I said.

"Let me ask you this, then, Rie." Ryoka said, "if Saki was alive. Do you think I would go and see her?"

I looked at Ryoka, who raised her face.

Her gaze met mine, determined for an answer.

"I would go to see her," I finally answered, "when I turned forty, with some white hair to prove my maturity. If I was to meet my old love now, I think we would end up staring at each other, like seeing a ghost, and have nothing to say. If I were to see her again, it would be so that we could reflect on our past, what had led us to where we ended up. Only when

I had that resolve, then I would go to see her, even if it was only to say goodbye."

"Rie," Ryoka said, "I think you are ready to go and see her now. And why shouldn't you? After what happened to us, I feel like all my hair has turned white."

We laughed. Then, we stopped.

The pain within my chest felt only slight. And I saw, too, that Ryoka felt the same pain. The pain in longing for the ones we loved.

"You're not the only one thinking about that, Rie," Ryoka continued. "Since that night, last year, when we gave each other hope. It feels like ten years have passed, since then. Often, I feel like walking into a dark wall that's a dead-end. And after long pondering, I always come to the same conclusion, that there is a thing still left to do. I must somehow bring myself to face my own past, for closure, or maybe a reconciliation. Anyway, that would serve best for me to finally free myself from an old ghost, to move on, to live."

"We are hopeless, aren't we?" I said, feeling warmth in my eyes.

"It's hard to forget the love we felt."

"Ryoka, I once asked you how you could get over Saki. I didn't realize until much later. How inconsiderate I was. After all, you—"

"I could never." Ryoka's tears came out, the same time as mine.

"Even though it hurts. We love them, don't we?"

We cried together. Ryoka held me as I held her in my arms. Both of us had lost someone we loved. But together, we managed to save each other.

"Let me tell you a story, Rie," Ryoka said after drying her tears. "Imagine a girl was drowning in the sea. She saw another person swimming her way—"

I wiped my tears while listening to the riddle till the end.

"Both of the girls already knew how to swim on their own." We answered simultaneously as we let go of each other.

"You cheat, Miss Himura told you that story, too?" Ryoka asked.

"It took me a while to figure out the answer."

"Rie," Ryoka's face expressed a peaceful smile when she spoke. "You no longer need me as your reason to live."

"And you no longer need me, Ryoka."

At long last, we were free, though not from our past, yet. At least we were now free from each other. However, the joy of freedom came at a price. I felt a wave of emotion surge up, and more tears came out. So I let myself cry some more, seeing that Ryoka, too, shed her tears. But once we finally finished crying, we gave each other a brave smile. Ryoka's smile as she was now, I thought, suited her best. So long as she could smile like that, she would be fine. And I, too, would be fine. We must. It's time we lived with our own strength.

The day would soon end. In the distance, the sun looked as if in flames, hanging just above the horizon.

"Rie, can we stay just a bit longer?"

I nodded, wiping the rest of my tears with the back of my hand. "Sure."

"So, now that we've graduated." Ryoka said, "what's your plan? Are you going to become a nun?"

"I will," I said, stretching my bare feet over the sand. "Aunt Risa insists, though, that I should earn a degree or useful working skill first. So I'm going to medical school."

"Sister Rie and Doctor Rie." Ryoka muttered, "nobody will die now."

"What about you, Ryoka? What are you going to do?"

"I'm going to university," Ryoka said, gathering dried sand in one hand and squeezing it. A pinkish blush showed over her face. "Miss Himura helped me get a scholarship. I will study to become a marine biologist."

"You've got a scholarship?" I said, "congratulations. I knew you were special, in your way."

"So are you, Rie."

The sun disappeared from the sky, but the warmth remained. Then the night came upon us. Stars appeared in the sky. Still, we lingered. I didn't want to leave this place. If possible, I would've liked time to stop. But I knew, as Ryoka too knew, that such a selfish wish would never be granted. Even though we might dislike it, even cry about it, the end was here.

"We should go," Ryoka said finally.

"Do we have to?"

Ryoka got up. And I, too, stood next to her. "I will leave first. Maybe that will make it easier," she said.

"Let's leave at the same time," I said, then felt a pain in my chest.

"Say, Rie," she said. "May be we don't have to end it this way?"

The prospect of us remaining as we were, tempted me.

"We have to, Ryoka," I answered finally. "Or in time, we would again burden each other."

Ryoka nodded, her brows knotted for a second. "Rie," her voice shivered, though clear. "In my life, often I blamed God for my misfortune. Then when little good things came my way, knowing not what to do with them, I mistreated those gifts. You are the most precious gift God ever gave me, that helped me learn better to live with more content. To know that you exist in this world, somewhere, I feel like I could finally make peace with myself, that my life, after all, isn't just a tragedy, but a story with love in it. I tell myself that this is enough. Yet, it's still hard for me to say goodbye to you, right in this place where we met."

"Ryoka, I take no joy in this either, that we have to say goodbye now. It's necessary. But it's still sad."

"Please, Rie," Ryoka's shoulders tensed, then she joined her hands together as if in prayer. "I know I have wronged you many times, that I don't deserve to ask you this. But if you could spare just a little bit of yourself that I can take away, as a memento, please Rie tell me at least. Are we friends?"

The pain in my chest shattered away. "Ryoka," I said, with joy filling my heart. "Of course, we are friends."

So long as we live, even though apart, you will always be my friend.

We stepped toward each other and passed by one another. I felt Ryoka's grip holding onto my hand, tightly, not letting me go. Our hands were still linked, our backs facing each other. Was this the only way? In my weakness, I wondered. But I knew that we could not waver. We couldn't return to the way we had been. All we could do now was to move on.

Our hands came apart—

"Goodbye."

I unlocked the pool gate, wanting to see it one more time, the place where everything started. The blue turquoise surface was still, without a ripple, reflecting the dull light of the late afternoon sun. One year more, ten years and this place would become like the faintest memory. The story that had happened here started and ended like a dream. And those who dream wake up in the end before all is forgotten.

No one would know what had come to pass here.

I stayed until the sun began to set. Then, I left and locked the gate, never to look back. Only a few students still hung around the courtyard when I arrived at the school buildings. Teachers had already left, from the look of it, all except her. I heard her voice from inside the office, talking to someone.

I knocked on the door before sliding it open. Miss Himura raised her eyes.

"I see, so that's what you have decided." Miss Himura spoke on the phone. "Call me once you get back, alright. Have a safe trip, Rie."

I found a seat and sat down opposite the desk.

Miss Himura finished her phone call and raised her eyes toward me. "Good evening, Saki." She said, "have you brought back what you borrowed?"

I handed her the pool key. "I had to see it one last time," I said before taking out a notebook from my handbag. Miss Himura accepted it and put mine on top of two others. She stood up and went to switch on the light. After they flickered to life, the office turned bright. Miss Himura asked me if I need a drink while pouring herself a cup of hot water. I declined the offer. The sight of the sky turning into night. My eyes paused over her desk, and the Bible that lay there.

"So, are you going back to the States soon?" She asked while getting herself a clean cup for a drink.

"I have been doing mail courses since last year. Then, I took a few months of absence. They will expel me if I don't return soon for the next semester.

Miss Himura poured the steamed hot water.

"Were you talking to Rie just now?" I asked.

"She said she's going to go travel." She said when returning to her seat, "her mind's made up, to go see that girl again."

"And you don't disapprove?" I said, "that it might undo everything she has accomplished."

"You don't think Rie's ready to face her past?"

"I used to know this girl in elementary, Miss, who got bullied. She grew up to be a strong and confident woman. And I met her not long ago at a class reunion. She came face to face with the girls who used to bully her. And her confidence was shattered, like a rabbit meeting a pack of wolves. Miss, things like confronting your past, I think, though necessary, it might threaten everything you have built."

Miss Himura placed down the cup. "You have read the Bible, right, Saki?" She said, "there is this wise man who said one thing I like, a narrow road often enough is the right path. Rie has lived through her choices between life and death. Now it's time to test if she has finally put the past behind her."

"I see," I admitted. "There is no other road but the hard road. Rie has to meet with that girl, even if it means to apologize and to say goodbye. Or else, the past will continue to haunt her, like an old wound."

Miss Himura sipped her water.

"Mom said you keep in contact with Sayo. How is she?" I decided to ask. "I heard her and Father talking to each other, that last year Sayo tried to break out of the institution, to come after me. Then she called to threaten you."

"I have made schedule to talk to her on the phone. She's become calmer, according to the doctor." Miss Himura said. "Saki, are you not going to see her again?"

"Miss, I have committed upon Sayo a crime," I spoke the last word, with my head hung low. "Her boyfriend, I drove him to death. Sayo herself went mad. And do you know what irony is? She couldn't even hate me for it, not really. Since we were little, she had known me to be a monster and still accepted me for who I was. And I made myself her burden, trying to keep her to myself, which led to tragedy. Ever since then, Sayo made herself my prison. She took out her hate on others around me, driving them away to protect them from me. Seeing my sister deteriorating, I found myself, for the first time, able to feel. It's like I had been sleep walking and swinging a knife. Then I woke up one day, and bodies already lay dead before me. And it hit me, oh, so this is feeling. But it was already too late. What have I done? I said, what have I done?"

Miss Himura listened until I finished. "You are a rare person, Saki," she said. "They say everybody is sinners. And to me, everyone is capable of hurting someone. Children bully each other, betray one another, and they grow up to be adults who do the same. But very few of them, such as yourself, come to recognize their own faults. It takes all the courage in the world to correct oneself, Saki."

"Please, Miss, I don't deserve the praise. After I have come so close to killing Ryoka, too."

"You saved Ryoka from drowning that night," said she.

I remembered it as if it happened yesterday. I had dragged Ryoka, who had gone unconscious, out of the water, and I had run for the nearest phone booth to call an ambulance. I returned home, and Sayo was furious with me. And my parents called Miss Himura in. Newspapers laid siege over our house. My family kept me hidden, so the press made a mistake, thinking that Ryoka alone survived and I died. They reprinted the correct version later. But Miss Himura had never let Ryoka know the truth, because I had asked her not to.

If Ryoka thought I was dead, she would be free from the obligation to look after me, and live.

So I had thought, back then.

"I love her, Miss," I said, with my face in both hands. "Ryoka, I love her. I thought that I could finally be like Prince Calaf, going to save Princess Turandot. But in the end, I could only be the cold Princess. My love came close to killing her, and then it almost broke her, like Sayo. When I first met Ryoka, my impression was that she was a lifeless shell, with suffering stuffed inside her. So I thought it was compassion that I was spending time with her, teaching her to swim. But then, a few weeks after our first meeting, that compassion-like feeling began to grow large. It became a new feeling that I had never known existed within me. It started to wriggle in my heart like a feeble form of creature. It made me want to reach inside Ryoka, to give her warmth as no one had ever done before. But then, after I slept with her the first time, I felt like I'd just committed an irredeemable mistake. So I tried, Miss, to get her to leave the house, leaving me for her own sake. But that didn't work. Then, Ryoka told me she loved me, and I—"

I struggled to continue. "I told Ryoka that I love her, too. I love her from the bottom of my soul."

Miss Himura continued to hold a calm look, like a priest with God's very compassion, listening to my confession.

"Ryoka asked me to run away with her. I couldn't resist my temptation. Being with her was my happiest time, sitting by the fire on that beach, resting my head in her lap. My heart wrinkled at the thought, how our happiness could end at any time. And then, Ryoka offered me a solution. Let's go to the sea together, her tone sounded so innocent and clear. And I felt peace at the prospect of her and me, together forever, in another world. So I told her that I would go with her. It's my fault, Miss. It's all my fault."

"Saki," Miss Himura finally spoke. "When you returned from the States suddenly, last year. You came to me, fell on your knees, and asked me to save Ryoka. And back then, I told you, to not intervene, because any reckless intervention could affect both Ryoka and Rie."

"I'm sorry, Miss, for not listening." I said, "I couldn't stop myself, seeing her with Rie at the market that morning. And I approached her. Before I knew it, I pretended to be Sayo."

"In a way, you helped." Miss Himura said, "and I thought it would take much longer for either Ryoka or Rie to seek to live with their own strength. You helped speed up what might have needed five or ten years to accomplish, into just two years. You have my thanks, Saki."

I looked up and saw Miss Himura's head bowing toward me.

"Please, Miss." I said, "continue to watch over Ryoka for me. I know I have asked so much of you already, but only this one last wish. Like Rie, who has grown strong. I want Ryoka, too, to do the same."

"You should say that to Ryoka yourself."

"Miss, you know I can't." I said, "the reason for me not revealing myself still alive, was for Ryoka's sake, to not try dying with me again."

"But Saki," she said softly. "Ryoka already knows."

My face raised in surprise. Miss Himura's gaze confirmed what she had spoken. "That," my lips opened, "can't be. How?"

"At the market when you showed yourself. You recognized the ribbon and its meaning. But the real Sayo shouldn't have known that."

A chill ran up my back.

"Ryoka told me this, Saki. That she once promised you, she would always believe you no matter what you said."

But then, me going to her at the apartment. What happened, what I did, what she did, all this time—

She knew.

A knocking startled me, and I turned around. Miss Himura's eyes fixed toward the door when I looked at her again. "I told Ryoka that an old friend was coming," she said. "And if she wants to, she could come as well."

The noise went silent.

"Ryoka."

"I've called her here because—" Miss Himura's voice raised, and I paused before getting up. "Because I want to give you two a chance, to do better than what you did that night."

I looked toward the door.

"I have meant to ask you two this for a long time." Miss Himura spoke, "why couldn't you wait? Sayo might have been in your way. But if you had hung in there for a few years, you could graduate, find jobs, and become independent. So long as you are alive, there will always be hope. So why? Why rush to your deaths?"

The silence that followed the question hurt.

"Because neither of you trusts your feelings," she continued. "In your heads, it must be now or never. You failed to see your surroundings, and you let your hearts make a choice. You ran away, dragging each other along and into death. Those are not the actions of those who love one another. It's just desperation, nothing more."

I felt Ryoka, too, was listening.

Miss Himura put the three notebooks on her desk and was preparing to leave. I turned away the moment she opened the door. "Saki," said her voice, "and you too, Ryoka. You two have gone a long way around to arrive at this point. No matter what you decide to do tonight, or in your future, I will have no part in it."

I heard the door shut, followed by Miss Himura's light footsteps moving away.

Silence returned.

I looked to where I felt Ryoka's presence. And I went, going to open the door when my hand paused as if being stopped by an unseen force. My breath grew heavy, and I ended up leaning against the door. I felt, too, another weight leaning against the other side. My hand poised at the door handle.

"Ryoka," I whispered.

"Saki," came the response.

Outside the window lay complete darkness. That night too, felt like this, like everyone else had disappeared from this world. I closed my eyes and heard from within my memory the sound of the roaring sea.

# AFTERWARD

Hello, Reina Sasaki here.

First, I want to thank you all who had read my book until the end. And I would like to thank my editor, Derek Murphy, whose harsh critics have helped me grow as a writer. Also, thank you to my book cover designer, the Creativindie. Without their help, this novel would never come to be.

Back when I was in school, the story of student suicide had always been in newspapers. And so, when I started this book, I had intended it to be the message of how one must never give up, despite how life could sometimes disappointed us. Although the events in this book were made up, I admit that some parts came from my own experiences in high school. I had gone to a Catholic school from elementary until graduating from high school. And I had been in the school's swimming club up until fifth grade. So the twenty-five-meter pool in the story took after the actual place. Also, the church's image in Rie's back story was based on my high school's church. The characters, however, are all fictional. If some should find any resemblances to actual persons, it's just a coincidence.

Upcoming next, *When God Says No* would get the audible version, I would include the following four special chapters.

- Miss Himura's Dream —The story of when Rie was nine years old and how Miss Himura first realized her dream to become a teacher.

- Rie's First Love— The additional backstory of Rie in Tokyo.

- Saki's Decision – How Saki first met Miss Himura.

- Ryoka's Christmas – The event after Ryoka saved Rie and before Saki reappeared.

To get an update on and read my other short stories for free, subscribe to the following page or look for me on https://reina-sasaki.mailchimpsites.com.

Until we meet again

Reina Sasaki

June, 2021

Made in the USA
Middletown, DE
27 June 2021

43122723R00253